CHASING
RAINBOWS

Text copyright © 2012 Kathleen Long
Printed in the United States of America.

Published by Amazon Publishing
P.O. Box 400818
Las Vegas, NV 89140

ISBN-13: 9781612184616
ISBN-10: 1612184618

CHASING RAINBOWS

by Kathleen Long

In life, you either choose to sing a rainbow, or you don't.

Keep singing.

CHAPTER ONE

— — —

Some people leave behind notes. Some leave behind journals. Some leave life lessons carefully documented for the good of future generations.

My dad left cryptograms.

Word puzzles designed to tax my brain cells.

As if I needed any help in that area.

"Were you expecting something different?" My mother barely glanced up from the bed where she sorted Dad's shirts and sweaters. Button-collared shirts. Flannel shirts. Crew-neck sweaters. Vests.

I wasn't half as organized with life as she was with death.

"I wasn't expecting anything at all." Hell, I hadn't been expecting him to die.

She emptied the contents of Dad's sock drawer next to a stack of cardigans. "It's the perfect time of year to get these to charities."

The bright note of her tone didn't fool me. She might be all perky determination on the outside, but inside her soul was just as shattered as mine.

Since my dad's sudden death a week earlier, I hadn't thought much could surprise me, but finding my mother here today, prepping Dad's clothes for charity, had.

Actually, *surprised* wasn't the best word.

Dismayed. Saddened. Stunned.

Any of those more accurately reflected what I felt.

My mother and I had sat with Dad for twelve hours after his aortic dissection, watching him slip away. Afterward, I'd driven her home, to the house where they'd spent more than fifty years together.

She'd stared out the windshield of my car, saying nothing. Her world had tilted on its side and I couldn't fix it, even though I wished somehow I could.

"I'll take good care of you, Mom," I'd said.

And she had answered, "I can take care of myself."

Her words hadn't been sharp or short, but determined. She'd always been one of those women who turned heads simply because of the energy she emitted. Strong. Poised. Classic.

A survivor.

Maybe clearing out Dad's clothes helped her cope, helped her survive.

On the other hand, I wanted to hold on to whatever I could.

I refocused on the pages of Dad's book, skimming his meticulous printing.

"Bernadette?"

I looked up from my study of Dad's perfect block lettering to Mom's heartbroken eyes.

"Where's Ryan?" she asked.

Was it horrible that my husband and I had separated three weeks earlier and I hadn't said a word? He'd stood beside me during the funeral. I owed him for that and not much more.

"He's working, Mom."

"He works too hard." She shifted her scrutiny to the piles on the bed and separated a rogue pullover from the stack of cardigans.

"You have no idea," I muttered.

I flipped back to the inside cover of Dad's book, where he'd written a single sentence beneath my name. I smiled, hearing the words in his voice, the words he'd spoken so often during my life.

In life, you either choose to sing a rainbow, or you don't.

What other words had he left for me? I'd never know until I deciphered the puzzles inside the book.

Cryptograms. I smiled, the sight of the encoded letters warming the cold space that had taken up residence inside me the moment Dad died.

Once upon a time, before college and work and marriage and life, Dad and I spent each morning at the kitchen table, racing to see who could crack the daily cryptogram first. He usually won, a master at analyzing letter patterns and knowing just where to start. There'd been a time, though, when I'd gotten almost as fast. Almost.

Mom tucked the ribbed top of one sock into another, neatly organizing gold toes for whatever stranger might sink his feet into the space where Dad's had once been. Her chin dipped slightly as she feigned complete absorption in her task. "I'm sure your father thought he'd have more time."

I blinked but said nothing, not trusting my voice.

What I wouldn't give to share one more morning with my dad.

My mother shook her head slightly. "I didn't even know he had that little book."

But I knew. I'd asked him to write down the stories he'd spun for as long as I could remember. The jokes. The adventures. The legends.

I'd always known this day would come. The day when he'd be gone. I had just never expected it to come so soon. So abruptly.

I'd asked for his words so that I'd never forget.

Instead, he'd given me cryptograms.

I clutched the book to my chest just the same, watching as my mother pushed away from the bed, headed toward the hall.

"I'll make some sandwiches," she said.

"Could I keep one of Dad's shirts?" My voice cracked.

My mother nodded, her features going soft. "I kept two of his flannels."

I sat on the edge of the bed after she'd gone, cradling the book of cryptograms as I stared at the walls, the family photos, the clothing piled on the bed. Then I set down the book and pushed to my feet, headed for Dad's bureau.

There on the corner sat the tray where he'd kept his extra pair of glasses, his loose pocket change, and his watch. Each item looked exactly the same as last week, last month, last year, with one exception.

Dad's gold wedding band now sat among his other belongings.

I'd never once seen the band off of his finger, so I reached for it, tracing the patterns of wear the years of marriage had left behind.

I shut my eyes and imagined Dad might round the corner at any moment, even though I knew he'd never round that corner again.

"Bernie, lunch," Mom called out from downstairs.

"There in a sec."

I kissed my father's ring and set it back on the tray. Then I reached for Dad's favorite plaid shirt and the book he'd left behind, grateful for any piece of my father I could call my own.

I'm sure your father thought he'd have more time.

Hadn't we all.

I'd been headed home from my mother's when my closest friend had called me with an urgent plea. Her period was two months late, and she'd finally taken a home pregnancy test. The good news was she hadn't started menopause. The bad news was she hadn't started menopause.

Diane's ob-gyn had squeezed her into the schedule, and I'd volunteered to pick up her daughter Ashley from school.

Why not? It was a good diversion from the fact my bereavement leave ended in the morning, and I could always count on Ashley to deliver sparkling teenage conversation—something sure to lighten the mood of my week. Also, time spent in her company was insurance I wouldn't lose touch with the latest slang.

I didn't even know if *slang* was the right word for slang.

I frowned.

"I'm sorry your dad died."

The teenager sitting beside me looked out the passenger window of my car as she spoke. Young enough to be blunt, she was apparently old enough to be uncomfortable with the topic.

"So, how does your heart split?" she asked.

She turned to face me, this question apparently worthy of direct eye contact. I slowed the car to a stop at a red light and returned Ashley's stare. There had been a time when I'd diapered this kid's naked behind. Now she sat next to me all long, sleek blond hair, braces, and curiosity.

I flashed suddenly on the image of her mother at the same age. Although a redhead, Diane had possessed the same slender image, while I'd struggled through body waves, hot irons, and crash diets.

Back then, I'd have done anything and everything to fight my hair and my tendency to carry extra pounds. Some things never changed.

I forced my attention to Ashley's question, wondering how long it would be before talking about Dad's death would be easier. "His aorta split. It's an artery in the heart. Not the heart itself."

She shrugged and shot me an expression full of impatience. "It's still his heart. Right?"

I nodded, squinting at her. Wouldn't it have taken far less effort if she'd simply said, "Duh?"

"Dad said he'll stick his head in the oven if Mom's pregnant. Then I'll have a dead dad, too."

I bit back an inappropriate laugh and pretended to check my side-view mirror out of respect for Ashley's fears. "That's a figure of speech, honey. I'm sure your dad wouldn't do that." Though I had to admit the image of David's head in an oven was not an entirely unpleasant one.

I mentally slapped myself. Bad, Bernadette. Bad.

I patted Ashley's knee just as the light turned green. "It'll be fine. You'll see."

"But what if my mom has a baby?" Her sharp, almost-a-woman-now tone dropped to a schoolgirl mumble. "What then?"

A lump tightened in my throat at the thought of a new baby. "Then that would be a miracle." I forced a quick smile. "You'll have a baby brother or sister."

She nodded. "What about Dad and the oven?"

"I think you're safe there." I pulled my car into Diane and David's driveway and shifted into park. "Your dad was never much of a cook. I have a feeling he wouldn't know how to turn on the oven."

Ashley giggled as she unbuckled her seat belt, and then inhaled sharply. "Mom's home."

Sure enough, Diane's minivan pulled in behind my car. Ashley launched into motion, and I followed close behind.

Tears glistened in Diane's eyes, her expression a cross between holy-shit-how-could-this-have-happened and I-thought-I'd-never-get-to-rock-a-baby-again.

"Ashley," I called out, knowing her mother wouldn't want to cry in front of her thirteen-year-old. "Aunt Bernie's cooking. Why don't you go order us two large pies? Whatever you want."

"All right!" Ashley reversed direction and headed into the house.

I refocused on Diane. "You okay?"

"Please." She shoved a hand through her too-long auburn bangs and rolled her eyes. "Like you have time for my troubles." A tear tumbled over her lower lashes. A matching drop followed down the opposite cheek. "Why couldn't this have happened for you?"

My heart hurt. Even though I had to admit I'd wondered the same thing myself, I hated that my inability to have healthy children had breached the perimeter of Diane's moment.

I shut the door on my old heartache, closed the space between us, and pulled her into a hug. "Stop it. What did the doctor say?"

"She said, 'Congratulations, Mrs. Snyder, that's one strong heartbeat.'"

"That's great," I whispered against her hair, while the traitorous voice inside questioned why it couldn't have been me. Why not? Just one more chance.

Diane sniffed so loudly my eardrum creaked. "I was kind of hoping for some major thyroid condition. That would explain the missed periods, and maybe she'd give me some pills to help me lose weight."

I couldn't help but laugh. It was refreshing to have a friend whose neuroticism matched my own. "Let's go." I hooked my arm inside her elbow. "Rumor has it David's going to put his head in the oven, and I want a front-row seat."

Later that night, I sat on the edge of my bed, staring at the large mahogany box that held the memories of Emma. Had it really been five years? I resisted the temptation to count the months and days for fear the past might devour me alive.

I hoisted the heavy object from the bureau and set it on top of the bed. I pulled open the lid and drew in a slow breath before reaching out to trace my finger across each precious keepsake.

Once upon a time—before I knew better—I believed grief faded over time. Now I knew it never did. Not completely.

Just when you thought you were fine, the pain and sadness came crashing back, grabbing some time on stage like a washed-up dance hall girl hoping for one last chance at fame.

That's how my grief for Emma announced itself in that moment, roaring back to life, linking hands with the numb fog that had swirled inside me ever since Dad took his last breath.

The two danced together, twisting their fingers into my heart and squeezing tight.

When had I last peeked inside the box? Touched her things? Read and reread the congratulation cards that gave way to notes of sympathy?

Emma's memory box had sat on my bureau for almost five years. In the beginning, we'd kept the box downstairs on an antique table that had been a gift from my grandmother.

Ryan and I grew tired of the sideways glances our friends and family tossed toward the box. They never asked to look inside, never asked to see the lock of Emma's beautiful, downy-soft brown hair. Never asked to see the tiny, crocheted booties a volunteer had donated to keep Emma's feet warm in the neo-natal unit.

They glanced at the gleaming mahogany box engraved with her name, then looked away.

Why should they do anything different? Once we moved the box upstairs, Ryan and I barely looked at it ourselves.

Maybe Ryan sneaked moments like I did, as if the grief might win if we opened the mahogany box together and let the heartache out.

Yet, the memories held their position in our bedroom and in our lives, taking up far more space than their one corner of the bureau.

I shut the lid and ran my finger across the engraved brass plate. Five days. They'd been the happiest of my life and the most horrible. I remembered coming home from the hospital without her. I always thought people only swooned in the movies, but that's what I'd done. I'd stood in her nursery and swooned.

And Ryan had caught me.

I reached for a pale pink card from inside the box and traced the inked image of Emma's foot. I scrutinized the tiny lines and gentle creases that had been the print of her chubby sole.

I lifted one multicolored pastel bootie to my nose, inhaling deeply. The yarn smelled like the inside of the mahogany box, no longer smelling of Emma, or of the detergent the hospital had used before they'd called us to pick up her things.

My heart had broken when I learned they'd laundered everything. Her tiny gown. Her blanket. Her booties. Each item scrubbed clean of any trace of our daughter, when traces were all we'd had left.

I flashed back on the piles of my father's clothes. Were they gone already? Or could I dash back and grab just one more shirt? A sweater? Something more to hold on to, even though I knew that soon all traces of my dad would vanish just as Emma's scent had faded away.

The minister had called Dad's passing a natural part of living, the beginning of the next phase of life. In my head, I knew he was right, but in my heart, I only knew my father was gone forever. Just like Emma.

After she died, I had cradled my tiny daughter until I realized I couldn't sit in the neonatal unit forever. Eventually they'd make me go home. They'd make me let go.

So I had.

After Dad died, I held my mother tight against my side as we made our way back through the emergency waiting room and out to the parking lot.

"We can't just leave him," she'd cried.

But we had.

I had thought about letting her go back, letting her sit with him a little longer, but then we'd only have to leave again.

The anguish of walking away without him once was enough. No one should have to make that walk twice.

My tears came.

For Emma. For Dad.

I stroked my finger over the tiny bootie, back and forth along the weave, across the tiny bow, the tiny heel, the tiny toes.

Life was fragile. Grief was resilient.

I hadn't quite figured out which had won during the years since Emma's death.

I thought of Ryan then and wondered what he was doing, what he was thinking. When he'd first moved out, I'd questioned when it had been that our marriage had begun to die. But as I sat staring at Emma's memory box, I knew the answer.

We'd buried our only child on a cold November day, and our carefully constructed world had begun a slow crumble.

Perhaps I shouldn't have been surprised he had walked out. Perhaps I should have been surprised he'd waited five years.

Life. Death. Marriage.

Each was fleeting. Each was enduring.

In life, you either choose to sing a rainbow, or you don't.

I gently pressed my lips to Emma's bootie and placed it inside the box. Then I wiped my damp cheeks and closed the lid.

As the sunlight slanted through the blinds the next morning, I opened my eyes and forgot. Forgot that Ryan had left me. Forgot that Dad was gone. In that moment of twilight sleep, I found myself at peace.

I rolled over and faced Ryan's pillow, empty except for the book of cryptograms. I'd tossed the journal there after my dismal attempt at the first puzzle. Reality rushed back, bringing with it a flood of memories. The voices. The faces. The loss.

I wondered how long this morning ritual would last. I couldn't remember how many days it took after Emma died before I woke in the morning remembering, knowing, hurting. I couldn't remember how long it had been before time had numbed the knife-like pain to a persistent, dull ache.

The alarm clock sounded, meaning only one thing. My bereavement leave had ended. The time had come to return to work and soldier on with the rest of my life.

I jumped into the shower, lathering the latest herbal wonder shampoo into my hair. Maybe this time the cosmetic company's promise of lustrous, tangle-free waves would come true. It could happen.

I forced my thoughts back to my job—the job I loathed. Yet, there I stayed…year after year after year.

Ryan had told me to branch out, to try something new, but I hadn't. He had suggested once that I could dream bigger, but at some point in my life, I'd become the kind of person who embraced the status quo, no questions asked. I didn't have the nerve to do anything about my job. And why would I? Sure, I might not like where I was, but I was safe there. I knew what I was dealing with, and—call me a cynic—I'd take the known over the unknown any day.

Just look at losing Ryan. Look at losing Dad. Look at losing Emma.

I wasn't sure losing Ryan had hit me yet, but losing Dad? Losing Dad had blindsided me, setting into motion what felt like the unraveling of my little corner of the world.

Poindexter, my border collie wannabe, barked, and I realized I'd never let him outside. I quickly rinsed off, wrapped a towel around myself, and hustled the poor dog toward the back door.

No sooner had I let him into the backyard than I heard a familiar noise—the low drone of an approaching airplane. Sure enough, Poindexter's ears perked up. He froze in the middle of the yard, tipping his head up. As soon as the massive plane cleared the treetops beyond our fence, he was off, racing from one side of the yard to the other, barking frantically.

Some people had dogs that chased cars. I had a dog that chased airplanes. Considering my house sat directly below the landing pattern for the Philadelphia International Airport, I had one busy dog. At least no one could ever accuse him of not dreaming big.

The phone rang on cue. I opened the door and hollered at Poindexter, but he was so deeply focused on his chase I was sure he never heard me.

"Hello?"

"Mrs. Murphy?"

I cringed. A card-carrying member of the school of formality, my next-door neighbor refused to address me by anything other than my last name. Granted, she called only to complain about Poindexter, which no doubt played a role in her tone of voice.

"Yes, Mrs. Cooke." I smiled, having read somewhere that smiling while on the phone could set a positive tone for the conversation.

"Your dog—"

So much for the smile theory. I rubbed my eyes. "I was headed out back to drag him in when you called."

"It's quite unacceptable at this time of the morning," she huffed into the phone.

"I apologize. I forgot to check the flight plan before I let him out."

"You can do that?" Her voice rose suspiciously.

"Oh, yes." I fibbed. "The airport makes their schedule available to all dog owners in the region."

This, apparently, rendered her speechless.

"Have a nice day." I hung up before she could say anything else.

Poindexter stopped barking, and when I reached the back door, he stood there waiting to come in, all wagging tail and panting joy.

I've heard people say dogs don't smile, but whoever made that statement had never seen Poindexter after a close encounter with a jumbo jet.

∾

I tried to hang on to Poindexter's positive mental attitude as I made my way through the employee door at McMann Shipping. I readjusted the waistband of my skirt one last time. Truth was, I hadn't been able to button the damn thing. Not even close.

I'd slipped a rubber band around the button, through the buttonhole, and back again to give myself the wiggle room I needed. Pathetic, but effective.

My coworkers greeted me in fairly normal tones, and I couldn't help but wonder if they likened my absence to some sort of bleak vacation.

"How was it?" Jane, in the next cubicle over, might ask.

"Lovely," I'd answer. "You should have seen the flowers...and the procession. There must have been forty cars."

"You don't say?" she'd reply.

"And did you hear Ryan and I split up a few weeks ago?"

She'd shake her head. "Boy, you really have been busy. Welcome back."

"Where's the Cooper file?" The voice of Blaine McMann, our CEO, sliced through my thoughts and signaled the official end of my allotted grieving period.

I swiveled in my chair to look up at him, and I mean up. The man was at least six foot six and he loved nothing more than intimidating his employees with his size. If anyone ever tells you family-owned businesses are lovely, warm, fuzzy places to work, run the other way...*screaming*.

"The file?" He glared down at me, a well-practiced part of his intimidation repertoire.

"It's in the pending customer files. Where I left it." I gestured to the black file cabinet against the wall. "I'll get it for you."

"Save your energy." His frown morphed into a smirk. "It's not there. Do you want to know how I know it's not there?" He patted his chest. "Because I looked. Then I had every employee in this office help look for that file. Your incompetence cost us valuable time and perhaps the account."

He stepped away from me, pivoted, and began to pace at the opening of my cubicle mid-rant. Back and forth. Back and forth. Like one of those moving targets at the boardwalk arcade. I wondered how many points I'd score for nailing him between the eyes with a rubber band.

I laughed a little bit. I couldn't help myself.

Maybe the emotions of the past few weeks had finally taken their toll, but I found it completely impossible to hold myself together.

I suddenly imagined all six foot six of Blaine McMann with a fuzzy duck head, and I laughed again.

He stopped and glared at me. "You think this is funny, Murphy?"

I nodded, unable to speak. As much as I tried to control myself, once I started laughing, I couldn't stop. And, the more I laughed, the more visibly angry Blaine became.

Truth was, he'd had it in for me ever since I had corrected him in front of a client. Company policy dictated the customer was number one, but apparently, if that meant catching the boss's mistake, the employee—namely me—had better be prepared for payback.

The missing Cooper file had given Blaine the taste of revenge he'd craved for months.

At one point he puffed out his cheeks in apparent frustration, but I was too far gone to care.

"Bernie." Jane shushed me from her side of our shared cubicle wall. "Knock it off."

Blaine stepped closer, towering over me. "Are you having some sort of breakdown?"

I shook my head, even though I thought he might be on to something.

Blaine launched into a spiel about separating personal issues from the office, and I stopped laughing long enough to ignore him and dive into my thoughts.

This might not have been the opportune time to give Ryan credit for much of anything, but he'd been right about one thing. I despised this job. Yet, I continued to put up with Blaine's shit, for lack of a better term.

Why?

Life is short. Wasn't that what Ryan had said when he'd left? And wasn't that what everyone had said when Dad died? When Emma died?

Good Lord. If I were to die right here, right now, would this be how I'd want to be remembered?

Hell, no.

What was to stop me from quitting? From walking out the door and never looking back?

I supposed there was the minor issue of income, but the new, soon-to-be-fearless me could surely handle finding a job. And even though Ryan and I were technically separated, he'd promised to keep up with his half of the bills, at least for now.

Everything else in my life had changed. Why shouldn't my job? Better still, if I quit now, at least I'd have one development in my life that happened on *my* terms.

There was a whole world waiting to be explored.

Poindexter had the right idea. I should find an airplane and chase it.

"Are you listening to me?" Blaine leaned so close I could feel his breath against my hair.

Our eyes locked and a sense of empowerment flooded through me. I did something I'd wanted to do since the first time Blaine McMann opened his mouth.

I told him to shut up.

I thought about climbing up on my chair to make the moment more memorable, but when I thought about the possibility of serious injury, death, or major embarrassment, I decided simply to stand instead.

Blaine's eyes widened behind his trendy rimless glasses. "What did you say?"

"I said, 'Shut up.'" I planted my fists on my hips and hoisted my chin.

Blaine narrowed his eyes. "I think you need to go home and give it another few days before you come back."

Blaine. What kind of parents named their kid Blaine?

"Are you listening to me?" he asked.

I shook my head. "I'm through listening to you."

He frowned. "I could put you on probation, you know."

I faked a shudder.

"Bernie." Jane peeked over the top of the cubicle wall. "Sit down and be *quiet.*"

I ignored her completely. "I quit."

The words felt natural, as if they'd been waiting on my tongue, hoping I'd use them.

Blaine said nothing as I plucked my purse from beneath my desk, gathered the pictures of Poindexter from my work area, and turned for the hall.

I stopped at the opening to my cubicle, turned back toward the black filing cabinet, and plucked the Cooper file from exactly where I'd left it. I slapped the folder on top of my desk and looked back at Blaine once. Just once.

As I marched toward the exit, I imagined my coworkers heralding my bold departure with thunderous applause. In my mind, I could hear them chanting, "Bernie! Bernie! Bernie!"

In reality, every last one of them sat slack-jawed in their cubicles as I marched past, stunned into submission by my uncharacteristic outburst.

I stepped out into the bright sunshine of the company parking lot and realized I could now do whatever I wanted to do. I could become whoever I wanted to become.

This was my time. My life.

My future was a blank slate, and nothing and no one could stop me now.

Not even the small, soft voice at the base of my brain wondering what in the hell I had just done.

CHAPTER TWO

— —— ——

"NTC RJBC MX EFXC FY PMN YM BIAT FP TMEQFPR J RMMQ
TJPQ JY LEJZFPR J LMMH TJPQ DCEE."
—T. N. ECYEFC

Poindexter and I had eaten every carbohydrate in the house by the next afternoon.

There are those who might think the massive upheaval of my life, combined with empty cupboards, presented the chance to fully reinvent myself, starting with my grocery shopping and eating habits.

I could work up a week-long menu balancing each day's consumption in an effort to increase energy, improve health, and decrease thigh girth.

I could shop smart, eat smart, and reap the benefits. Or, I could eat junk food.

Five minutes later, I pulled into the Walgreens parking lot. After all, Rome wasn't built in a day.

I didn't notice my footwear faux pas—one spotted slipper and one clog—until I'd shuffled halfway down the cosmetic aisle.

Was my life in such disarray I could no longer select matching footwear?

Apparently, yes.

I lifted my focus from my fashion-challenged footwear to the activity buzzing around me. Fellow shoppers chattered and browsed, scanned and purchased. They walked and talked at hyperspeed, self-contained bursts of energy and purpose.

The blur of faces and voices dizzied me, and I fought the urge to tap someone on the shoulder.

"Yes?" the perfect stranger would reply.

"My father died," I'd explain.

The stranger's brows would crumple. She'd cluck her tongue sympathetically and pat my shoulder, nodding to a passerby.

"Her father died," she'd say, and the new stranger would mutter comforting words, cluck her tongue, and stop yet someone else.

I imagined things would continue on this way until clucking and patting strangers surrounded me. For the first time in days, I felt loved and comforted, wrapped in the imaginary embrace of countless Walgreens shoppers.

Just imagine what would happen if I tossed in Ryan's desertion on top of everything else. Hell, the manager would probably make an announcement over the public address system.

Dumped mourner on aisle six. Please stop by on your way to the register to cluck and pat.

"Lady." An impatient voice interrupted my mental tangent—too close and too real to be part of my fantasy. "You're blocking the cotton balls."

I focused long enough for the woman's annoyed frown to register. So much for my imaginary world of comfort.

"Sorry," I mumbled as I sidestepped toward facial creams. I grabbed a pore-reducing mask then headed for the candy aisle. After all, I might be in shock, but I wasn't stupid.

An hour later my face hurt, my stomach hurt, and I'd dug my wedding video out of the deep dark recesses of the hall closet.

I'd made another attempt at the first cryptogram in Dad's journal, giving up after a solid three minutes of concentration. I'd chosen to revisit the past instead. After all, things had seemed so much brighter back then.

I fast-forwarded through the video, freezing the screen at my favorite moment. My waltz with Dad.

I remembered the moment as if it were yesterday. We'd fumbled through our dance, Dad counting off the steps under his breath as I concentrated on smiling up at him instead of looking down at my feet. We practiced night after night in my parents' living room in the weeks before my wedding to Ryan.

I pressed the play button on the remote and tossed back a handful of chocolate as Ryan cut in, beaming down at me as if he'd never love anyone the way he loved me at that moment.

Sometimes the happy moments of life came in a rush, over-whelming in their lightness and brightness. Sometimes those same moments lingered in the recesses of memory, assurances that no matter how bad things might seem, happier times would come again.

And sometimes...sometimes those happy moments served as a reminder that there were no guarantees in life, in happiness, in anything.

My throat closed up and I choked. Choked on the reality my wedding video no longer meant a thing.

After all, what would I say if someone stumbled across the tape during a party? Assuming I ever gave a party again.

"Community theatre." I'd wave my hand dismissively. "A little play that ran for a while after college."

The phone rang, and I squeezed my eyes shut, tired of seeing the smiling faces on the video and not wanting to look at the Caller ID on the phone.

"Mrs. Murphy?" A clipped voice spoke as soon as the answering machine's beep sounded. "It's Pat Diller from the Canine Academy."

Dread rolled in my stomach and I glared at Poindexter. He tipped his head from side to side, apparently trying to make sense of the talking voice emanating from the machine.

"We held our weekly staff meeting this morning and decided it best that Poindexter doesn't return to class. Your full refund will be in tomorrow's mail."

The dial tone sounded briefly before the machine disconnected, and I narrowed my gaze on the dog. He rolled over onto his side, settling back into his daily routine, totally oblivious to the fact he'd just been booted from his fourth obedience school for his inability to sit, stay, and refrain from tormenting the other students.

I didn't know why I held on to fantasies about recreating my life when I couldn't even train the dog.

At least this time we were getting a refund. My luck had either changed or the folks at the Canine Academy figured returning my money was a small price to pay to ensure Poindexter never set a paw inside their school again.

Hoping my luck *had* changed, I rapped my knuckles against the distressed oak of the coffee table. Poindexter charged the front door, fangs bared, barking like a fool.

"It was me, you goof."

He tipped his head in my direction, squinting as if I were the fool. He retrained his focus on the crack between the door and wall, a low growl rumbling from deep inside his throat.

Perhaps I should have spent more time with the dog and less time with Ryan. Maybe then at least one relationship in my life would fall into the success category.

Poindexter left the door, jumped back up on the sofa, and snuggled into the pillows, apparently spent from his guard dog exertion. Napping was not an unappealing idea, but I had a better one.

I uncorked an ancient bottle of wine at the precise moment Diane let herself in the front door.

"So now you're not answering your door *or* your phone?" she asked.

I'd left her a message after I quit my job, but I hadn't picked up the phone since then.

Pink splotches covered Diane's chest and throat. She'd flushed like this for as long as I'd known her.

One time in third grade, Mrs. Haberstadt had sent Diane to the principal's office for chewing gum, and the principal had sent her home sick with no punishment or warning.

Diane had broken out into so many spots on the way to the school office, the principal had wanted nothing more than to get her the hell off school property before she spread whatever rare disease he thought she'd contracted to the entire student body.

"Are you listening to me?" Diane's blotches marched north, threatening to overtake her cheeks.

I nodded without saying a word, trying frantically to remember the last time I'd seen her so emotional.

She yanked the bottle of wine from my hand. "Are you drunk?" One fist landed sharply on her hip and she glared at me.

I shook my head.

She pinched her lips into a tight line then jerked her thumb toward the television and the mess of junk food strewn across the coffee table. "Cookies. Ice cream. Wedding video. Wine. You have every right to feel sorry for yourself, but bingeing isn't going to help anything."

I shrugged. So I felt sorry for myself. Shoot me. "Is this lecture going anywhere or are you in one of those moods where you like to hear yourself talk?"

Harsh, I knew, but years of experience had taught me that Diane's rants were best stopped before they could get started.

She glared at me then like I'd never seen her glare before.

Poindexter launched himself from the sofa and careened toward the kitchen at a full-out sprint. The dog was not only obedience-challenged, but he couldn't stomach conflict in any shape or variety.

"I"—Diane splayed one hand against her chest as if she had a plan to save the world—"am here to keep you from falling into a funk."

"Funk?" Now she was pissing me off. I returned her glare and straightened my spine. "What's the matter? Is my shitty mood offending you somehow?"

Diane's eyebrows lifted toward her hairline. "Don't take this the wrong way, sweetie, but the fact you're in any mood at all is a good sign. Now we just have to channel that energy into moving forward."

She gestured toward the front door as if she intended to shove my old life out in order to make room for the new one. *Zip. Zip.* Piece of cake.

"First of all, don't call me sweetie. Second of all, what are you trying to say? I've been a zombie or something?" I squinted at her.

Diane shrugged. "If the robe fits."

Her blotches had merged, giving her the appearance of a lobster with a hot flash.

"Just how strong are those prenatals they put you on?" I tightened the sash on my terry-cloth bathrobe. I was not without my dignity, after all. "And you can't tell me how to feel."

"That's great." Diane moved to the coffee table and systematically gathered my junk food into a pile. "Been watching Dr. Phil during your down time?"

"So what if I have?"

She hoisted the pile into her arms and pivoted on one heel, headed straight toward the kitchen.

Shock and disbelief tapped at the base of my brain. "Where are you going?"

"To the mall. And you're coming with me." She disappeared around the corner and I heard the distinct click of the trash can lid hitting the wall.

That got my attention.

"Don't you dare—" The swoosh of my dietary staples sliding into the trash stopped me midsentence.

"Now then." My soon-to-be-ex-best friend reappeared in the hall and wrapped her fingers around my elbow. "You're getting a shower and I'm going to pick out some clothes." She gave my stomach a quick pat. "If you haven't already eaten yourself into the next size."

"Bitch," I mumbled beneath my breath.

"Damn right."

We stared at each other then, two friends who had seen each other through just about everything two friends can see each other through.

Much as I longed to run to the kitchen and pull my chocolate from the trash, I stood my ground, staring into Diane's eyes.

Her gaze softened, and tears welled in my vision.

She pulled me into a hug and I leaned into her, wrapping my arms around her waist, willing her strength and determination to seep into my body. "Sorry I called you a bitch."

"That's okay." She spoke softly against my ear. "It's an unwritten rule that you can call your best friend a bitch when you're out of your mind with shock and sugar." She pushed me to arm's length. "You'll feel better after you get some fresh air. I promise."

I wasn't sure a trip to the mall constituted fresh air, but I was in no shape to argue, especially not when Diane was on a mission.

"You'd better hurry up"—she tipped her chin toward the dent on the sofa where Poindexter had been—"otherwise we won't have time to shop and be back for obedience class."

I made a face and shook my head.

Diane pressed her lips tightly together. "Oh, honey. This is so not your month."

In that moment, I realized I didn't need the clucking and patting strangers at the store. Diane had stood by me through new math, training bras, driver's education, losing Emma, and now—apparently—she planned to help kick-start the reinvention of my life.

She whistled as I climbed the steps in front of her. "Damn, Bernie. How much *have* you eaten?"

Sometimes, you simply needed an old friend to give you a kick in the ass.

One stylish—and previously too large—velour lounging outfit later, we were on our way to the mall. While Diane blathered on about second chances, starting over, and rediscovering life, I stared silently out the passenger window.

The feeling of detachment I'd felt since Ryan left clung to me still. I found myself wishing I'd changed the locks the moment he left, not so much to keep him from coming back, but to keep my well-meaning—but highly annoying—friend out.

Much as I loved Diane, her insistence that life should go on had me considering just what it would take to drive me to homicide.

As I understood it, Diane believed any proper rebirth, and mine in particular, should begin with a makeover. I could hardly wait.

Even worse, she wasn't about to settle for a department store cosmetic counter. No. She'd set her sights on the mother of mall cosmetics, the Rediscover You kiosk.

I shuddered as we neared the cart in the center of the mall. Diane's sensible heels snapped smartly against the tile floor while my sneakers squeaked along a few hesitant feet behind her.

I sensed impending doom the moment one of the salesgirls looked up…and winced. I focused on her name tag, hoping for a gentle, sensible name like Helen, or Mary, or Anne.

I squinted as I read the engraved type.

Brittany.

Great.

Brittany cleared her throat, no doubt trying to assess how much commission she was about to earn from my less-than-perfect appearance. "Can I help you?"

I shook my head, but Diane pinched my arm. Hard.

"Yes," Diane answered with her most serious tone. "My friend has been on the receiving end of some rather bad news lately and she deserves a little pick-me-up."

Rather bad news. I supposed that was one way to sum up the implosion of my life.

"What were you thinking?" Brittany peered closely at me. Too closely.

I fought the urge to cover my face with my hands and run screaming.

Diane tipped her head to join in the scrutiny, and I wondered if it wouldn't be easier to turn on a huge spotlight and ask every shopper in the mall to rate my pores.

"I'll take a lipstick then I'm out of here."

Diane arched a single brow—a move I hated, probably because I couldn't do it. "She'll start with some skin care."

A second salesgirl sidled up to Brittany. This one's name tag read Tiffany, but they might as well have been twins. Their flawless complexions glowed, their long blond hair shone like waterfalls of honey.

"Prevention or recovery?" Tiffany asked.

How about grief? I wanted to say. *How about impending divorce?*

I stared into their luminous faces and wondered how they got to work each day. Surely they weren't old enough to drive. Did their parents drop them off? Did they take the bus?

"Um…" Brittany tipped her head to one side, still studying me.

Definitely not the bus, I decided. Hell, they probably had drivers.

"Prevention?" I guessed, wanting to end my misery.

Both heads shook in matching condescension. *Great.* So far my shopping excursion was doing wonders for the rediscovery of my self-esteem.

"Definitely recovery," Tiffany offered.

"Definitely," Brittany agreed. She tipped her head to the other side. "Have you been under a lot of stress or something?"

"Or not sleeping?" Tiffany asked. "Your skin looks like it's seen better days."

Heat began to blossom in my cheeks and Diane placed a hand on my arm.

I'd always been the sort of person who kept her thoughts to herself, at least in public. I decided then and there that decorum was overrated.

"Are you this helpful to all of your customers?" I narrowed my gaze first on Tiffany, then on Brittany.

"Oh yeah," Tiffany answered, jerking her thumb toward a sign hanging on the kiosk wall. "It's our motto."

I read the sign and winced.

You are our most important feature.

I scrubbed a hand across my eyes. "I was being sarcastic, just so you know."

"Oh," Tiffany said, as if she had no idea what that meant.

"You really shouldn't rub your face like that," Brittany piped up. "You're going to make your wrinkles even worse."

I bit my lip and counted to ten.

"Maybe we should go," Diane murmured under her breath, her grip tightening on my elbow. "This might have been a bad idea."

You think?

Tiffany nodded and wrinkled her nose. "Maybe you should be shopping at one of the mall anchor stores. Rediscover You might be a little too young for your needs."

That straw broke this camel's back.

I'd held it together...all right, basically held it together... through Ryan's departure and my dad's funeral, but I had zero intention of holding it together for some little smart-mouthed chippie who needed to be put in her place.

"What did you say to me?" I leaned menacingly across the counter, and both girls went slightly pale.

I'm not ashamed to admit my sense of power was more than a little heady.

Diane, no doubt anticipating my impending loss of self-control, tugged on my arm. "Bernie. Let's go."

I shook her off, leaning so far across the counter my feet dangled. The stunned kiosk counter duo said nothing.

"I asked a question. Polite society dictates you answer." I pursed my lips. "Or did they not cover manners yet in your pre-school class?"

"*Bernie.*" Diane hooked one hand into the waistband of my velour lounging pants and yanked.

I released my grip on the counter long enough to swat her away.

Brittany and Tiffany huddled together, sidestepping toward the register, no doubt making a move for the help-there's-a-middle-aged-wrinkled-woman-threatening-us silent alarm.

They morphed into something far more sinister than Rediscover You employees at that moment…at least in my eyes. To me, they represented every perfectly coiffed, perfectly perfect specimen of the female race, including the woman I liked to think of as PSB—pregnant slut bimbo—also known as Ryan's new love.

To this day, I don't know how I did it, but I hurdled over the counter. I jumped up, pivoted on my velour-encased derriere, and dropped down into the inner sanctum of flawless-skinned cosmetic sales.

I felt a bit like Jack Nicholson's character in *The Shining* at the moment he chops through the bathroom door with an ax. Determined. Focused. And most likely, out of my mind.

"Know what you need?"

Both girls shook their heads, and I couldn't help but notice the way their lustrous tresses reflected the glow of the overhead lights. Had I ever had lustrous tresses? I shoved a hand up into my unruly rats' nest.

No.

Brittany lifted a phone from its cradle. "You'd better stay back."

"Or what? You're going to knock me senseless with the receiver?"

She shook her head again. "I'm calling security."

"Again," Diane said sweetly, trying to reach me across the counter, "she's been under a lot of stress." She uttered her next statement in her most threatening tone. "Bernie. Let's go. *Now.*"

I shot her a warning glance and she backed off. I refocused on my targets. "Where's the prevention cream?"

While Brittany dialed, Tiffany pointed to a row of boxes to my right. I won't deny how happy it made me to spot her nervous swallow.

I plucked one box from the shelf and then a second, ripping open fancy cardboard tops and slamming expensive glass vials to the counter. "You two have no idea how much you need prevention cream." I nodded as I worked. "Trust me. Otherwise, those superiority complexes of yours are going to leave permanent marks."

I crooked my finger, encouraging them to come closer.

A voice from the loudspeaker called a code something-or-other to kiosk number fourteen.

"Bernie."

I lifted my gaze to Diane's and blinked. If I'd thought she'd been blotchy earlier, I'd been wrong. She'd moved beyond blotchy, beyond lobster, to full-out, flaming, fire-engine red.

I wondered if the kiosk twins had a cream for *that.*

"Get. Out. Of. There. Now."

I thought about her request for a full second. Honestly, I did. Her tone was so convincingly authoritative I almost caved to her will, but then Brittany made a fatal mistake.

She spoke.

"Yeah. Get out of here now. You don't belong here."

Her words weren't so much what pushed me over the edge. It was her tone. Her I-will-never-lose-my-perfect-figure-or-my-flawless-skin-and-my-husband-will-never-leave-me tone that sent me lunging for her creamy throat.

Unfortunately, the security guard grabbed me from behind at the precise moment I made my move.

An hour later, Diane and I were escorted out of the mall. She'd received a warning and I'd received a lifetime ban, but that didn't scare me. I mean, what were they going to do, post my picture at every entrance? Hey, maybe they'd use those little red circles with the lines through them.

Actually, the thought was rather funny.

Then I realized something.

I was *smiling*.

Maybe Diane had been right about feeling something. *Anything.*

Sure, our mall excursion hadn't exactly left me happy, but it had left me feeling alive, and alive was good.

"You know what?"

"What?" Diane's exasperated tone had persisted since I'd scaled the counter.

"You were right." I nodded. "We should do this more often."

Later that night I attacked the first cryptogram again. This time, I copied the encoded letters onto a sheet of paper and tried to remember how I'd worked these things once upon a time.

The process came back to me slowly…very slowly. I guessed at word patterns and placements, arbitrarily assigning the letter *E* where I thought it belonged. The solution took shape at a snail's pace, but after almost an hour, there it was.

I studied the words, savoring the quote Dad had chosen just for me.

While the message itself was a little too borderline cheerleader for me, I knew what Dad had been trying to say.

I slept soundly that night, as if my dad himself had told me somehow, someway, everything would be all right.

"The game of life is not so much in holding a good hand as playing a poor hand well."
—H. T. Leslie

CHAPTER THREE

—— —— ——

*"IYWSLUK OC NJK LSN YR HKOXU NJK YXBZ YXK TJY
PXYTC ZYW'SK CILSKG NY GKLNJ."*
   —KLSB TOBCYX

Late the next afternoon, I sat on the floor, watching my brother, Mark, touch Dad's sport coats where they still hung in the closet. He touched each sleeve, each lapel, as if the fabric might disintegrate beneath his touch.

He'd arrived not long after I had. He'd never been much for the pop-in, but my mother's smile was evidence of how much his surprise visit meant to her.

She disappeared downstairs to make a snack, leaving Mark and me alone in the master bedroom, no doubt hoping we'd somehow discover the closeness we'd never shared growing up.

I'd lived in awe of my brother—older than I was and seemingly wiser in every way. With eight years between us, he'd always seemed just out of reach. I'd had the sense he tolerated me, counting the days until he could leave his annoying little sister behind.

I'd been failing miserably at mastering roller skates when he was learning to drive. Once he left for college, he never looked back. The years spent apart showed in the awkwardness that invariably stretched between us.

We might have had the same parents and been raised under the same roof, but Mark and I shared no similar experiences until now.

Now, we shared our grief.

I pulled my knees to my chin. "He'd love you to have those, don't you think?" I forced a bright tone into my voice as I looked away from the jackets, trying hard not to focus on the fact Dad would never wear them again.

When I glanced back at my brother, I realized the hint of gray that had once peeked only from Mark's sideburns now covered his entire head, mixing generously with his short, dark brown waves.

I had never mastered the air of confidence my brother seemed to effortlessly exude. As long as I could remember, I'd envied him for that, but today he looked defeated, broken.

His profile hadn't changed, but the heartache plastered across his face mirrored my own.

He reached for a navy-blue jacket, letting his hand linger against the lapel.

"Did you know that was his favorite?" My overly cheery tone bordered on used-car-salesman slick.

Why was I so determined to foist one of our father's jackets on my brother? Did I need to prove Mark needed Dad as much as I had? That he felt as awash in loss as I did?

Yes.

Mark pulled the hanger off the rack and held the jacket in front of him, his arms outstretched as if the sleeves might strangle him at any moment.

"Surreal." He uttered the word flatly and looked at me.

I met his sad gaze and forced a tight smile. "Surreal." My heart gave a squeeze.

Mark's eyes shone with unshed tears. "He wasn't even sick."

I shook my head. "Not sick."

He hung the hanger back on the rack and crossed the room in a few quick strides.

I scrambled to my feet. "Where are you going? Aren't you going to pick something?"

"Not now."

Mark didn't stop to look back. Didn't stop to say good-bye. He rounded the upstairs railing and took the steps two at a time on his way down.

"I'll call you later, Mom," he hollered a split second before the front door slammed.

I sank back onto the worn carpet of my parents' bedroom, staring at my father's jackets. Alone. Unwanted. Soon to be forgotten.

"Come get something to eat," Mom called out from downstairs.

I crawled across the floor until I could reach the closet door and push it shut. Sometimes it was easier not to see the realities you weren't quite prepared to face.

After I inhaled cheese, crackers, and a fistful of grapes, I contemplated the small piles of paperwork Mom had organized on her kitchen table.

The funeral home had dropped off ten copies of my father's death certificate and all that remained now was the task of wiping Dad's life out of existence—at least that's how it felt to me.

There were insurance papers to be filed, retirement accounts to be notified, banks to be called. As I scribbled each item onto a yellow tablet, I began to think the list would never end, but finally it did.

"Why won't Mark pick a jacket?" I asked.

Mom frowned, apparently displeased with the shift in topic. "Everyone grieves differently, Bernie."

I shook my head, unwilling to let her dismiss my question that quickly. She countered before I had a chance to deliver my follow-up.

"He calls every night to see how I am."

Hurray for Mark. Through some deep-seated logic I'm sure went back to my childhood, I took this statement as criticism of the fact I, on the other hand, had not called my mother every night.

I dropped my focus to the yellow tablet, my eyes seeing none of the words, my brain concentrating on the fact I should have called her every night. She'd just lost her soul mate, for crying out loud. Why hadn't I called her every night?

"How's Ryan?" she asked.

Boy, the woman sure knew how to push the buttons, didn't she?

My feelings of inadequacy morphed into feelings of abandonment.

How *was* Ryan? Deceitful. Despicable. Worthy of cold-blooded revenge.

I didn't see the need to fill her in on either Ryan's departure or the recent change in my employment status. As far as she knew, I was still on bereavement leave.

The woman had enough on her plate.

"He's fine, Mom. He sends his love."

"He's working hard?" Her voice climbed a few octaves, and I realized she wasn't one hundred percent sold on my response.

I forced a bright smile. "Absolutely."

"Everything all right?" Her dark brown eyes narrowed.

I'd seen the look a million times. The woman could see right through me. Always had. I had to change the subject...and fast.

I wasn't about to confess my failure to stay married. Not now. Maybe not ever.

"Let's talk about you. You sleeping? Eating?" Genius. I could match her interrogation skills question for question.

She nodded. "There was an incident at church."

I hesitated before I asked the obvious question. "Like what?" What sort of incident could happen at church? Seriously?

She answered without meeting my gaze. "I punched an usher."

I blinked. "Pardon me?"

"Punched an usher." My mother gave a shrug of her slender shoulders as if her statement should come as no surprise. "Split his lip." She blinked. "He got a bit too close when he passed the collection basket." She gave another shrug. "I may have overreacted."

"You think?"

Apparently the insanity was genetic. And here I thought I'd merely lived in New Jersey for too long.

I bit my lip and tried very hard not to snicker, but come on. The visual was priceless. It seemed we Carrolls threw decorum to the wind under stress.

"Split his lip?" I repeated.

She nodded, then let out a quick sigh.

"Boy, too bad Dad missed that." I said the words without thinking, without stopping to realize Dad was the reason my mother had slugged the poor usher to begin with.

As much as I missed Dad, I couldn't begin to imagine how lost my mother felt.

Her eyes filled with tears. I gathered the paperwork into a single pile and set my yellow tablet on top of the various forms and notes. "Why don't I take this home?"

She nodded, not speaking, probably not wanting me to hear her voice crack or wobble.

"How about a walk?" I asked. "The fresh air might do us both good."

Mom nodded again and I pushed back my chair, heading toward the closet to grab our jackets. A few minutes later, we walked in silence, eyes squinting against the bright afternoon sun.

"You should ask Ryan to help with the paperwork," Mom said. "He's very good with things like that."

"We'll see," I said. *Not a chance*, I thought.

My mother snapped her tongue. "It's too much for you to handle alone."

This was the perfect time to tell her about Ryan, but I couldn't quite bring myself to do it. She loved Ryan. *Loved* him.

Why shatter her illusions by telling her he'd not only lined up his rebound relationship, but had moved right ahead to his rebound offspring?

We walked in silence from that point on, soaking in the warm sun and crisp autumn air. I kicked haphazardly at the piles of orange and red leaves gathered along the sidewalk in front of the neat suburban houses.

It spoke volumes about our relationship that even at a time when I knew we'd both like to scream and cry, or rant and rave, we remained calm, quiet, controlled, numb.

A better daughter might have known what to say or how to act, but I didn't have a clue. I said nothing. I did nothing.

When we stepped back inside my mom's house, I headed for the kitchen. "I'm going to grab this paperwork and go, Mom. Maybe I can get ahead of rush-hour traffic."

"Oh." A note of surprise sounded in her voice.

"What?" I turned to look at her as she studied herself in the hall mirror. "I can stay, if you'd rather—"

"My earring's gone." My mother's voice dropped to barely more than a whisper. She slipped the remaining earring off and cradled it in the palm of one hand. "Your father gave me these. Before we were married."

Damn.

"I'll find it." I slapped the paperwork down on the table and flipped on the overhead hallway light. "I'm good at finding things. Really. Just ask Ry—anyone."

We searched for several minutes in the hall, next to the closet, under furniture. We searched every inch of her windbreaker before I made her untuck her sweater and shake that out as well.

We found nothing. Not a blessed thing.

"It has to be here somewhere." I couldn't deny a tiny bit of panic squeezed at my insides even as I did my best to sound confident.

Mom shot me a weak smile. "It's okay."

I'd never seen her look so…lost. I yanked open the front door. "I'll find it."

The breeze had picked up and the sun had dipped lower in the late afternoon sky.

"You'll catch a chill." She placed a hand on my shoulder. "Let it go, honey."

But I couldn't let it go. Not now. I might not know what to say to ease her heartache, but I could find her earring. "I'll be right back."

Forty-five minutes later, I'd picked through every inch of ground we'd covered, flipping leaves and running my now-numb-with-cold fingers through the edge of every carefully manicured lawn. The grim realization I'd over-promised on my ability to find the earring began to sink in.

I dropped to my knees and let out a frustrated breath. I was out of sidewalk. I'd failed.

That's when I saw it. A flicker of gold beneath one crinkled point of a dried-up maple leaf. The back of Mom's earring.

Excitement whispered through me as I carefully checked the surrounding leaves, flipping over each one until I spotted the object of my search, an amber stone lying next to its dented gold setting.

As I raced back down the sidewalk toward my parents' house, I remembered being five years old, running down the street, carefully cradling the first tooth I'd ever lost in the palm of my hands. I'd been so proud, full of happy anticipation, imagining my mother's smile and her words of praise.

This time when I handed her the tiny object I cradled in my palm, she pulled me into a long, silent hug. And that meant more to me than words ever could.

I left for home feeling oddly buoyed by the simple act of finding Mom's earring, but the closer I got, the more I realized I wasn't ready to face my empty house. Not yet. The only things waiting for me there were the obedience school drop-out and a dozen rolls of positive affirmation paper towels Diane felt I couldn't live without.

I experienced a moment of guilt about not rushing back to Poindexter, but based on the snores that had come from the sofa that morning, the drama of the past several days had taken its toll.

I had no particular destination in mind until I spotted Genuardi's supermarket coming up on my left.

I'd never been one who enjoyed grocery shopping. *Never.* Yet, suddenly, the thought of spending an hour tossing food items into a squeaky-wheeled cart felt promising. I'd begin the rebirth of my life right there...in the nutrition-rich, calorie-laden aisles of my neighborhood grocery store.

I shifted my car into park and stared out the windshield. Other shoppers busied themselves—loading SUVs, pushing carts, herding children across the traffic lanes.

They moved through the steps of their lives effortlessly, flawlessly, while I sat and stared, knowing I could never measure up. Not then. Probably not ever.

I don't really know how long I sat there, but the pace of life in the parking lot became more than I could handle.

I drove home, opened a bag of peanut butter M&Ms, slipped into my dad's plaid shirt, and plucked the cryptogram book from my underwear drawer.

I hunkered low in my favorite chair, reached for a pencil, and concentrated, hoping I could lose myself in the process of solving another puzzle.

But when a knock sounded at the front door and my soon-to-be-ex-husband stood on the other side of the peephole, all thoughts of cryptogram solving flew off my radar screen.

I flashed on the last time Ryan had been here—inside the home we'd planned to share forever. I'd been expecting a normal evening at home—Ryan watching television while I read a book—but instead he'd made the face, the one that meant he had something *significant* to say.

Sure, I'd seen it before, but it had always been directed at someone else.

That night, he'd directed the face at me.

"I met someone," he said.

For better or for worse.

The memory of our vows raced through my mind, juxtaposed with the words he spoke. I wrapped my arms tightly around my knees, bracing for impact. "Do I know her?"

He shook his head. "No."

Ryan had done his best to look remorseful even though I knew he wasn't sorry at all.

In sickness and in health.

I remembered thinking I could be a better wife. I could cook more. Clean more. Laugh more.

"She's pregnant, Bernie," he said.

Pregnant. That one I couldn't do.

My disbelief had stunned me then, but now...now Ryan's hey-won't-you-let-me-in smile threatened to push me past the limits of rational thought.

I shook off the remembered images and muttered a few choice words as I unlocked the door. Poindexter raced upstairs, apparently unwilling to risk whatever confrontation might follow. At least he knew better than to greet the traitor who had deserted us.

"What's the matter?" I asked as I opened the door. "Forget where you live?"

Ryan gave a slow shake of his head. "Your mother called me."

Shit. This was not how I wanted her to find out about the demise of my marriage. I was the worst daughter in the world.

"I didn't tell her." He tipped his chin toward the living room. "Can I come in?"

I hesitated, but he squeezed past me before I could decide whether or not to step out of his way.

"She said you might need help with your dad's paperwork."

"So you dropped everything and dashed over?" I stiffened. "I can handle it myself."

"Why don't you let me run through everything with you?" Ryan squinted and nodded as if I he knew the task would be beyond my ability.

I pulled myself taller and planted my fists on my hips. "First of all, I don't need *your* help. Secondly, my family's business is no longer your business."

I'd like to say he looked hurt. I'd like to say my words hit him like a slap, but apparently they didn't faze him in the least. Instead he stood there looking *kind*. Asshole.

"I want to help you, Bernie. You and your family are important to me. I can understand if you feel—"

I had no intention of letting him finish whatever line of bullshit he was about to deliver. "Maybe you should have thought about my family before you and your pregnant slut bimbo started your little affair."

Ryan's entire body tensed. "Don't you ever—"

I grabbed his arm and steered him toward the door. "No. Don't you ever come here unannounced again. This is my home, not yours." I pounded my fist against my chest. Heat flowed in my cheeks. I think I actually saw red. "You chose your bed, go lie in it."

Ryan paled momentarily, and I realized my little outburst had taken him by surprise.

He frowned. "Maybe I should stay until you calm down. I've never seen you like this. Are you sure you're not having some sort of breakdown?"

He was the second person to ask me that question this week. Maybe they both knew something I didn't.

I opened the front door and pointed toward the driveway. "If I am, I certainly don't need you around to watch."

I slammed the door the second Ryan cleared the threshold. My trembling started even before the rumble of his car's engine filled the night. At least I'd gotten him out of the house before my newly found bravado crumbled.

I sank onto the steps, shivering with emotions that had battled inside me for weeks.

Then my gaze fell to the wedding band I still wore.

If I'd had any sense at all, I'd have hurled the gold band at Ryan the night he first left. I suppose denial had become such a large part of my life, I'd grown comfortable with the act of doing nothing.

Three wiggles later, I held the ring in my palm.

Once upon a time, the simple gold circle had stood for all of my hopes and dreams—love, a family, Ryan. Now, it stood for nothing.

Till death do us part.

I studied the indentation on my finger. Fourteen years had left one hell of a mark.

Poindexter trotted down the stairs behind me, settled at my side, and measured me with huge, worried eyes.

I jerked a thumb toward the door. "That, my friend, is how you handle confrontation."

Then I wrapped my arms around him, buried my face against his furry neck, and cried.

"Courage is the art of being the only one who knows you're scared to death."
—Earl Wilson

CHAPTER FOUR

— — —

*"HRA BKANHAQH EFQHNYA CVS MNP ENYA FP WFTA FQ
HV LA MVPHFPSNWWC TANKFPB CVS ZFWW ENYA VPA."*
—AWLAKH RSLLNKX

I tossed and turned all night, the events of the past several days playing through my mind like a movie reel on fast-forward.

When the morning light filtered through the blinds, I let out a sigh. I was wondering how in the hell I was going to rebuild the rest of my life when Poindexter body-slammed the bed.

"I'm sleeping," I mumbled, unable to summon the energy necessary to lift my mouth clear of the pillow.

He responded by slamming the bed again and again in an apparent effort to keep our morning routine on schedule.

I tossed back the covers and cringed when my feet hit the cold floor. I shrugged into my favorite sweatshirt—you know the kind—where the cuffs are worn and torn and all signs of elasticity have long since disappeared.

Whether I wanted to admit it or not, the sweatshirt symbolized the person I'd become—well-worn, a bit beat-up, and hanging by a thread.

I operated on autopilot, following the dog down the stairs and through the kitchen to the back door. Poindexter no sooner made it outside than I heard the roar of a jet engine overhead.

"Shit," I muttered, just as the barking began and the phone warbled from behind me. I picked up the receiver but said nothing.

"Mrs. Murphy?" Mrs. Cooke's voice reached across the line.

"I'm sorry." I spoke using my best recorded-voice imitation. "No one is available to take your call at the moment. Please leave a message after the beep."

"I know you're there," Mrs. Cooke said. "Your car's in the drive. You need to get a muzzle for that—"

"Beep!" I drew out the word until I heard the unmistakable clunk of my next-door neighbor hanging up in my ear.

Maybe she wasn't a morning person. But then, who was?

Poindexter stood waiting for me as I eased open the back door. "What part of no barking before eight o'clock in the morning don't you understand?"

He graced me with a happy dog wiggle before he trotted over to the kitchen counter where I kept his treats. He sat, nose tipped toward the counter, left front paw in the air. If nothing else, the dog had a flair for the dramatic, and who was I to say no to that?

I shook two treats out of the box and tossed them into Poindexter's bowl.

Now that I was up before seven and had nowhere to be, a major decision loomed before me. What on earth was I going to do with myself?

I waited for the coffeepot to finish its cycle, filled a mug, and chugged a steaming mouthful before I ran through my options.

I could go for a jog.

I shook my head. Too much, too fast. I needed to pace myself.

I could draw up a goal poster, update my resume, surf the web for charities that needed volunteers. I could sign up to work the food line at the local soup kitchen, offer to read to the blind, take meals to the homebound. Or, I smiled, a flicker of determination lighting inside me, I could purge.

I knew just where to start.

Back upstairs, I stood at the door to the smallest bedroom in our house—the room Ryan had used as a home office.

I'd spent the past few weeks fantasizing about tossing a gas-soaked rag and a match into the space, but the rational part of my brain kept reminding the irrational part that my homemade firebomb would take out all of my belongings as well as those belonging to he-who-sleeps-with-pregnant-slut-bimbos.

Ryan hadn't taken a thing from his office, and I couldn't help but wonder when he would. Once he took his things, my fate would be sealed, but the truth was, my fate had already been sealed. Any emotional connection between us had snapped a long time ago. Ryan was gone.

I was alone. At my age, chances were pretty good I'd stay that way.

Don't get me wrong. I still had moments in which I wished I could reset my life. My dad would be alive. My marriage would be intact, and Ryan and I would find a way to fix what we'd let break. My life would be what it had been before I fell into the chasm of personal chaos.

After all, if *Dallas* could write off a whole season, shouldn't I be able to write off a few weeks?

I slouched against the doorframe and stared at the shelves next to Ryan's desk. Framed certificates. Plaques. High school swimming trophies.

Swimming.

That seemed an appropriately passive-aggressive sport for a guy who'd grown up to cheat on his wife while pretending to rough it on business trips. Not that I had anything against swimmers as a group.

The crack in my heart began to fuse, fueled by the anger suddenly boiling inside me. The morning sun shimmied between the blinds in the office, gleaming off the crystal trophies I'd worked so loyally to keep dust-free. Day after day. Year after year after year.

I sneered at the little men in their little Speedos.

I'd never nicked or scratched or chipped a single one.

Just look at them. Spotless. Perfect. *Extremely* fragile.

I snatched one from the shelf and held it, testing its weight. Poindexter tipped his head from side to side, studying my every move. When I tossed the trophy from one palm to the other and then back again, understanding lit in the dog's eyes. He turned and ran, disappearing beneath the bed in my room.

I tapped the trophy tentatively against one corner of Ryan's mahogany desk.

Nothing.

I banged.

Nothing.

Then I slammed the perfect replica of the cheating male species against the desk with all my might.

The crystal remained intact. The desk...not so much.

A whisper of disappointment slid through me. I peered at the dent in the desk and frowned. While damaging Ryan's desk gave me a small measure of satisfaction, I wasn't sure whether he or I would get the piece ultimately, so I decided to pursue Plan B.

I cradled the trophy in the crook of my arm then piled the additional trophies on top. Two. Three. Five. Seven.

Perfect.

I hurried out of the office and into the hall. Poindexter stuck his head out from beneath the bed, took one look at me, and ducked back out of sight.

I made it down the steps, to the back door, and out onto the patio in record time. A pair of squirrels paused midfrolic, watching as I lined the trophies along the back wall of the house. I hoisted the first above my head, and the squirrels dashed for the fence, scaling the vinyl and disappearing over the top.

Everything around me grew still, as if my impending rampage had lowered the cone of silence. No birds chirped. No tires squealed. No horns honked. No planes soared overhead.

When I released the crystal statue, I heard nothing but the satisfying crash of Ryan's cherished prize shattering against the concrete.

Then my conscience kicked in. Loudly.

I'd looked away to protect my face from flying glass, but as I turned back, the glistening shards provided none of the gratification I'd expected.

Shame and guilt tangled in my gut.

Was trashing Ryan's trophies that much higher on the maturity scale than burning his office? And what had the trophies ever done to me? None of *these* little swimmers had impregnated the future Mrs. Murphy.

"Is everything all right?"

I winced as Sophie Cooke's voice sang over the hedge that divided our properties. Did the woman miss nothing?

Was everything all right? I stared again at the countless splinters strewn before me, the perfect symbol for just about every facet of my life.

"I'm fine, Mrs. Cooke." *Liar.* "Just dropped a glass."

Ten minutes later, I'd swept up every last trace of my transgression. But instead of carrying the surviving trophies back up to Ryan's old office, I set them on the kitchen table. Then I tracked down a sturdy box and a roll of bubble wrap in the garage.

Carefully, meticulously, I wrapped each swimmer as if somehow I could make up for smashing their counterpart into smithereens.

When I finished, I placed the sealed box next to the front door. After a few minutes of sitting on the steps staring at the taped-up cardboard, I knew I'd made a mistake.

The box looked pathetic waiting for Ryan to come back.

Poindexter settled on the step behind me and rested his chin on my shoulder.

"What do you think, buddy?"

He nudged my cheek with his cold nose, and I nodded in agreement.

"You're right."

I crossed the foyer, hoisted the box into my arms, and carried my cargo to the garage.

I cleaned off a shelf and placed the box in its new home. I scrounged around for more empty boxes and totes before I headed back inside.

I worked the rest of the morning, packing, padding, purging.

Poindexter studied my every move as I cleared and cleaned each surface in Ryan's office.

Once the boxes sat stacked in the garage, I returned to the office, now empty. The paint had faded, leaving marks where Ryan's diplomas had hung.

I couldn't sort out whether melancholy or satisfaction welled inside me. In the end, I decided it was loss—not hope—that consumed me still.

I didn't know what the future held for the office any more than I knew what the future held for me. I smoothed my hand across the empty desk, then left and shut the door behind me.

Maybe closing the door would make my new life a bit easier to find. If nothing else, there would be one less reminder of the life my husband had left behind.

By Friday afternoon I knew I had to do something to fill my time or I really would have a breakdown. I'd be damned if I'd let that happen. After all, I had zero intention of proving either Ryan or Blaine McMann right.

I scanned the online job listings and found nothing matching my skills, so I headed for the only business where I knew the owners—Diane and David's ice-skating rink. Diane's car wasn't out front when I pulled into the lot, but I found David in the office.

"She's not here"—he shook his head—"said she didn't feel well." He twisted up his mouth as if her pregnancy symptoms were harder on him than on her.

"Well, it can't be easy, David. She's forty-one years old. Maybe you could be a little more sympathetic."

He scowled. I hated it when David scowled. He'd been scowling at me ever since I'd convinced Diane that a few shots of rum the night before senior finals would help her study.

"You think it's easy on me?" He patted his chest. "I need her here."

I narrowed my gaze on him. He couldn't be this selfish. Could he? Didn't he realize how lucky he was to be expecting another child?

"Do you know what I would…"

I caught myself before I said it. *Do you know what I would give to be pregnant?*

I'd put on a pretty good front when it came to Diane and David's pregnancy. I wasn't about to blow the illusion now—especially not in front of David.

I tried again. "…what I would do?" I gestured grandly toward the rink, empty now that the local hockey league practice had ended. "I'd get some temporary help."

He scowled again. This was really growing old.

"You think it's easy to find the right person just like that?" He snapped his fingers. "Plus, that would mean another salary."

I tapped my chest, knowing I had a solution that could help us both. "I could do it…for *free*." I was desperate for direction in my life and, if nothing else, helping at the rink would achieve my first two life goals. Keep busy. Get out of the house.

As far as life goals went, mine might not be up there with say, saving the world, but they were a start.

David's expression tightened. I hadn't thought it possible. "What the hell are you talking about?"

I cleared my throat, pulled myself up taller, and bolstered my resolve. "I'm taking a sabbatical from work. I could help you out in the afternoons."

One brow lifted. "I heard you got fired."

David had always believed the worst of me. I shook my head and decided to rise above the temptation to argue semantics. "I quit."

"Shouldn't make big decisions right after a major life change… or two."

This time I was the one sporting the scowl. "Where'd you learn that? Daytime television?"

"I know things, smart-ass."

"You don't say?" I rubbed my chin as if I were impressed by David's enlightenment.

He smirked. "You're serious about helping?"

I nodded.

"When can you start?"

"Right now."

"Great. Ashley needs a ride to some bead party thing."

We were barely out of the ice rink parking lot when Ashley let loose a sigh that rattled the car windows.

"Did they tell you they want to sing at my school family night? *Sing.*"

I winced. On the grand scale of parental embarrassment, that had to rank right at the top.

"I'll die, Aunt Bernie. Die." She gasped. "Sorry."

"No problem, honey. In this case, it's a well-deserved use of that particular figure of speech." I chose my words carefully. "Other parents must be performing, right?"

Ashley shook her head. "I don't care. You've got to stop them." She gestured wildly. "If they sing in front of the whole school, I'll…I'll…"

She turned to me dramatically, leaned across the console, and spoke slowly and clearly. "I'll never be able to go back there again. I'll have to change my identity or something."

I worked to keep my expression as controlled as my response. "Ashley, it can't be that bad."

"Have you ever heard them sing?"

Sadly, *yes*. "Not since college. They used to sing this old Sonny and Cher song." I laughed. "Lord, they were awful."

Ashley blew out another sigh and slumped against the passenger door.

I blinked. "They're not singing *that*, are they?"

She nodded. "In costume."

Okay, so the kid had reason to panic, and suddenly, I couldn't help torturing her just a bit more.

"Hey, if you want real talent, your mom and I could do our 'Super Freak' dance routine."

The heat of the kid's glare singed my cheek. "You're not helping."

I bit back my grin. "I'll talk to them."

"Thank you."

The instant relief in her voice made me smile. "So, tell me about this party."

Ten minutes later I'd gotten a blow-by-blow description of every girl attending the birthday party. Apparently, this was Ashley's first invitation into an "in-crowd" gathering, and she was scared to death.

"What if I blow it?"

I patted her back as we walked toward the entrance to the shop. "You won't blow it. Relax."

As soon as we pushed through the door, the sound of teenage giggles and squeals carried from somewhere out of sight.

"Are you here for the party?" A young woman looked up from a table where she worked, beads and tools strewn in front of her.

Ashley nodded.

"In the back." The woman smiled. "Have fun."

Ashley's expression suddenly lost her usual I-can-do-anything confidence. "Don't leave, Aunt Bernie."

"You're going to have a great time. Stop worrying."

She swallowed. "But, I don't really know these girls. What if they don't like me?"

I gave her shoulder a squeeze. "How could they not like you?"

She frowned.

"I'll stay," I said.

"You're welcome to try beading a bracelet or necklace." The young woman sitting at the table barely looked up before her dark gaze dropped back to her handiwork, her focus intent. She tucked her long, smooth mahogany hair behind her ears and a pang of hair envy flickered through me.

I watched for a moment as she wove a fine silver wire into an intricate design. As much as I'd like to fantasize about my ability to do something similar, I had no problem admitting my shortcomings.

"I don't have a creative bone in my body."

Then I thought of the cryptograms from Dad. How was I going to reinvent myself if I was afraid to bead jewelry?

"It's easy." Ashley gave my elbow a shove. "That way you'll be right here in case we need to bolt."

"We're going to work on that confidence," I called after her as she sauntered away. She didn't turn back, already deep into her I'm-too-cool-to-acknowledge-you cover.

"Come on," the young woman coaxed. "I'll set you up for a bracelet."

She placed a tray in front of me then clipped a length of some sort of flexible wire from a spool and handed it to me. I held it as if it might explode. "I meant what I said. I've never done a creative thing in my life."

"Here." The woman held up a matching wire, threaded on a clasp, then wove one end in and out of some sort of silver bead.

"This is the crimp bead. You tighten your wire like so"—she pulled the wire taut, holding it in one hand while she reached for a small tool with the other—"then you use these to squeeze the bead." She looked up and gave me a dazzling smile. "Like that."

After five mangled attempts I managed to crimp the bead. The result wasn't pretty, but the wire held long enough for me to bead the ugliest bracelet ever known to mankind.

In the end, I decided to check jewelry designer off of my list of possible future careers, yet I still managed to spend far too much money on far too many supplies that would, in all likelihood, never witness life outside of a kitchen drawer.

Maybe I'd been caught up in the warmth of Ashley's thank-you hug at the end of the party, lost in the moment she wrapped her arms around me and smiled.

I stared at my purchases later that night before I slid the kitchen drawer closed. Chances were good I'd forget about the beads completely. After all, my brain wasn't operating at peak efficiency these days.

But who was I to argue with the possibility I might someday make something beautiful.

"The greatest mistake you can make in life is to be continually fearing you will make one."
—Elbert Hubbard

CHAPTER FIVE

— — —

*"ZRUM KCEIMJ TJ ICM IWKWJJUGTXL MRW JTDW CO MRW
VCH TI MRW OTHRM, TM'J MRW JTRW CO MRW OTHRM
TI MRW VCH."*
—VZTHRM V. WTJWIRCZWG

I was halfway to the ice-skating rink on Monday afternoon when
Diane called my cell phone.

"Whatcha doin'?" Her voice chirped across the line.

"You sound like Mary Poppins on speed." I groaned inwardly.
This was just what my day did not need—a perky pregnant
woman.

"It's the hormones," she answered. "Up and down like you
can't imagine."

Silence beat across the line.

"Sorry." All traces of perk left her tone.

"Knock it off," I answered as I took a left on Maple.

"I wasn't thinking."

"Stop it." Frustration welled inside me. "The statute of lim-
itations is up on avoiding all pregnancy talk. You're allowed to
wallow in glee." I squeezed my eyes shut at a red light, hoping I
sounded sincere. "I want you to wallow."

"Waddle?"

"Wallow…in glee."

A noise came across the line that sounded suspiciously like a sniffle.

"Are you crying?"

"No."

But she couldn't fool me. I'd known her for thirty-five years. I could pick up on a sniffle no matter how much space stretched between us. "What's the matter?"

"I don't deserve you."

The light turned green and I pressed down on the accelerator—gently—even though I felt like leaving a trail of burnt rubber in my wake.

"Trust me." I swallowed down a sigh. "No one deserves me."

More silence.

"Where are you?" I finally asked.

"The mall."

"I thought you were having a rough time with morning sickness. Isn't that why you haven't been at the rink?"

"Oh, that." Diane chuckled. "David bought that one hook, line, and sinker."

I narrowed my gaze, working to focus on the traffic. "So what *have* you been doing with yourself?"

"*Shopping.*" She breathed the word as if she'd never shopped before.

"For?"

"Purses." Her voice whispered across the line like a seductress working her target.

"Purses?" My voice, however, hid not a stitch of my disbelief. "You're shopping for purses?"

"Isn't it great?" Her voice jumped so high her last word squeaked. "Each time I make a new find, I'm overcome by the most amazing joy."

"Great." But even as I tried to muster up some measure of disapproval for Diane's little ploy, I couldn't. If she wanted to shop for purses, she should shop for purses. "You know, normal pregnant women crave pickles."

"Well, I never claimed to be normal."

"No kidding."

"Want anything while I'm here?" Her teary moment passed and shades of Mary Poppins returned.

"A new life," I answered before the filter on my mouth could stop me.

"Tell David you're sick and come meet me. I know exactly what you need."

Visions of the Rediscover You fiasco flashed through my mind. "I'd hate to leave him hanging at the last minute," I fibbed.

In a choice between the rink with David and the mall with Diane…well…I couldn't believe what I was thinking, but I'd choose David.

"All right," Diane answered, "but don't tell him you spoke to me."

"Mum's the word."

"Literally." Her shrill laughter sounded in my ear as she disconnected the call.

Heaven, help me. I wasn't sure I could survive seven more months of Diane's hormones, but after everything she'd put up with from me over the years, I intended to try.

A few minutes later, I studied David's latest scowl.

"She's not answering her phone." He shook his head, his annoyance palpable as he scrubbed down the snack bar counter.

I had never been a good liar, and covering for Diane fell soundly into that category. After all, I knew exactly where she was. I'd become an accessory after the crime...during the crime... whatever.

"Maybe she's napping." I gave a quick shrug, hoping my feigned ignorance would cover for the fact his wife had gone to the mall to satiate a sudden craving for purses. "Probably turned the ringer off," I added. "I'm sure she's fine."

"I'm not worried about that." He scowled. "I just want to know who's going to run the Zamboni tonight."

I blinked. He'd honestly planned to have a hormonal, pregnant, middle-aged woman operate heavy equipment. I should have known he was only concerned about how Diane's absence might inconvenience him.

"Aren't you the least bit concerned about the health of your wife and your unborn child?" I asked.

His scowl deepened. Then he stopped midswipe and lifted his gaze. "You'll have to do it."

Was he kidding me? "Are you kidding me?" I shook my head. "No way."

"It's either that or flip burgers, and I've tasted your cooking."

Now it was my turn to scowl, and I couldn't help but notice the tiniest hint of amusement at the corner of David's mouth.

"Funny." I faked a laugh.

He shook his head and returned to his work. "There's nothing funny about your cooking."

I leaned against the counter. Surely David didn't think our conversation complete. "Seriously. There's nobody else here who knows how to drive the Zamboni?"

"Diane, me, and Ashley."

"Ashley." I said her name a bit too enthusiastically and did my best to rein in my relief. "Ashley knows how to run"—I shot a glance toward the motorized monster in question—"that?"

"Any moron could run it." David's impatience had begun to show. He'd turned his back on me, probably hoping I'd develop a sudden fascination with operating massive, potentially life-threatening equipment and leave him in peace to scrub counters and flip burgers.

"Gee, thanks."

"You always say I don't have any faith in you." He shrugged, still keeping his back to me. "I have faith in you."

Faith or no faith, I had no plans to drive a machine that could squash me like a bug.

Just then Ashley breezed through the door, illuminated by the outside light as if she'd merged with the brilliant rays of the sun. When the door slammed shut behind her, she stood for a moment, blinking.

"Couldn't you turn up the lights in here?" I directed the question to David's back.

"Now what? Your Internet degree in ice rink management come through?"

"Funny, again."

I waited for Ashley to make her way to the snack bar before I hit her with the question of the day. "I hear you know how to drive the Zamboni?"

She shrugged, the move a perfect carbon copy of her father's. "Any moron could run it," she mumbled.

I shuddered. "Gee, I wonder where you picked up that pearl."

Ashley tucked her hair behind her ears and dropped her gaze to the concrete floor. When she offered no typically indignant teenage rebuttal, my Aunt Bernie radar chimed deep inside my brain.

"Something happen at school?"

She shook her head, still looking down.

I closed the gap between us and hooked my fingers beneath her chin. She looked up at me, her young eyes far more serious than they should be.

"Spill it."

"I got invited to a party this Friday night."

I frowned, doing my best not to give away the confusion I felt. "Isn't that a good thing?"

Ashley rolled her eyes. "A boy-girl party."

I made a face. "Isn't that even better?"

"Dad won't let me go."

"Why?" I gave a quick lift and drop of my shoulders. "It's not like you're having sex."

Ashley's eyes popped wide, à la Bambi in the headlights. Fear gripped my insides.

"Are you?" I asked.

Her features twisted as if she'd sucked on a lemon—a really big lemon. "Gross."

I relaxed a smidge and dropped my hand from her chin. "Then what's the problem?"

"I need Mom to soften him up. Convince him I'm old enough to go."

"So ask her to help."

"She doesn't have time for me anymore." Ashley drew in a ragged breath and shifted her focus once more to the floor. My heart ached just looking at her defeated posture.

"Now you're talking crazy." I gave a little laugh to try to lighten the mood. "Your mom lives for you."

"Have you talked to her lately?" Ashley shot me an incredulous glare. "She lives for the baby and purses. Period."

I bit my tongue. The child had a point.

I held my breath and tried to think this one through as fast as I could. If I called Diane to give her a heads up on the situation, I'd be forever branded as a spy in Ashley's book. If I helped Ashley without saying a thing to my dearest friend, I might be forever branded as a traitor.

But chances were pretty good Diane would understand, and just in case she didn't, I could always stop by the mall and pick up a faux-croc tote on my way home.

"I could talk to your dad."

Ashley's head snapped up.

"And drive you to the party," I continued.

"Really?"

I gave her shoulder a squeeze. "And maybe we could go by my house first and you could borrow something from my closet. That would be cool."

Ashley's nose crinkled.

"I'm not that out of touch, Ash."

"Aunt Bernie." Her nose crinkle turned into a full-out scrunch.

"Okay, but I am killer when it comes to spiral curls."

I caught her staring at my natural frizz, and I self-consciously smoothed a hand over the mess I reluctantly called my hair. "On other people. Killer curls on other people."

Her facial scrunch morphed into the warmest smile I'd seen on her face since Santa brought her Tickle Me Elmo for her fourth Christmas.

She leaned forward and kissed me on the cheek. "Thanks, Aunt Bernie."

I did my best to project nonchalant coolness as she sashayed away, when I really wanted to jump up and down. For the first time in days I'd actually said something right. At least, I think I'd said something right.

As I stood there watching Ashley effortlessly operate the Zamboni, I realized she might be a whole lot younger than I was, but we weren't all that different.

I may have been caught in the transition between married and single, and between having a dad and surviving a dad, but Ashley was caught in a transition of her own. The transition between childhood and womanhood.

And while I may not have known a thing about how to drive a Zamboni, flip a decent burger, or survive *my* life transition, I knew how to help Ashley through hers.

The thought of lending Ashley the benefit of my experience gave me the same glimmer of purpose I'd felt when she'd hugged me at the bead shop.

I, Bernadette Murphy, had finally found someone to whom I could make a difference.

I looked at Ashley and waved.

After all, how difficult could it be?

Later that night, I sat up in bed, staring at the walls. Sleep eluded me.

Poindexter, however, yipped and growled in his sleep as he sprawled across his dog bed, no doubt giving some obedience school trainer a piece of his mind.

I slid out of bed and grabbed Dad's book from my bureau. I climbed back into bed, plumped my pillows, and flipped the pages open to the next puzzle.

What felt like hours later, I stretched and studied the cryptogram's message, proud I'd managed the solution but a bit sad my father had felt the need to gather these messages for me.

Had I become so pathetic he thought motivational quotes were the only way to save me?

I read the message again and realized Dad was trying to tell me he didn't think me pathetic at all.

I smiled.

Then I shut the book, closed my eyes, and fell asleep.

"What counts is not necessarily the size of the dog in the fight, it's the size of the fight in the dog."
—Dwight D. Eisenhower

CHAPTER SIX

— — —

*"JG ZVA UVX'F WXVK KIDMD ZVA'MD CVJXC, ZVA NPZ
NJHH JF KIDX ZVA CDF FIDMD."*
—AXWXVKX

On Halloween, David told me to skip coming over to the rink.
There weren't too many kids who'd choose ice-skating over trick-
or-treating.

I prepared for the onslaught of costumed kids the only way I
knew how—by buying six bags of candy when experience told me
I only needed five. If everything went according to plan, I'd keep
my chocolate consumption to two thousand calories or less, yet
still be on a satisfying sugar high by the end of the night.

As daylight turned to dusk, however, I was partway through
my second bag and the laws of supply and demand indicated the
kiddies might be in for a disappointment.

The crowds were heavier than in years past, and the little
ghosts and goblins and vamps seemed to have three hands each.
I'd never seen such efficient grabbing. Every mother had perfected
her delivery of the phrase "Just one, honey" using a high-pitched,
singsong voice, but not a one fooled me. The way I saw it, each kid

had been coached to grab whatever he or she could get to ensure an ample supply for Mom and Dad at the end of the night.

After all, that's the way I'd handle it.

Halloween never failed to be a rough night for me. I did my best not to imagine what Emma might be wearing, but it was impossible not to.

I had never thought she'd go the traditional princess route. I imagined her rather as a throwback to the classics. Maybe a cowgirl, complete with lasso.

Her dark hair would be bobbed adorably short, smooth waves curling up beneath the rim of her pink cowboy hat. Poindexter would play the part of her loyal pony. He, of course, would wear a cowboy hat of his own, complaining not in the least.

I embraced the mental picture as a pair of little girls waved happily to me and took off with half of my remaining stash. When a car pulled into my driveway, I frowned.

The car wasn't one I recognized, and I hadn't ordered a delivery of any sort. Surely trick-or-treating by automobile was outside the parameters of acceptable behavior.

The driver's door opened and a lanky man unfolded himself from his seat, leaving the lights on and the car running as he approached the front door.

"Can I help you?" I asked, still clutching what was left of my basket of miniature candies.

"Bernadette Murphy?" He stopped just short of where I stood, studying me.

I nodded. "That's me."

He held out a folded document, and I took it in my free hand, still frowning.

"Consider yourself served."

The stranger pivoted on one heel and made it back to his car and out of my drive before the reality of what had just happened registered.

I'd been served. And I had a pretty good idea of with what.

I dropped to the front step and set the basket on the walkway. The motion set off the skeleton I'd hung from the shepherd's crook I'd never gotten around to hanging flowers on over the summer.

When you go out in the woods tonight…

I sucked in the deepest breath I could manage and unfolded the document.

…you're in for a big surprise.

Ryan Murphy vs. Bernadette Murphy.

My head bobbed as if it were suddenly too heavy for my neck.

"Trick or treat."

I looked up from the papers. A three-foot-tall fireman stood before me, but I found it impossible to coax my mouth into forming words. I picked up the basket and handed it to him, pushing myself to my feet.

He stared at me, wide-eyed beneath his fireman's hat.

"Take it." I managed to whisper, afraid that if I tried to do or say anything more, the anger and shock I fought to control might explode, and I didn't want to scar the poor kid for life.

He stood, frozen to the spot, clutching the basket as I launched my numb body toward my front door. The last thing I heard as I pushed the door shut behind me was his mother's voice. "Just one, honey."

I flicked off the light, threw on the deadbolt, and sank to my knees in the middle of the foyer.

Divorce papers. On Halloween.

How could he?

I wasn't sure how long I'd been in that position when the phone rang, but it took a few rings before I could make my knees cooperate with my brain's desire to stand up.

When Ryan said hello, I realized I'd been sucked into one of those Halloween thrillers where the villain never dies. The kind where you think the bad guy has inflicted all the damage he possibly can, only to find he's reared his ugly head one more time.

"Bernie?" Ryan's voice filtered across the line as if this were a day like any other, and not the day he'd chosen to have me served with the papers signaling the end of our marriage.

"Don't you Bernie me." I growled the words, startling myself with the intensity of my tone.

"Oh." Ryan grew silent for several long seconds. "I wanted to give you a heads-up."

I laughed—a tiny, bitter burst of breath. "Perfect timing, as usual."

"I'm sorry."

I shook my head, even though I knew he couldn't see me, blinking back tears as I struggled to find the words I wanted to say to him.

"I don't think you're sorry at all. I think you're probably ready to dance with joy."

"Bernie—"

"No," I interrupted him. "You don't get to talk. Not now. Not ever. Just leave me alone."

"I wanted to make sure you're all right."

Disbelief welled inside me and I pressed my lips together, hoping the move would somehow stem the sound of my anguish before I spoke. "You should have thought of that before you cheated on me."

Silence stretched between us, and I was just about to hang up when he delivered his parting shot. "I know this is a tough week for both of us. I'll be thinking about you."

A tough week.

Emma's birthday.

"I hate you." I hung up the phone and stared at it for a long time, suddenly unable to cry. Too stunned to react in any way, shape, or form.

I hate you.

I did hate him. I hated him for cheating instead of telling me he was unhappy. I hated him for not giving me a chance, for not giving us a chance. I hated him for falling in love with someone else. I hated him for being able to have a child without me.

I hated him for leaving me behind.

I thought of Emma and wondered how different our lives might have been if she'd survived.

That's when my heart broke.

Again.

After Ryan's call, I had every intention of eating the leftover Halloween candy. Then I remembered I'd given the entire basket to the tiny fireman. I cracked open my front door to see if he'd left anything behind, but there was no trace of the basket or the chocolate.

I imagined his mommy at home, crafting the perfect autumn centerpiece out of my attempt at fashionable candy distribution while she ate my chocolate.

I walked to the calendar I kept in the kitchen and flipped it open. There it was.

November third.

Emma would have been five.

Damn.

Every year, the date sneaked up on me like a car that blind-sided me just when I thought the coast was clear. Last year, I swore it wouldn't happen again. I swore I'd be ready.

I must have forgotten to check the side-view mirror.

In the five years since Emma was born, some of the details had faded. I always thought every moment of every day of her life would stay forever embedded in my mind, but they hadn't. I wasn't sure if that made me a horrible person or an even more horrible mother. Yet, some things were still as vivid as if they'd just happened.

Our next-door neighbor and I had been pregnant at the same time. She delivered a healthy baby girl a few days after we buried Emma.

I could still picture the ten-foot stork anchored into the line between our properties.

I didn't begrudge our neighbors their happiness, but I couldn't help but think fate had a pretty dark sense of humor.

On the day I decided to drag Emma's crib out to the garage, our neighbors brought their daughter home from the hospital. The crib didn't fit through the interior door, so I wrestled it outside to use the overhead garage door instead.

I was halfway down the sidewalk when four cars pulled up bearing family, friends, and gifts for the new bundle of joy next door.

The memory swirled through my brain, churning the Halloween chocolate in my stomach. I barely reached the bathroom in time to be sick. Then I sat back, rested my forehead against my knees, and held on tight.

I was into my forty-eighth hour of wallowing when the phone rang. I let the machine pick up and pulled one of my pillows over my head, expecting to hear another of Diane's pep talks. When I heard Ashley's voice instead, I sat straight up in bed. Poindexter lifted his head, staring at me as if I were some alien creature—a human who actually moved.

I plucked the phone from the nightstand, interrupting the message Ashley had been leaving. "I'm here, what's up?"

"Dad said I can go." There was a lightness and brightness to her tone I hadn't heard since Diane had announced her pregnancy. I smiled with relief.

"To what?" I climbed out of bed and stretched, not wanting to throw my body into sudden shock by actually trying to walk.

A loud, annoyed sigh blasted across the line. "The party." Ashley drew out the word's last syllable as if she were a kid going over the top of a roller coaster.

The party.

I blinked. How could I have forgotten? What had happened to my resolve to channel my energies into helping Ashley?

"I remember." I crossed my fingers, convincing myself it wasn't a total lie if my fingers were crossed—a definite throwback to my own teenage years. "What time should I pick you up?"

"An hour?" Her inflection went up, turning her statement into a question.

I walked toward my mirror as we spoke, holding the cordless to one ear as I stared open-mouthed at my reflection. I'd always known my hair had a life of its own, but this was ridiculous. Long, wiry sections zigged and zagged away from my face at angles a geometry professor would be proud of.

My face was worse. Sheet marks so deeply lined my left cheek, not even a series of Botox injections could save me now.

I leaned close to the mirror, scrutinizing my eyes—my red-rimmed, sleep-encrusted, swollen-beyond-recognition eyes.

"An hour sounds good," I answered. "I was just working out, so I'll grab a quick shower and come get you."

There was a pause from Ashley's end of the phone, and I imagined her making that squished-feature face she made when she doubted every word from some adult's mouth. "You sound like you were asleep."

"It's the endorphins," I countered. "Very relaxing."

Another pause. "They make you hyper, Aunt Bernie, not sleepy."

I rolled my eyes. Didn't they have better things to teach kids in school these days? "Are you going to keep yapping, or are you going to let me get out of my sweats and get ready to come get you?"

I fingered the hem of my rattiest sweatshirt. At least that wasn't a total lie.

"Can you pick me up at the mall? Food court entrance? Then we can go straight to the party."

A twinge of something I couldn't quite put my finger on eased through me. Suspicion? Disappointment? Fear of the mall security guard?

"No spiral curls?" I asked.

"That's asking too much of you," Ashley answered sweetly. Too sweetly. "Just a ride would be great."

"And your parents are okay with this?"

"Who do you think dropped me at the mall?"

I blew out a resigned breath. "Okay, see you in an hour. Just don't make me come in to look for you, deal?"

"Deal."

I headed for the shower determined to rediscover the sense of purpose I'd felt just days earlier.

"If you don't know where you're going, you may miss it when you get there."
—Unknown

CHAPTER SEVEN

— —— —

"ICRP MWKV VC PAQWEK, MCA YM PAQWEK PYQ, RYMQ YK RYXQ W NACXQS-UYSDQR NYAP VIWV TWSSCV MRZ."
—RWSDKVCS IJDIQK

Precisely an hour later, I sat in my car, parked along the curb outside the food court entrance. Ashley was nowhere in sight.

I waited impatiently for what had to be two or three minutes, drumming my fingers on the steering wheel, then I turned on the car's emergency blinkers and pushed myself out of the car.

Fortunately, I'd pulled on one of my better sweatshirts after my shower, this one sporting a roomy, identity-disguising hood. I snapped the soft fleece up over my head and slipped on my sunglasses, imagining other mall shoppers might mistake me for a glamorous movie star and not some crazed beauty kiosk attacker who'd been banned from the mall for life.

I stood at the entrance to the food court and realized two things. One, every young girl sitting around gabbing with her friends and sipping soda looked exactly like Ashley. Two, I hadn't eaten in forty-eight hours.

Suddenly famished, I scanned the menu signs above the sea of food counters, looking for that perfect something to fill the empty pit in my stomach.

Salads, no.

Smoothies, no.

I wanted nothing good for me. Not now. Probably not ever.

My gaze landed on the Taco Bar and I made my move, walking confidently toward the line of people waiting to order. I forced myself to look straight ahead and not nervously over each shoulder as if the mall security guard posse might move in at any second.

As I took my place in line, I studied the menu carefully. This wasn't a selection to be made lightly. After all, this was the first meal of post-divorce-papers life. And then I saw it.

The super-size taco deluxe.

My stomach growled so loudly the woman in front of me grabbed her child's hand and stepped between us, like a mother bear protecting her cub from the hungry wolf.

I rolled my eyes.

Several minutes later, I'd just taken my first bite of perfectly seasoned meat, lettuce, tomato, and soft taco when I heard footsteps snap to a stop at close range. Unless Ashley had taken to wearing combat boots, this might spell trouble.

"You." A voice boomed behind my left ear.

I spun around, almost spitting out my food when the recognition set in. The security guard who'd apprehended me at the Rediscover You counter glared at me, obviously none too pleased.

I shifted the food into my cheeks and stammered incoherently. "This isn't what you think."

He frowned, obviously unable to understand a word I'd said. My mother had always warned me about stuffing my mouth so full of food I couldn't talk.

The guard hoisted his walkie-talkie to his lips. "I need backup at the Taco Bar."

Ashley appeared in my line of sight and broke into a jog, no doubt realizing the sight of her aunt faced off with a security guard could only mean one thing. Embarrassment. She skittered to a stop beside me.

"I'm just picking her up. Honest." I swallowed my food, tossed out the rest of the taco, put my hand on Ashley's back and pushed. "We're leaving now. No need to call in the guards. Minor misunderstanding. I didn't realize *banned* included the food court. Scout's honor. Have a nice day."

Ashley giggled and I picked up the pace, forcing her to trot along beside me.

"You look like one of those smash-and-grab guys they show on the news."

So much for my illusions of celebrity chic.

"You keep it up and I'll have them ban you too," I whispered.

Nothing struck fear into a teenager's heart faster than the threat of being banned from the mall. She didn't so much as make a peep until we were in the car, and even then her only words were those necessary to guide me to the party. She didn't even roll her eyes or sigh when I imparted what I was certain were invaluable boy-girl party tips.

Ashley assured me she'd made arrangements for David to pick her up at the end of the night, so I headed home, content I'd done my good deed for the week. I felt useful, when useful was something I hadn't felt in a long time.

My only regret was tossing out the taco in my security-guard-confrontation panic. Live and learn.

When the phone rang at two o'clock in the morning, I was happily watching an old Hepburn and Tracy movie and eating a cold slice of pizza left over from the pie I'd ordered earlier.

The pizza did a slow roll in my stomach as I reached for the phone. History showed phone calls in the middle of the night rarely brought good news. This one was no different.

When I answered, Diane shrieked so loudly I had to hold the phone away from my head to keep my eardrum from exploding.

The hysteria level in her voice was higher than I'd ever heard it, and when you've known someone since first grade, that's saying something.

"What's wrong?" Fear now tapped a rapid beat in my chest.

"What's *wrong*?" she repeated, her voice climbing even higher still. "You drive *my* daughter to a boy-girl party without permission and you ask *me* what's wrong."

Without permission.

I'd kill the kid.

Then the fear hit me. "Is she all right?"

"Yes," Diane snapped. "No thanks to you."

"She told me you and David said it was fine. I mean, where did you think she was going when you dropped her at the mall?"

"We didn't drop her at the mall." Ice dripped from Diane's words. "Apparently she walked. All part of her little master plan— which you fell for."

I rubbed a hand across my eyes and wished my glass of water could morph into something stronger—like grain alcohol. "I'm sorry. I never thought she wasn't telling the truth."

"You never thought." Diane's exasperated exhale registered loud and clear in my brain.

I knew exactly what was coming next.

"Maybe you'd have *thought* differently if you actually had children, Bernie. You think you know it all, but you don't know anything. You don't know what it's like to be a mother and wonder where in the hell your daughter is when she doesn't come home."

I drew in a deep breath, working to keep my anger and hurt at bay. There were so many things I wanted to say, yet I said nothing.

I wanted to tell her I might not know what it was like to have my child miss curfew, but I knew what it was like to hold my daughter as she took her last breath. I wanted to tell her I knew what it was like to bury my child in a casket that looked like a damned Styrofoam cooler.

I wanted to tell her a million things, but I didn't. I let her rant and rave, but I tuned her out. I didn't have it in me to listen.

Of all the things Diane could say, this was the worst, and she knew it.

Maybe once she calmed down I'd tell her she'd hurt me. Then again, maybe I wouldn't. Maybe once she calmed down I'd tell her she needed to start balancing out the scales in terms of how much attention she paid to her kids. At this rate, she'd be asking "Ashley who?" by the time the new arrival cut his or her first tooth.

If she thought lying about a boy-girl party and staying out half the night was the worst a thirteen-year-old could do, she'd better think back to our own teen years. Hell, I often wondered how we'd survived at all.

When Diane paused to take a breath, I repeated my apology then pushed the disconnect button. I picked up the slice of pizza I'd been eating, but suddenly the smell only made me queasy.

I turned the volume back up on Hepburn and Tracy, but even they no longer provided a warm, fuzzy escape. Instead, their banter represented everything smart, together, witty, and wonderful that I wasn't—and I didn't need the reminder.

Diane was right.

I should have known better. Hell, I couldn't even drive a kid to a party without knowing enough to check with her parents first.

What was wrong with me?

I clicked off the television and went upstairs, slipping Dad's book out of my underwear drawer. I cracked open my closet and pulled out Dad's shirt, savoring an instant sense of warmth and security as I pushed my arms through the sleeves.

Then I settled beneath the covers, determined to achieve the one thing I knew I could do.

I could solve the next puzzle.

I worked with a determination I hadn't felt for a long while. It was almost as if I'd taken Diane's harsh words as a challenge—a challenge to prove I was good at something…this thing.

I methodically decoded the puzzle then studied the cryptogram's solution and frowned.

Tears stung at the back of my eyelids and I drew in a slow breath. My throat had constricted to the point of choking me.

Once upon a time, I'd had big dreams—dreams of life and love and family and hope. Dreams of becoming something special. Now I had no idea what any of that meant.

When had my dreams become unimportant to me? After all, I hadn't missed them. It was easier simply to be, easier to let life happen than it was to work for something I might have once wanted.

I stared at Dad's printing and felt a sense of loss beyond the physical.

When I was growing up, Dad never failed to find me when I was scared or upset.

Here he was, finding me now, even though he was gone.

While I might not understand everything he thought or the quotes he'd chosen, I understood one thing. He loved me enough to reach out. He'd seen in me a light still flickering in the darkness, a potential not yet extinguished.

If only life were as simple as solving a cryptogram. Then I realized the two were not that different.

Only if I quit, would I fail.

I'd quit after Emma died. I'd shut down. I'd let life go on all around me.

Now that Ryan was gone and Dad was dead, I could quit again. Or, I could dust off my dreams and try.

Success might take a while. Success might take forever.

But as long as I refused to quit, I just might succeed.

"Hold fast to dreams, for if dreams die, life is like a broken-winged bird that cannot fly."

—Langston Hughes

CHAPTER EIGHT

— — —

"MUMDORCM SPR WRV SPMDM PM FT PIY VR ZMWFC SPMDM PM SIT."
—DFNPIDY J. MUICT

When I woke up the next morning, I knew exactly where to start.

The days of neglect and inactivity and less-than-ideal food choices had taken their toll. I felt like a blob.

I was due at Mom's that afternoon, so I sketched out an exercise and eating schedule, deciding there was no time like now to put my plan into action. The inches weren't about to melt away, but with any luck at all, I'd be able to fit into something other than my stretchy sweatpants in time for the holidays.

I stepped into the bathroom, intending to weigh myself, but one look at my full-faced reflection in the mirror told me everything I needed to know. Seeing the numbers on the scale wouldn't do anything but send me running for the Walgreens candy aisle.

No worries. Today was the first day of the rest of my life, and I would never be this heavy again. I frowned, remembering this was the exact speech I'd given myself the last three times I'd decided to get in shape.

I fumbled through the medicine cabinet until I found the little gem I'd bought last year.

A pedometer.

I held the cobalt-blue beauty in my hand and relived the promise of the infomercial. Ten thousand steps a day would ensure a new, slender, energized me. How difficult could that be to achieve?

I shimmied into my baggiest sweatpants, pulled on my favorite sweatshirt, and shoved my feet into my well-worn sneakers. Eyeing my hair in the mirror, I considered the options for taming my out-of-control waves and decided there was no hope. I leaned over at the waist, shook my head, and then straightened.

I carefully programmed the pedometer to measure my stride, then I headed out, full of enthusiasm and vigor.

If nothing else, getting some exercise would help keep my mind off of Emma's birthday and my argument with Diane. Losing the weight I'd gained might actually be easier than negotiating a truce.

Five minutes later, however, I fantasized about calling a cab to take me home.

No matter.

Surely I was well on my way to racking up my ten thousand steps. I pulled the pedometer off the waistband of my sweats and glared at it.

Three hundred and fifty-seven steps. That was it?

Let's see now. Three hundred and fifty-seven was a hell of a long way from ten thousand. At this rate, I'd have to do what I'd just done another…another…how many times?

I had no idea.

Sweat blossomed on my upper lip. I dragged my sleeve across my face, refastened the pedometer, and marched on.

My feet hurt, my hair had grown big enough to be visible in my peripheral vision, and I had a catch in my side that couldn't be good.

When I stepped on a pebble and twisted my ankle, I did an about-face and headed for home. I might have failed at my first attempt to hit my goal, but there was something to be said for self-preservation.

As I rounded the corner of my street, I dared another peek at the pedometer from hell. Each time I'd checked it during the walk, the readout had proclaimed far fewer steps than I knew I'd taken. How could I rely on an inaccurate pedometer?

I squinted at it now. Eighteen hundred. I blinked and looked again, thinking I'd missed a zero.

Still eighteen hundred.

Who could actually do the ten thousand, and why would they want to?

I bounced the little cobalt-blue device in my palm, considering my options.

I glanced around. The only sign of activity on the street was a van parked a few doors down.

I made my decision and took action, letting the pedometer slip between my fingers. It hit the sidewalk and bounced once before I stomped down, twisting my foot, crushing the tiny plastic torture device to pieces.

All of the emotions of the previous days and weeks joined forces, morphing into anger—hot, raw, unadulterated, glorious anger.

Heat fired in my chest and face, and I knew the sensation had nothing to do with exercise.

Unlike Ryan's crystal swimmer, the sound of the pedometer meeting its end filled me with satisfaction—misguided, perhaps—but satisfaction, just the same.

"Did you need some help?" A male voice rumbled from somewhere close by.

I squatted and tried to scoop up the shattered pieces of the pedometer as I searched for the source of the voice. A man I'd never seen before ambled toward me, the upturned corners of his mouth suggesting he'd seen the entire pedometer desecration.

"Aidan Kelly." The stranger stopped close to where I still squatted and held out his hand.

Countless childhood warnings about talking to strangers flew through my head, but I took his hand just the same.

He pulled me to my feet then shook my hand. "I'm moving into number thirty-six. And you?"

I wondered if I'd be smarter to offer up an excuse for what I'd just done, or if I should say nothing.

I chose nothing.

"Number thirty-two," I answered, working up a polite smile. "Bernadette Murphy."

"Nice to meet you, Number Thirty-Two."

He nodded to the pedometer pieces in my opposite hand. "What is it?" He grinned, the move lighting up his dark blue eyes. "Or rather, what was it?"

"A pedometer." I wrapped my fingers around the shards of plastic to hide them. "Must have fallen off my waistband."

"Must have." But, the glint in his eyes suggested he was not a man easily fooled. "You run often?"

"Pretty regularly." I nodded. Why go for honesty now when I was handling the fabrication so smoothly?

"Great morning for it," he said, and I kept nodding.

Suddenly, I remembered how I'd looked when I left the house. I could only imagine how incredibly scary my appearance must have been by then, while the man standing before me looked anything but scary.

His gray T-shirt had gotten smudged with something black, probably from loading or unloading the moving van. His dark brown hair was long enough that he'd shoved it behind his ears, but it was his smile that captured my stare.

I couldn't remember the last time one of Ryan's smiles had reached his eyes. Number Thirty-Six's smile not only reached his eyes, it crinkled the skin around them.

"You live alone at number thirty-two?"

My back stiffened instantly. Why in the hell would he ask me that? "No...er...yes. I mean. Now I do."

I wanted to say something a bit more coherent, but this was the first time I'd had to address the issue of living alone.

The reminder of my newly found marital status rocked me to my core. Then I thought of something I'd forgotten.

"I have a dog."

Number Thirty-Six nodded slowly, his probing gaze never leaving mine. "I have a cat."

A *cat*? This guy looked nothing like any cat person I'd ever known.

Damn. He'd said something and I missed it. "Pardon?"

My new neighbor's grin widened and the move shifted his entire face from alluring to...well...*wow*.

"I asked if you'd like to stop by for coffee sometime." He nodded at the smashed pedometer in my hand. "Maybe after one of your runs."

I bit back my laugh. *Runs.* Good thing he'd only caught the last part of today's little show.

I realized a good neighbor would invite Number Thirty-Six to her house, seeing as he was in the middle of unpacking. I, however, was not a good neighbor.

"No thanks." I spoke a little too sharply and the man's smile faltered. "I mean, no coffee for me. Doctor's orders, but thanks anyway."

I jerked a thumb toward my house. "Better get going. Don't want to keep you from your unpacking. Welcome to the neighborhood."

The grin returned to his face, and I had to admire the man's ability to remain charming after his encounter with…well… me.

Truth was, if Ryan hadn't left me, I'd have no problem sharing coffee with Number Thirty-Six. I'd be perfectly comfortable, because I'd be married, and I—unlike the man to whom I'd once pledged my love—had never considered being unfaithful.

But now I was available, and I didn't want any part of that realization. Of course, Number Thirty-Six most likely didn't want any part of my availability either. He'd merely been neighborly, and I was about to run like a scared girl.

"Nice to meet you," I mumbled as I turned for the safety of my house.

"See you later, Number Thirty-Two."

I gave a quick wave over my shoulder and picked up my pace. I could feel Number Thirty-Six's eyes burning into the back of my head, but I didn't look.

I concentrated only on making it to my front door, wondering how many more steps I'd accumulated in the process.

A pair of feet showed beneath the bumper of my mother's car when I parked in front of my mother's house later that day.

"Mark?" I asked as I climbed out of the driver's seat.

"How's it going?" my brother answered.

"Good." I shrugged, not that he could see me. Whatever he was doing had him so preoccupied, he didn't move from his position. "You?" I asked his feet.

"Same. Mom's inside."

The front door sat slightly ajar, so I pushed my way inside. My mother appeared from the kitchen, pressed a kiss to my cheek, and wrapped me in a hug. If she could bottle and sell the security and love I felt just then, she'd make a small fortune.

"What's Mark doing?" I straightened and jerked my thumb toward the driveway.

"Someone hit my car up at the market. He's trying to bang out the dent and touch up the paint." She looked through the storm door and smiled at my brother's feet.

"So why is he *under* your car?"

"I'm sure he knows what he's doing."

An irrational bubble of emotion sprang to life inside me, a mix of jealousy and guilt. Mark had apparently rushed right over to help my mother fix her car when I still hadn't looked at the paperwork I'd promised to take care of.

I cut my eyes toward the top of the stairs, hoping Dad would appear from his office, reading glasses in one hand, crossword puzzle in the other. He'd smile and tell me not to worry so much, and that thought just made me miss him more.

Silence hung over my mother and me, as if she knew exactly what I was thinking.

I wondered how many times she had stood in this same spot and stared up at the door to the office, praying she'd imagined everything that had happened. Wishing Daddy would appear at any moment—alive and laughing.

"You won't believe the nightmare I had," she'd say, and then they'd happily sit out back on their porch and listen to big band music as they read the paper.

"You ready to go?" Her voice cut through my thoughts, her tight, choked tone not escaping my notice.

I nodded as she gathered up a pair of rubber gloves, a small jug of water, and a bucket she'd left by the front door. I didn't ask her what they were for. I already knew.

Once, when we visited Emma's grave, the brass marker had been caked with mud, and the sight had brought me to my emotional knees. It was hard enough to visit the cemetery, but the dirt and unkempt marker had added insult to injury.

My mother had gone prepared to scrub ever since.

I wondered if I would have been that sort of mother if Emma had lived. I hoped so.

"Where are you two going?" Mark called out as we climbed into my car. He emerged from beneath Mom's Buick and stood frowning at the fender.

"Running some errands," my mother answered. "We'll be back in a little bit. There's lunchmeat in the fridge if you get hungry."

"Why don't you tell him the truth?" I asked after we both shut our doors and sat safely out of earshot, inside my car. "Tell him today's his niece's birthday and we're going to the cemetery. She's my daughter, Mom, not an errand."

I regretted my sharp tone as soon as I spoke the words, but my mother merely gave me a tight smile and patted my knee. "Everyone grieves differently, honey."

No kidding.

"Did he pick one of Dad's jackets yet?" I was not about to let this go. It felt good to sink my teeth into something, even if it was at my brother's expense.

"Give him some time."

Our family had done an oddly polite dance around each other for as long as I could remember. Sometimes, I wanted to scream, but my mother's voice was so flat when she answered me, I knew I'd better shut up.

"Sorry," I mumbled.

"Nothing to be sorry for." But she turned her head toward the window, as if she didn't want me to see her face. "And don't mumble. Nothing drove your father crazier than your mumbling."

I rolled my eyes and pulled the car out onto the street.

We didn't say another word to each other until I'd parked along the side of the lane next to Emma's cemetery section. My mother and I climbed out. She grabbed the bucket and gloves as I reached for the water.

We walked wordlessly up the small hill to the spot where the brass marker rested, one corner covered by a patch of thick grass that had grown up and over the marble base.

Mud had been caked onto the engraved poem and the date of Emma's birth.

I swallowed, frozen to the spot.

Mom dropped to her knees, reaching back for the water jug, but I didn't hand it over. Instead I dropped to my knees beside her and reached for the scrub brush.

"It's okay, Mom. I'll get it."

But tears swam in her eyes as she lifted her gaze to mine. "It's not okay."

I remembered calling my parents' house after Ryan and I had gotten home from the hospital. I'd never forget the pain in my father's voice when I told him Emma was gone, much like the anguish that spread across my mother's face now.

I studied her features, the pain and love so blatant in her eyes.

I wasn't the only one who'd lost Emma. Ryan had lost her. Dad had lost her. Mom had lost her. I wasn't alone in my sorrow. I wasn't alone in my life.

Suddenly, I had no idea why I hadn't picked up the phone to call Mom the moment Ryan walked out.

"Ryan left me," I said.

Mom nodded, her eyes still moist with unshed tears.

"You knew?" I leaned toward her, staring intently into her dark eyes. They softened as she looked at me, as she reached for my cheek.

"I'm your mother."

The emotion of the moment grabbed me by the throat and held tight.

Why *hadn't* I told her sooner? She was my mother, and she'd do anything for me. Much like my argument with Diane, that realization made me realize the time had come to do some things for myself.

Mom patted my cheek and reached for the scrub brush, but I covered her hand with mine. "I can do this."

"I know you can." Her tone lost its soft edge, growing sharp and determined.

When her eyes met mine this time, I knew she wasn't talking about scrubbing Emma's marker.

She was talking about life. My life.

I only hoped she was right.

On Sunday afternoon, I knew the time had come to face the paperwork I'd promised to handle for my mother.

I thought about Mark working on Mom's car and my vow to face life head-on. I stared at the piles spread across my coffee table.

I separated the papers and notes into categories. Retirement account. Life insurance. Banking. Pension. Health insurance. Utilities. Homeowner's insurance. Car insurance.

The manila envelope holding the copies of my father's death certificate sat farther away than anything else. I'd shoved it to the end of the table as if it were a cobra waiting to pierce my heart with its lethal bite, yet my gaze continued to land on the words scribbled in handwriting I'd never recognize as my own if I didn't know better.

Death certificates.

The enormity of the task threatened to swallow me whole. I couldn't help but wonder if this wouldn't have been easier before my shock and denial wore off. Now that I'd become aware and determined, my heart ached as if an elephant sat on my chest.

This to-do list would be emotionally devastating if the paperwork had been for anyone, let alone for my dad.

I understood life ceased at the moment the heart stopped beating, but as far as the rest of the world was concerned, life stopped at the moment they received a completed form, a properly worded letter, and an official copy of the death certificate.

My gaze traveled again to the manila envelope and froze there. The contents all but dared me to peek inside, to see if this time I'd be strong enough to study them without dissolving into a puddle of tears.

I traced a finger along the edge of the envelope then released the clip that held the flap closed. I reached inside, sliding the neat

93

stack of ten notarized certificates from within. I swallowed, a vain attempt to fend off the sob mercilessly snaking its way up my throat.

I skimmed the words typed onto each page. Name. Social security number. Time of death. Cause of death.

The words blurred and I wiped at my cheeks before the tears tumbling from my eyes could drip and mar the pristine pages— pages that screamed what my heart knew but still wanted to deny.

Dad was *dead*.

And at that particular moment in my life, that one fact—that one morsel of understanding—seemed almost more than I could bear.

I pushed the envelope away and fell flat on my back, staring up at the textured ceiling and the line of recessed lights. One bulb sat dark and I frowned. When had that happened? Today? Yesterday? Last week?

I squeezed my eyes shut, trying to stem the steady trickle of tears, trying to regain my composure, but I couldn't. Tears streamed from the corners of my eyes down the sides of my face, running into my hair and my ears. Slick. Wet. Cold.

A cold nose nudged the side of my face and I blinked my eyes open. Poindexter hovered above me, probably more concerned over whether or not I'd be able to provide for his nutritional needs than he was about my emotional state. But then his expression changed. I mean, I think it changed. Maybe my imagination was simply more active than usual, and that was saying something.

Poindexter frowned a little, tipped his head to one side, and dropped to his belly. He sprawled beside me on the carpet and lowered his chin to my stomach. I looped one arm around his neck, sinking my fingers into his fur.

We stayed like that for a long time. I'm not even sure for how long. It seemed like hours, but could have been just minutes. All I knew was that Poindexter loved me. His actions may not have been entirely unselfish, but I liked to think they were.

He loved me enough to flop down with me on the family room floor while I succumbed to my latest wave of grief. And for however long we stayed there, Poindexter's nearness comforted me, soothed me. Sure, I had a momentary flash of realization that this was what my life had come to—me in tears, comforted by the dog.

Then I realized, just as I had the night before, that only by lying like a slug in the middle of my floor would I be a complete and total failure. All I had to do was get up.

Get up.

I gave Poindexter a squeeze before I headed for the kitchen. After I tossed him a treat and put on a fresh pot of coffee, I decided I was ready to face my dad's paperwork. Ready to face whatever else life had to dish out. Though I sincerely hoped the surprises were through for at least a little while.

I carried my steaming mug back to the coffee table, took a deep breath, and reached for the first pile.

"Everyone who got where he is had to begin where he was."
—Richard L. Evans

CHAPTER NINE

— —— —

"UBO QODU HPSUKPF PN G ZGF'D RKNO KD BKD RKUURO,
FGZORODD, JFSOZOZQOSOY GTUD PN IKFYFODD GFY
RPAO."
   —*EKRRKGZ EPSYDEPSUB*

I turned on the television a little after one o'clock in the morning.
I'd been unable to sleep. My mind had shifted into overdrive trying to process my new normal.

Separated. Fatherless. Unemployed.

Now, there was a winning combination if ever there were one.

I sighed, exhaustion easing through me, my body fatigued,
my brain set on obsessed.

I missed Diane.

We'd had our share of arguments over the past thirty-six
years, but this was the hardest she'd ever thrown the kid card.

I realized I couldn't have my cake and eat it too. I hated when
she gave me the pity face, hated when she tiptoed around my
inability to have more children. There was also a very real part
of me that hated the fact she'd become pregnant at age forty-one
without trying. It smacked of sacrilege.

Don't get me wrong. I was happy for her. I knew once she got over her compulsion to shop and David got over his compulsion to be a grouch, they'd work along with Ashley to integrate the newest arrival into their family.

They'd achieve a new sense of balance—a new sense of reality—and hopefully I'd be part of that, as I always had been.

The thing was, Diane had never spoken to me as she had after I'd driven Ashley to the party. And she'd been right. I didn't know what it was like to sit up at night wondering where my child was. I'd always known exactly where Emma was. In the neonatal unit.

I'd sat up at night wondering if she'd keep breathing, if the hole in her heart had healed, if she was in pain. If she knew how very much we loved her—how much we'd fought for her life.

I never got a chance to worry about all the other things in a child's life—the teething, the eating, the first bike ride, report cards, chicken pox, boys. You name it. I only had a tiny taste of just how much a child stole your heart.

So there I sat, staring at the television, hoping the talking heads could lull me into dreamland and away from my racing mind.

An overly enthusiastic woman touted the benefits of shoving my linens into plastic bags and attaching the vacuum to suck out every ounce of air.

Interesting. My closets were in a terrible state of disarray, and this was the perfect time to spend money I didn't have on making over every bedroom in the house—all two of them. I could buy new sheets, new blankets, new comforters. Then I could shove the old ones into bags and suck out the air.

As I watched, the woman submersed one of the miracle bags into a bathtub full of water. I watched slack-jawed as she checked the gaudy comforter inside. Dry as a bone. Now there was a feature no one should be without, because you never knew when you might need to submerge your bagged linens in the tub.

All skepticism aside, I picked up the phone and dialed. What the hell? A little waterproof organization couldn't hurt me. While the sales representative took my order, he offered me the opportunity to toss in a set of knives.

I agreed, energized by my mini buying spree. I wondered whether the superstrength plastic bags could withstand an attack by the bonus knives. Maybe I'd save that experiment for clothes Ryan had yet to take out of his closet.

An odd sense of excitement filled me as I hung up the phone. If I could remove the air from my linens, think of the other magic items I had yet to discover in the land of infomercials. The possibilities were endless—simply, wonderfully endless.

At last, I had something tangible to cling to. Life-changing inventions that could be mine in three easy payments or less.

But *wait*, there was more.

I followed the bag purchase by calling for the Deluxe Whitener for teeth. After all, if Mary Tyler Moore could turn the world on with her smile, so could I. And I certainly wasn't going to pass up the chance to own even more Billy Banks Tae Bo DVDs I'd never open, so I ordered a set of three.

I passed on buying the Snuggie. Call me crazy, but it seemed to me I could put my robe on backward and save myself twenty bucks.

Yet, when the most beautiful and graceful woman I'd ever set eyes on began a belly-dancing demonstration, I sat mesmerized, unable to tear my gaze from the television screen. She explained the toning and fat-burning benefits of the ancient moves, and I was a goner. Sold to the woman with the wild hair and bunny slippers.

My excitement morphed into downright euphoria.

I added a juicer and a flashlight that never needed batteries to my list of purchases, and then I spotted the pièce de résistance. Crab cakes from Maryland.

If all else failed, at least I'd never go hungry.

I clicked off the television a little after four in the morning. As it was, the UPS guy would probably want my head on a platter as payback for the packages he'd have to deliver.

Boxes and boxes full of promises.

Whiter teeth. Flatter belly. Sharper knives.

Things were looking up, and that was something I hadn't thought in a very long time.

I sat in the café at Genuardi's the next morning and sipped a grande chai latte.

There was something to be said for observing life in a grocery store. While I wasn't ready to become an active participant, the simple act of sitting and watching validated my life…or rather, the fact I had a life…or would again someday.

Perhaps my wallow was officially over, at least for now. I'd woken up craving life much like an addict might crave a drink, or Diane might crave a new hobo bag. I'd been frantic to shower, dress, and get out of my house. I needed air. I needed space.

I needed to start making things happen.

Something.

Anything.

Even if that something was only a trip to Genuardi's café.

Poindexter didn't wait for me to leave before he jumped up on the sofa, doggy bliss plastered across his face. I imagined any day

I didn't drag him to a new obedience school was a good day in his book. I also imagined he was ready to spend a bit less quality time with me. After all, even dogs had their limits.

So there I sat in the grocery store, pondering life, when it hit me. I watched as a young woman reached a box down from a top shelf for an older woman. She smiled brightly and the look of sheer surprise on the older woman's face took my breath away.

Surprise.

She'd been surprised a stranger not only performed a kind act, but smiled as she did so.

I pulled out the notebook I'd brought along with Dad's book of cryptograms and fished in my purse for a pen. Then I began to write.

I considered the quotes Dad had chosen about dreams, about life, and I remembered how once upon a time—when I'd been young and full of hope—I wanted to write so badly I spent every spare moment scribbling in my diary.

How funny that my dad's collection of writing inspired me now, reigniting a fire in my belly I thought long dead.

The words poured out of me. Words about kindness and love and the simple acts that make us human, make us loving creatures, and connect us. I wrote briefly about Emma and all she'd taught me, all she'd taught her doctors, but every word came back to the same thing.

Kindness.

Was it really so difficult to be kind to each other? To smile at each other? To look out for each other? I didn't think so.

I'd just put the period at the end of my closing thought when I heard a shriek. A young, shrill, hauntingly familiar female voice that said, "I don't want to go to school. I'm excused. Leave me alone."

My suspicions were confirmed when I stood up and leaned to my left to gain a clear view past a display of brightly colored mugs. There she stood.

Ashley.

Hands on hips. Lovely young face twisted with an emotion that looked a lot like fear, even though her words suggested otherwise.

I sprang into motion, leaving my belongings behind. I didn't think there was a big resale market for fathers' journals or the ramblings of a dumped, middle-aged woman, so I wasn't worried either would vanish and reappear on eBay.

"Is there a problem?" I asked as I neared the spot where Ashley and the store employee faced off. Ashley gripped a can of peas in one hand, and I sincerely hoped she hadn't threatened to use them.

"Aunt Bernie?" Her expression was a mix of happy recognition and what-on-earth-are-you-doing-here?

I moved to her side and anchored an arm around her shoulders. When she didn't squirm away, but rather leaned into me, a bubble of warmth burst inside my chest and spread outward. I gave the store clerk my warmest smile and squinted at his nametag.

"Is there a problem"—I repeated, this time tacking his name on to the end of my question—"Geoff?"

"This young lady should be in school." He pointed at Ashley as if she'd just knocked over the ATM machine, his finger trembling so badly I shifted Ashley behind me to keep her out of his reach.

"Right." I nodded. "We realize that, but she needed to pick up some peas"—I nodded toward the can she still gripped, searching for a reason that might sound valid—"for an art project. We're running a bit late."

I kept talking, having learned a long time ago my babbling could render even the most determined male silent. "So, we'll be on our way. Won't we, Ash? Here we go." I sidestepped her toward the café and looked back over my shoulder at Geoff, again with the biggest smile I could manage. "Thanks for your concern."

"You want to tell me what's going on?" I muttered beneath my breath as I slipped Dad's book back into my tote bag.

Ashley's fingers brushed against the edge of my notebook, her eyebrows knitting together. "Did you write this?"

I slid the notebook out of her reach, then stashed it in my bag. "Just some of my thoughts. Nothing important. You're avoiding my question." I gave her my sternest look—at least I thought it was my sternest look—but I obviously was mistaken, since she completely ignored me.

"What did you write?" She looked up at me, eyes sparkling. "An article? A story?"

"Letter to the editor." I shrugged. "Maybe. About being nice to each other. Kind. You know?"

"Yeah." A slight chuckle slipped from between Ashley's glossed lips. "You should let my parents read it. They could use a lesson."

The comment snapped me back to my original focus. "Right. You need to tell me what you're doing here today, and then you need to tell me why you lied to me on Friday."

Ashley winced. "Sorry, Aunt Bernie."

I anchored my tote over my shoulder and hooked my arm through hers. "Let's go. You can tell me in the car."

I paid for Ashley's peas, and then dragged her toward the parking lot, not saying another word until we were both settled in the car, seat belts clicked into place.

"Start talking."

"Do you have a can opener?" She gazed lovingly at the can of peas. Her avoidance technique could use some work, but you had to give the kid points for trying.

"No." I plucked the can from her grip and set it behind her seat. "Why aren't you in school? How did you get here? Do you have any idea how angry your mother is with me?"

Silence stretched between us as she stared straight ahead, her eyes growing wide. When she turned to face me, I expected a full confession. *Wrong.*

"Can I run back in for a can opener?"

"What is so urgent about the peas?" I'll admit I let her pea fixation sidetrack me from my inquisition, but the whole thing was downright weird.

"They make me happy." Ashley shrugged her petite shoulders.

"*Peas* make you happy?" My disbelieving tone climbed a few octaves higher than normal. "You can do better than that, Ash."

She shook her head as if her life depended on those peas. "No, I mean it. They make me happy. I need them, Aunt Bernie. I *need* them."

Either the kid suffered from a serious vitamin deficiency or she was simply a freak in the craving department. But then, look at her mom. Maybe the apple didn't fall too far from the tree.

"What's wrong with a good old chocolate bar?"

Ashley wrinkled her nose as if I'd suggested chicken liver. "Gross. Just peas, thank you."

I started the ignition and backed out of my parking spot. "I'm sure your mother's got a can opener at home."

"She'll kill me."

"Should have thought of that before you cut school."

"Can we go to your house? Please? I'll tell you everything."

The promise of a full confession made my decision an easy one. "Afterward, we're calling your mother."

Ashley slumped back against the passenger seat as if I'd told her she had only two hours to live. "Fine."

I bit back my smile. She might make you want to strangle her more often than not, but the kid had spunk, and spunk was a very good thing indeed.

"The best portion of a man's life is his little, nameless, unremembered acts of kindness and love."
—William Wordsworth

CHAPTER TEN

— — —

"RLANGZANR ZG ZR QZUUZBFCG GL IJLE EPL ZR IJLBIZJK—
LHHLOGFJZGW LO GNAHGTGZLJ."
  —FJIJLEJ

I left a message on Diane's cell phone when we reached my house. Ashley sat at my kitchen table, jumping at the slightest noise as if her mother were going to send a team of truancy enforcers through the door at any moment.

Poindexter's chin sat planted firmly on Ashley's knee and, if I wasn't mistaken, the dog was smiling. He'd probably thought the world had ended and he and I were the only two creatures left alive. The look of relief in his eyes had been unmistakable when Ashley walked through the door.

She spooned in a mouthful of peas, then eyed her bowl as if she might lick it. "Do you have any more?"

Peas? Not in this lifetime.

"I'll look." But I knew better. If the kid wanted nacho chips, popcorn, or chocolate in any shape, size, or form, she'd be in business. But peas?

I stared into my pantry, past the zillion boxes of doggie treats. It was immediately apparent who ate better in this house. Back in the far corner of the middle shelf, I saw something shiny. Something round. The top of a can. Soup, I guessed, but I guessed wrong.

I lifted the can out of the pantry and screwed up my face in surprise. Peas? In my house? Maybe Ryan had put them there. Or maybe they'd been there since the previous owners had moved out.

I checked the can for any sign of rust or dents or bulges or whatever else you were supposed to check for. I also checked for an expiration date, but couldn't find one.

Ashley swallowed, her eyes fixated on the can in my hand as if she were a vampire and I held the longest, most tender neck in town.

"I'm not sure about this." I shook my head. "Your parents are angry enough over my driving you to the party. If I gave you botulism, they might really be pissed."

Ashley didn't say a word, her eyes never leaving the can.

The kid was starting to freak me out.

Thankfully, the phone rang. I snatched up the receiver, tossed the can into the pantry, and flattened my back against the door to prevent any attempt on Ashley's part to open the obviously lethal can of peas.

"I see you're really becoming a great influence on my daughter." I hadn't heard this note of disgust in Diane's voice since I'd cut off her bangs in high school. And I mean cut off. To the scalp.

"You're just lucky I was there," I answered, frowning into space. "If she'd beaned the clerk with the peas—no pun intended—you'd be looking at assault charges on top of truancy."

Ashley's eyes widened at my words, like she'd seriously considered clocking Geoff.

But all Diane said was "peas" in vacant tone of voice. "She loves her damned peas."

I shrugged, not that she could see me. "So the kid has a fetish. So what? It's not like you haven't conducted a commando raid on every purse department in town."

Diane's gasp filtered through the phone line, and Ashley pulled herself up straighter in her chair, smiling. I winked at her. So what if the move wasn't part of the support-parental-authority handbook. It felt right. Hell, it felt good.

"When will you be bringing my daughter home?" Diane asked. "Or was there another party you two planned to hit on the way back?"

I smirked, wanting very badly to say a few choice words to my friend but drawing the line at saying them in front of her daughter.

"In about a half hour." I leveled my gaze at Ashley. "We've got a few things to talk about first."

I expected Diane to tell me a half hour was too long. I expected her to tell me she needed to see her firstborn immediately. But that's not what she said at all.

"Listen, Macy's is having a one-day sale, so if you get to the house before me, use your key."

I blinked. Not that I was the poster child for rational thinking, but my old friend had her priorities completely out of whack.

"Got it." I hung up the phone and sat down across from Ashley.

"The peas?" Her eyebrows shot up hopefully.

"We'll stop at 7-11 on the way to your house and get some more. Fair enough?"

She nodded. "Was she mad?"

I nodded back. "A bit. We'll meet her at home. She has to stop at the mall for something."

Ashley sighed and my heart hurt for her. She was old enough to realize her mother was more than a little distracted by her pregnancy.

"It's normal for women to get a little weird when they're pregnant." I reached over and gave her hand a quick squeeze. "She'll snap out of the purse thing, honey. You'll see."

"It's not that." Ashley's voice dropped low, flat.

"What, then?"

"She's moved on to outfits that 'accentuate' her belly."

My stomach caught for a variety of reasons, and I tried to ignore them all.

I shifted my grip to hold her hand, and she amazed me by not pulling away. "Want to tell me what's going on?"

"Nothing." She shrugged, but the sadness around her eyes was undeniable.

"Ash?"

"She's so busy showing off the baby, she doesn't know I'm alive." The words spilled out of her as if she'd held them bottled up for weeks.

"That's not true. She loves you like you can't believe. We all love you."

Poindexter moved to the corner of the kitchen and let out a loud, window-rattling sigh.

"Just look how you've captivated the dog."

I spotted the slightest lift at the corner of Ashley's mouth.

"I saw that." I pointed.

"What?" She narrowed her gaze, her features falling serious.

"The smile."

She shook her head. "I didn't smile."

I shrugged. "Wouldn't kill you if you did."

Her gaze darted from me to the tabletop to the pantry. "Forget it."

She blew out a frustrated breath.

"Listen." I gave her hand a squeeze. "I know things are kind of crazy right now with your mom being pregnant." And insane, but I didn't say that. "You're at a tough age." I smiled. "Just remember. If you need someone to talk to, I'm here. Talking is good. Expressing yourself is good. Keeping everything inside is not. Got it?"

She nodded, looking as if she had her doubts but she'd humor me by agreeing.

"But"—I shifted my tone to serious, very adult—"don't lie to me again, and don't cut school again. Hear me?"

Ashley looked as if I'd slapped her hand instead of holding it.

"If anything had happened to you, no one would have known where you were, and we all love you too much for that, okay?"

Her throat worked and tears glistened in her eyes. "Aunt Bernie?"

"What, honey?"

"Do you think I could have a hug? I've kind of had a rough week."

A smile spread wide across my face as I pushed out of my chair and she did the same. I wrapped my arms around the little girl who was becoming a young woman before my eyes, and I held on tight.

"I can't think of anything I'd rather do."

"You're the best," she whispered against my shoulder, and my heart caught.

"You're not so bad yourself," I answered as I planted a kiss against her downy soft hair. "Ready to go?"

She nodded, but pulled away suddenly to pin me with an intent gaze. "Are you going to send that letter to the editor?"

I uttered a slight laugh. "I'm no writer, Ash. It was just something to do."

"Can I read it?"

Could she? I didn't see why not. "Sure." I nodded. "Let me get it."

She sank back onto her chair, and I retrieved the notebook from my bag. Ashley devoured the words on the page, never looking up until she'd finished.

"Wow, Aunt Bernie."

"Wow, what?" I hoped she hadn't picked up on how many octaves my voice jumped in my anxiety over whether or not she liked what I'd written.

"You have to send it."

"You liked it?"

Ashley smiled the loveliest smile I'd ever seen. "Call the paper and get their e-mail address." She brightened even more.

I realized then that the smile on Ashley's face meant far more to me than the fact she'd liked the article.

"I'll make you a deal." I slid the notebook away from her and met her gaze. "I'll send this in if you promise to come to me or call me, any time of day or night, if you need anything. Anything at all. Fair enough?"

"Fair enough."

With that, we set out toward Diane's house. I only hoped negotiating a truce with my purse-crazed, hormone-driven friend would be as painless as talking to Ashley had been.

Somehow, I had my doubts.

I pranced through the door of Diane and David's rink on Wednesday afternoon as if I owned the joint and hadn't skipped work for almost a week. Part of me hoped David would ignore my absence and say nothing about what had happened Friday night.

That part of me was an idiot.

I should have known he'd be angry with me based on the icy reception I'd received from his wife the day before.

Diane had ushered Ashley into the house while she planted her arm across the threshold to keep me out. I'd driven the whole way back to my house wondering when it had been that she and I started stuffing our feelings.

In the old days, we'd have thrown all of the hurt and anger out in the open, but last night had been different. Last night we'd merely given each other polite nods, held our thoughts and feelings inside, then turned our backs on each other.

But I couldn't blame Diane. I was equally to blame. After all, I'd kept my mouth shut when she called on Friday night, and I hadn't done a thing last night to force the issue.

I'd put just as many bricks in the wall building between us as she had.

"So, I understand you're working your corruption skills on my daughter now." David's sharp tone shattered my thoughts before I could stew any further.

I squinted at him, narrowing my eyes to tiny little slits. "I was trying to *help*."

"Good one." He let out an annoying laugh and shook his head. "Ashley's got sneak skills you didn't perfect until college."

I resented that comment. "I was never sneaky."

"Right." David smiled—a look rarely spotted on his face, and one to be noted while it lasted.

"Well, Ashley's not sneaky. She's just upset right now. That's all."

David shrugged. "Women."

His typical scowl returned to his face, and I fought the urge to slap it off. Truth be told, I'd wanted to slap it off for as long as I could remember.

I clasped my hands together to avoid any possible assault charges.

"Is that all you have to say about it?" I gave a quick lift and drop of my shoulders. "'Women?'"

"She'll get over it," he answered. "Whatever *it* is."

Maybe men really were from Mars.

He tipped his chin in my direction. "What brings you around?"

Was this a trick question? "Work."

David made a loud snapping noise with his mouth. "You don't work here anymore."

I sagged as if he'd let the air out of me. "What do you mean?"

"You. Don't. Work. Here. Anymore." He spoke emphatically and distinctly.

"I understand the words. I don't understand why."

He shook his head and smiled again. He was enjoying this, the rat. "You don't show up for three days, you're fired. You haven't been here since Halloween. Company rules."

"What if I was sick?"

"Too sick to dial the phone?"

He had a point. "You're not even paying me. Can't you make an exception? Really, I don't think it's too much to ask. I'm ready to do my job. I need this job, David."

His eyes began to glaze over. My babbling was working its usual charm.

"I don't tolerate slackers." He scowled anew.

So much for babbling.

I rolled my eyes at him. I knew that drove him nuts.

His scowl intensified.

"I'm in the midst of a major life upheaval, you know."

He laughed. The man's mood swings were making my head hurt. "I'm forty-two years old, my wife's pregnant, and my teenager's cutting school to buy peas. I'll see your life upheaval and raise you twenty."

Well what did you know? The man actually had noticed his family's issues. There might be hope for him yet.

"I could make some fries." I used my best you-can't-live-without-me-and-I-cost-you-nothing voice, but David was visibly unimpressed.

"No."

"Drive the Zamboni?" I choked a bit on that last word, but if that's what it would take to smooth out my little pity-party absence, I'd do it.

"No."

I needed this job. Heaven help me, I *wanted* this job. Without the ice rink in my daily schedule, I had nothing but an obedience-challenged dog and my dreams of reinvention to fill my time.

I shrugged. "I give. What'll it take to get back into your good graces?"

"Go clean the bathrooms."

I jumped back a step. "You have got to be kidding me. Don't you pay someone to do that?"

His scowl morphed back into a smile—an evil smile.

"All right," I mumbled. "But I'm lodging a complaint with Diane."

"If you toss in a purse or some maternity clothes, you might have a chance with that."

Surprised, I blinked at him. "You know about the shopping?"

"I'm not stupid."

Not stupid, I thought as I walked toward the restrooms. Who knew?

David called to me just before I turned the corner. "Supplies are in the closet. Don't forget to glove up."

When I got home that night, it was still unseasonably warm for early November. I'd left the screen door in my kitchen cracked open for fresh air, but it had been pushed off its track.

My heart seized up in my chest. My dog had made a run for it. He'd no doubt taken off in search of a nonwallowing, well-adjusted human.

I raced out into the yard and whistled. I should say I tried to whistle, because that trick had never been my forte.

Poindexter was nowhere to be found. Even worse, the back gate stood wide open to the athletic fields behind my house. I began to run, aimlessly at first, then methodically from yard to yard, checking every inch of ground fringing the edge of the field.

Cold tears stung my cheeks, but I slapped them away. I was tired of crying. Poindexter was obviously *very* tired of my crying.

I had to pull myself together, and I had to find my dog.

Sure, he had issues. He chased airplanes, he avoided confrontation like the plague, and now, apparently, he'd developed escape tendencies, but I needed him.

He might be an obedience school dropout, but he was *my* obedience school dropout.

I dropped to my knees, not caring that they sank into what I hoped was mud. I threw back my head and I yelled. Yelled like I'd never yelled before.

In public.

In my family, we didn't yell. Plain and simple.

But I let my voice fly, bellowing in the middle of the huge field while the windows of my neighbors' houses looked on. Not caring who saw me, who heard me, or what they might think.

Then I closed my eyes and prayed with all of my heart.

I stayed like that for what felt like forever until I heard a sound, faint at first, then clear and close.

Footsteps. The jangle of dog tags.

"Lose something, Number Thirty-Two?"

My new neighbor's voice jolted my system like a shot of electricity. I opened my eyes, twisted in his direction, and spotted Poindexter barreling straight toward me, all happy innocence and doggie glee.

I opened my arms and choked on tears of joy, having switched instantly from desperation to euphoric blubbering.

"Wh...what happened?" I wrapped my arms around Poindexter's neck and held him to me so tightly it was a wonder the dog could breathe.

I looked up at Number Thirty-Six and the kindness in his eyes sucked every ounce of air from my lungs. He shook his head. "Mrs. Cooke knocked on my door. Said your dog was loose in the field, barking up at the sky. She was afraid something might happen to him."

Disbelief did a slow tumble through my system. "Mrs. Cooke?"

My new neighbor nodded and extended his hand. I dropped my focus to his fingers, remembering our first encounter. I loosened my grip on Poindexter and dragged my sleeve across my face, shuddering momentarily when I realized I must look like a very bad Halloween leftover.

"Come on," Number Thirty-Six said. "I won't bite."

Promises, promises.

I slipped my fingers into his and scrambled to my feet, doing my best to ignore the warm brush of his skin against mine. Poindexter jumped up on me, sending me staggering to one side.

"Sit," Number Thirty-Six said in a deep, authoritative voice.

I fought the urge to plant my butt in the mud, but Poindexter did exactly what he was told. I stared at him, stunned.

"How did you do that?" I pointed to the dog, sitting on command.

My neighbor shrugged. "He's a great dog. When did you teach him the commands? As a pup?"

I narrowed my gaze, staring at Poindexter. "Commands?" Maybe this wasn't my dog at all. Maybe this was a pod dog that had been grown in some basement down the block.

"Sure." Number Thirty-Six nodded enthusiastically. "He sits. He shakes. He plays dead, and he loves to roll over."

Roll over?

I shot a frown at Poindexter, and I could have sworn the dog shrugged. Was he actually so smart he'd wanted to get thrown out of obedience school after obedience school after obedience school?

"Amazing," I muttered.

"Yes, he is."

He grinned, and I realized I was still holding his hand. I jerked my hand away as if his touch had scorched my palm. "Thanks for taking him in."

"No problem."

We walked together, side by side, back across the field. Poindexter trotted happily along as if he were the most well-trained dog in New Jersey.

"You look like you could use a cup of coffee," Number Thirty-Six said, the skin around his eyes crinkling with sincerity.

I shook my head, sudden nerves sliding through me. "I only drink tea," I fibbed.

"Sure you do."

He smiled a really great crooked smile then tipped his head toward the back of his house.

"I'm only two doors away if you ever want some lessons."

"Lessons?" My voice squeaked like a chipmunk on speed.

For a moment, my mind raced with the possibilities. Just what sort of lessons did Number Thirty-Six feel qualified to teach?

"For the dog." He laughed a little as he turned and walked away.

Poindexter began to follow him and I cleared my throat. When the dog looked back at me, I shot him my most threatening glare. He turned sharply and headed for our house, racing ahead of me even as I called to him to heel.

A jumbo jet appeared over the top of the trees and the chase was on. Poindexter raced beneath the belly of the plane, barking up at the sky.

I watched Number Thirty-Six head toward his house then snapped myself back to reality.

Lessons. *For the dog.*

Imagine that.

"Sometimes it is difficult to know who is knocking—opportunity or temptation."
—Unknown

CHAPTER ELEVEN

— — —

*"T PAFY FG T ATLWBL FP PTHK, WIU UATU FP GBU DATU
PAFYP TLK WIFQU HBL."*
   —OBAG T. PAKEE

Three weeks later, the UPS man had grown sick of delivering packages to my front door, and Diane and I still hadn't spoken. Truth be told, I missed her. A lot. She might be a hormone-crazed purse fiend, but she was also the one constant in my life. At least she had been.

After my sixth voice mail went unanswered, I stopped calling.

The night of the family talent show arrived, and even though I wasn't speaking to her mother, I'd promised Ashley I'd go.

Diane and David had been unwilling to perform without their Sonny and Cher costumes and Ashley wanted all of the moral support she could get.

I cruised the school parking lot, hoping for an available parking space. Glancing at the dashboard clock, I realized I was ten minutes late.

Even when I had no life I couldn't get somewhere on time.

Relief eased through me when I cleared the threshold of the foyer and spotted the flashing overhead lights. My relief, however, quickly gave way to sensations far different.

Ryan stood on the far side of the lobby, his palm planted possessively against the small of another woman's back.

My face went hot. My face went cold. I was torn between the desire to run and the desire to vomit.

I squeezed my eyes shut and willed myself not to shriek or faint or in any way call attention to myself, but he spotted me just the same. Ryan possessed a sixth sense when it came to me, but the realization he still felt my presence didn't do much to console me as I looked at his companion's swollen belly.

He met my gaze then whispered something in the other woman's ear. She glanced in my direction and smiled. A tight, uncomfortable smile. A smile that said she knew exactly what she'd done to my marriage. Hell, to my life.

She turned away, but as Ryan made his way toward me, I studied her, not believing what I saw.

I'd pictured young and gorgeous. I'd pictured radiant skin and perky breasts. I'd never pictured someone my age with two teenagers in tow. I glanced again at her baby bump and swallowed.

I hadn't been prepared for being replaced by someone just like me—only fertile.

"We met in the parking lot when I gave Ashley a ride to one of her dances."

Ryan's voice sounded close beside me. When his fingers closed around my elbow, I jerked my arm free and took several steps away from him.

I nodded as if his explanation made perfect sense. "Does Ashley know her?" Even more importantly, "Do Diane and David know her?"

Ryan shook his head. "They'll meet her for the first time tonight. I promise."

Lucky, lucky me. Just in time to be a happy witness to the couple's first public appearance.

"Your promises don't go too far with me, Ryan."

He nodded, letting his focus drift to his shoes. Then a crease formed between his dark brows and he shifted his attention back to my face.

Maybe it was the shock of seeing Ryan, or the shock of seeing the other woman, but sudden tears swam in my vision. Much to my dismay, a traitorous drop slid down my cheek.

Ryan reached for my face, and I captured his hand in mine. "Don't."

I thought he might seize the moment to tell me he was sorry for everything that had happened, but he didn't.

"I'd better get back." He turned to walk away, but hesitated, pivoting to face me once more. "I'm taking flying lessons."

"Flying lessons?" He could have knocked me over with a feather.

Pride danced in his eyes. "I always wanted to fly."

I nodded. "But I never thought you'd do it."

He gave a quick shrug. "Why not?"

Why not? I returned his shrug. "Why not?"

"How about you?" He tipped his chin. "Any new tricks?"

I thought about the belly-dancing DVD still safely sealed in its cellophane, the Maryland crab cakes frozen before I'd tasted a single one, and Number Thirty-Six's offer of lessons for Poindexter. An offer I'd soundly ignored.

"A few." I nodded, lying through my teeth.

"Good." Ryan's smile spread wide across his face, lighting up his features. "You deserve to be happy."

"We all do." I answered flatly, unable to wrench my stare from the uninhibited joy plastered across his face.

Maybe he'd needed someone to light the dark places inside him I couldn't reach. After all, how can you illuminate another when your own shadows run so deep?

"She listens to my dreams, Bernie." Ryan spoke the words softly, as if he were afraid to hurt me. Before I could respond, he turned and walked away.

I studied his back. Then I measured what he'd said.

I couldn't remember the last time I'd listened to his dreams.

I stood frozen to the spot as he interlaced his fingers with those of his new love and steered her toward the theatre doors.

Apparently I hadn't been listening for a very long time.

I stopped off at the all-night convenience store on my way home from the high school. I'd like to say I bought nothing but healthy foods—skim milk, yogurt, fresh fruit. But that would be a total lie.

In reality, I walked out of that store carrying every sweet and salty snack my increasingly chubby arms could manage.

Somewhere around two o'clock in the morning I began to feel queasy—really and truly queasy.

I'd been binging on caramel-filled chocolates and watching a *Hart to Hart* marathon. This seemed like a perfectly reasonable course of action until the chocolate tangled with the nacho chips I'd layered into my stomach during the previous hour.

The gangs in *West Side Story* had nothing on the junk food battling it out inside my gut.

I burped, more than a little unladylike. Poindexter hoisted his head from the sofa to glare at me before he tucked his nose behind a pillow.

I blew out a deep sigh and sank back against the cushions, turning my focus from my dog to the pile of empty wrappers strewn across the coffee table.

No wonder my clothes didn't fit.

If I kept this up much longer the only thing I'd achieve was proving a person actually could explode.

I clicked off the television and moved to stand. My over-sugared limbs protested, so I rolled off of the sofa instead. I crawled toward the DVD player and reached for the belly-dancing DVD, still secure inside its wrapper.

Getting the cellophane off the case might have been a work-out, but it was the DVD itself that blew me away. Had I been born a double-jointed, swivel-hipped, rubber band woman, the moves might have been doable. But, because I had been born...well... me, the moves were anything but.

I'm sure my gyrations weren't easy to watch. Matter of fact, five minutes into the beginner routine, Poindexter groaned and left the room.

I paused for a moment, watching the dog's departure.

What did it say when even man's best friend could no longer take being in same room with you?

I worked out for...oh...another five or six minutes before the stitch in my side became more than I could bear.

Not a problem. I had a plethora of infomercial purchases to choose from in search of my next activity.

I started with the flashlight that needed no batteries. The instructions clearly stated a simple shake would magically cause the flashlight to illuminate. Quite frankly, the beam of light was about as weak as my atrophied muscles.

I tossed the flashlight aside and reached for my next victim.

The space-saver bags.

I started with the linen closet upstairs, ignoring the groan of protest from Poindexter, now firmly ensconced beneath my bed.

I cleared the shelves, stuffing extra sheets, towels, and blankets into the assortment of bags that had come in the deluxe package.

Next, I dug the vacuum cleaner out of the guest room, plugged it in, and used the attachment hose to suck every ounce of air from the bags.

I was left with an empty closet and the sinking realization the sense of accomplishment brought on by the sight of flattened storage bags was the most satisfaction I'd felt in a long time.

I pulled myself up, tossed the bags into the closet, and shut the door, vowing to take drastic action.

I cleaned.

I tore the house apart from top to bottom, from kitchen cupboard to garage shelves. By the time the sun rose, the pile of discarded items on the curb resembled a mini Kilimanjaro and oddly, I didn't care what the neighbors thought.

My house sparkled, purged of the old and unused. Scrubbed clean of accumulated cobwebs and dust.

I planted my fists on my hips and smiled.

Poindexter tentatively poked his nose from beneath the bed and studied me. Then he studied his surroundings, the look of amazement blatant across his furry face.

"This is how we're going to do things from here on out," I said, nodding my head in his direction. "No more hanging on to crap. No more letting clutter overwhelm us." I pumped my fist into the air. "We're going to face life head-on and we're going to deal with whatever happens."

The dog moaned and backpedaled out of sight.

I confidently marched into the master bathroom and reached for the thing I feared the most.

The scale.

I drew in a deep breath, steadied myself, and placed the scale in the middle of the tile floor. I pressed the button to activate the electronics and waited for the series of zeros that were my cue to step aboard.

I closed my eyes as I waited for the beep, seriously unprepared for what I saw when I looked at the readout.

One hundred and fifty-one pounds.

I blinked. I rubbed my eyes. I looked again.

Damn.

This was a new all-time low...er...high.

I peeled off my clothes, layer by layer, until I stood in the middle of my bathroom buck-naked.

I reset the scale and tried again.

One hundred and fifty.

Holy cow.

Without thinking, I jerked open the bathroom window and hurled my most hated possession toward the pile of trash below.

The scale hit the sidewalk in an explosion of glass and metal.

"Rough night?"

I winced.

Number Thirty-Six.

Didn't this guy ever sleep?

I peered out the window, frowning at the sight of the man walking his cat on a leash.

Who the hell walked their cat on a *leash*?

When his eyes popped wide, I remembered a key point.

I dropped to my knees and pressed my naked back to the wall.

With any luck, the entire episode would be blanked from Number Thirty-Six's memory by the terrifying vision of my bare breasts.

I pressed my face to my palms and muttered a string of expletives.

Just when I thought I had it all together, I was forced to realize I was, in fact, hopeless.

The trill of the telephone gave me a welcome excuse to crawl across the bathroom floor toward my bedroom.

The shock of my new weight, the sugar crash from the night before, and the look of sheer terror on Number Thirty-Six's face combined to trigger a sharp pain above my left eyebrow.

I reached for the phone just as the machine prepared to click into action.

"Yes."

Granted, the sharp bark was not my typical greeting, nor was it particularly appropriate for the impending holiday season, but it summed up exactly how I felt—mortified, overweight, and in no mood for sales calls or conversation.

"May I please speak with Bernadette Murphy?" Try as I might, I couldn't place the deep male voice on the other end of the phone.

I frowned, automatically expecting the worst.

A bill collector.

Neighborhood trash police.

Indecent exposure investigator.

I steeled myself. "Speaking."

"Ms. Murphy, this is Jim Barnes, the op-ed editor for the *Courier Post*. I received your letter to the editor and I'd like to run it, with your permission."

"Run it?"

I winced as soon as the words slipped between my lips. My voice had grown so tight with surprise I sounded like a startled parrot.

"Yes," he answered, his patience palpable across the line.

"In the paper?"

Parrot.

Startled.

Asinine.

Mr. Barnes's soft chuckle was unmistakable. "Yes. In the paper."

"No shit."

This time I squeezed my eyes tight and cringed. "Excuse me. I'm just a bit…"

"I apologize. I shouldn't have called you this early."

I waved one hand, as if he could see the gesture through the phone. "Not a problem. I guess you get this reaction all the time?"

"Not really." I could hear the kind smile on his face. I'd never met Mr. Barnes, but I liked him instantly. "I was impressed with not only the content of your letter, but your style. We'll be giving the article a byline."

I pressed my lips together so tightly I no doubt resembled a mouthless Keanu Reeves from *The Matrix*. I made a noise without opening my mouth, afraid of what I might actually say.

"May I take that as a yes?"

Another noise.

"Very well then. We'd like to run this on Sunday as part of our special holiday issue."

My letter.

In the paper.

Sunday.

With a byline.

I nodded, incapable of doing anything else.

"Ms. Murphy?"

"Yes." I shook myself out of my stunned silence. "Thank you. Yes. I'd be honored."

I pulled an oversized sweatshirt over my head before I headed back to the bathroom. I stared down at the pile of trash I'd once thought necessary pieces of my life.

Number Thirty-Six was nowhere in sight, but a pair of early morning walkers had paused to shake their heads at the mess I'd made.

Oddly, I felt nothing but happy amazement.

Maybe sometimes you had to clear out the old before you could make space for the new. And maybe once you did, the new was like nothing you'd ever imagined.

Maybe it was even better.

"A ship in a harbor is safe, but that is not what ships are built for."
—John A. Shedd

CHAPTER TWELVE

— —— —

*"MWVFAOBS NE OAB HSVEA OAWO ERBBQE WRWZ OAB
DCHRBHE CX OAB ABWSO."*
—*LCSO RWMGBS*

I never imagined the resolution of my disagreement with Diane
would take place over a sale rack of Dooney & Bourke hobo bags,
but there we were.

She'd ignored me for weeks, zipping right past Thanksgiving
and zeroing in on Christmas and New Year's.

When I hung up after the phone call with Jim Barnes, I realized the person I wanted to tell more than anyone else was Diane.
Sure, Ashley would be over the moon with excitement for me, but
there are some things a woman needs to share with her best friend.

This was one of them.

David helped me track his wife to Macy's by analyzing the
recent pattern of spending on their credit cards. Diane might be a
genius when it came to sniffing out a bargain, but she apparently
had a lot to learn about subterfuge.

I hesitated when I saw the size of Diane's abdomen. She'd
popped since our last encounter, and I instantly regretted the
time we'd lost over an inability to air our grievances.

She acknowledged me over a brown suede hobo, but just as quickly returned her focus to the rack in front of her.

I thought about turning away, moving on, ignoring the pang of sadness I felt every time I reached for the phone to call her before I remembered we weren't speaking. Maybe learning to face life included learning to face your own weaknesses and mistakes.

"I was wrong," I said softly.

She squinted at me and frowned.

"I shouldn't have taken Ashley anywhere without checking with you first." I casually inspected the zipper of a patchwork bag as I said this, knowing the trick to making the first move was to appear nonchalant.

"I might have been a little harsh." Diane's typically strong voice filtered weakly through the hanging straps of leather and suede.

You think?

But I didn't say it. I thought it, and then I tucked it away.

Arguing with Diane wasn't going to get me anywhere. Besides, she was pregnant and she was the mother of a teenager. She had a right to yell at me. Bottom line was that she knew what she was doing when it came to kids. I hadn't a clue. Five days does not an expert make.

"I'm sorry." I lifted my gaze to hers and smiled at the puzzled expression on her face. Then I laughed. I couldn't help myself.

Even though we were speaking softly to each other, she was obviously tense. Red blotches had exploded across her cheeks and down her neck, making it look like a mutant strain of chicken pox had taken over her face.

"Is it bad?" she asked.

I rounded the rack and linked my arm through hers. "Nothing a tropical smoothie won't cure."

She raised her brows and tipped her auburn head from side to side. "There is that."

And as we headed out into the mall, the tension I'd carried since the night we'd argued began to ease. Relief spread through my muscles and bones.

"I'm sorry, too," Diane said. "I saw you at the talent show."

The talent show.

I flashed back on my conversation with Ryan and then on Diane and David's performance.

"What did you think?" Her voice jumped an octave, the note of hope ringing loud and clear. "Be honest with me."

I rolled my eyes. From years of experience, Diane knew exactly what that meant.

"That bad?"

I rolled my eyes again.

Diane shook her head. "Ashley shaved off her eyebrows in protest."

I stopped dead in my tracks. "She what?"

"Shaved off her eyebrows."

But before I could say anything more, I spotted the security guard from hell. Unfortunately, I was fairly certain he'd spotted me as well, based on the way his eyes morphed into angry slits.

I squeezed Diane's arm, dropped my chin, and steered her toward the food court.

"Shaved her eyebrows?" I asked the question softly, still unable to picture Ashley without her typically arched brows.

Diane giggled, the sound growing from a slight chuckle to a full-out belly laugh. She stole a glance over her shoulder at the security guard.

"He's on his walkie-talkie. Maybe we could try to blend in with the crowd."

I pressed my index finger to my chin dramatically. "You're big as a house, covered in red spots, and laughing like a hyena." I shook my head. "I really don't see blending in as a possibility."

We were still laughing as the guard escorted us out of the mall, smoothies in hand.

But, we had a firm grasp on our friendship as well as our drinks, and that was worth any humiliation the mall security flat-foot could dish out.

When I got home that afternoon, I planned on taking a long, hot shower, changing clothes, grabbing the Christmas gifts I'd purchased, and heading to my mother's house for a family dinner.

I didn't plan on finding a note taped to my front door.

Come ring my bell. I've got something for you.

Those two short sentences were so loaded with double entendres, I smiled in spite of myself. The note-writer hadn't identified him or herself, but I had a strong suspicion of just who he was.

Number Thirty-Six.

After all, the only thing Mrs. Cooke would like to give me was a noise violation citation or a visit from animal control.

Before I had time to do much more than lift the note from the door, a Christmas tree made its way up the sidewalk. The telltale pair of work boots sticking out from below the trunk ensured the tree-bearer wasn't Mrs. Cooke.

Heat flushed my cheeks at the thought of the last time Number Thirty-Six and I had been face-to-face, so to speak. The memory of my less-than-clothed state still stung, and the last thing I needed was a stark reminder of my stark nakedness.

"What are you doing?" I had to admit my tone was less than receptive.

The tree trunk slammed to the front walk beside me.

"Bringing you a Christmas tree."

I tried to arch a brow but failed miserably. "What if I don't need a Christmas tree?"

"Everyone needs a Christmas tree."

"What if I don't want one?"

His single brow arch was far more effective than mine had been. "Are you going to open the door, or am I going to have to do everything myself?"

"I suppose this is going to cost me."

His amused expression turned to one of disbelief. "Like how?"

"Well, I can't imagine you'd go to this much trouble out of the goodness of your heart."

He thinned his lips, shook his head, and hoisted the tree into the air. "Then you don't have much of an imagination. Open the door."

I did as he instructed, moving out of the way to allow room for man and tree to pass.

"Where's your stand?" he asked as he held the tree balanced over a bare spot in the middle of my living room.

I held up one finger then dashed for the garage. Please Lord, don't let me have tossed the stand along with every other piece of clutter in my life.

But there it was, in all of its faux-antique glory.

Stand in hand, I raced back into the house, carefully sliding the heavy metal object underneath the trunk. Five minutes later, the tree stood majestic and straight.

I smiled.

Number Thirty-Six smiled.

"Seriously. What do I owe you?" I asked, widening my gaze.

Number Thirty-Six's smile slipped and his eyes turned sad. "Not everyone has an agenda, Number Thirty-Two." He forced a parting smile. "Merry Christmas."

He crossed the room and was out the door before I could say another word.

"Merry Christmas," I muttered to no one as I watched him stride away.

I sat on my staircase and stared at the tree for a long while after Number Thirty-Six left.

He hadn't said a thing about the scale incident, as I'd come to think of it. He hadn't said a thing about seeing me naked. He hadn't said or done anything except bring me a Christmas tree.

Not everyone has an agenda.

I was fairly sure most everyone I'd ever known had an agenda, but then, Number Thirty-Six wasn't like most everyone I'd ever known.

Matter of fact, Number Thirty-Six wasn't like anyone I'd ever known at all.

And that scared the shit out of me.

Mom, Mark, his wife Jenny, their three children, Poindexter, and I gathered around Mom's dining room table later that day. Christmas had loomed on the horizon for weeks and the moment of truth had finally arrived. The first Christmas without Dad.

His chair sat empty, shouting from the head of the table that he was gone forever.

I wondered why someone didn't make life-size cutouts of deceased loved ones for all major holidays. The thought wasn't entirely crazy.

There must be plenty of grieving relatives who'd like to see their loved one's smile one more time across the dinner table, or next to the Christmas tree, or over the Easter basket.

Maybe I was on to something, maybe even something that could be parlayed into a new career, because heaven knew my job at the ice rink wasn't getting me anywhere.

Of course, maybe I was also a bit insane, which was a distinct possibility.

"Bernie?"

My mother's voice jolted me from my mental development of the dearly-departed-cutout marketing plan. I lifted my gaze and realized everyone was staring at me.

My mom made the get-with-it gesture with her eyes that told me I'd missed something vital.

"I'm afraid I might have been daydreaming."

She rolled her eyes. "It's your turn to say what you're thankful for."

I squinted at her.

Was she kidding? "Are you kidding?"

My dad had died. My husband had left me. I'd quit my job, and my dog would never earn his obedience school graduation papers.

Plus, this exercise typically took place around our Thanksgiving table—a meal we'd all skipped this year. I supposed my mom had postponed the inevitable, saving this oh-so-uncomfortable moment for Christmas instead.

"Bernie."

Her tone left no room for excuses. She wanted an answer and she wanted it right then.

"I'm thankful for—" I paused for several long seconds while I searched my brain for a suitable answer. But then I had it.

My answer.

"I'm thankful for all of you. And Poindexter. And my health."

I wasn't thankful for the extra ten pounds I'd socked on, but this probably wasn't the time to nitpick.

Then I looked at the empty chair. Dad's chair. My voice cracked as I forced out my next words.

"Most of all, I'm thankful for Daddy and the years we all had together."

As we worked our way through the ham and scalloped potatoes and green bean casserole, I stole periodic glances at Dad's empty chair.

I could almost picture him there. Laughing. Entertaining us with a story from his youth or asking for an update on our lives.

Most of all, I could picture his smile. And his eyes.

I missed them.

I missed him.

During an uncomfortable lull in the conversation, Mark told a rather lame joke and everyone laughed a bit awkwardly.

Before too long, we each attempted a joke or a story, and in the end, our polite quiet faded away into a sea of laughter—the laughter Dad had loved so very much.

In my brother's laugh, I heard Dad's laugh.

In his eyes, I saw the same twinkle that had shone in Dad's eyes.

Our family didn't need a life-size cutout. If we looked hard enough, Dad had left his mark on each of us.

And that was truly something to be thankful for.

"Laughter is the brush that sweeps away the cobwebs of the heart."
—Mort Walker

CHAPTER THIRTEEN

— — —

"QTS AYWW BT VTTWYUE NEYIJU, HSN BT NEZD AYNE ZINESUYXUD."
—KTWZNNZ

Why I agreed to go back to the mall with Diane, I'll never know. After all, the last time she got it into her head to improve my life through shopping, I ended up on the receiving end of a lifetime ban.

Minor details aside, Diane promised me this excursion would be life-changing.

A doubt or two...or ten...danced through my brain as we headed out the front door.

"I really don't think this is necessary."

She waved her hand dismissively, effectively silencing me with a simple gesture.

"What if I can't afford this?"

Another wave. An added *shush*.

"But I don't think—"

Wave. "Shh."

"What if—"

Wave. "Shh, shh."

"Maybe we should—"

"*Hello.*" Diane's voice dripped sensuality, her comment quite apparently directed elsewhere.

I squeezed my eyes shut. Please don't let her see Number Thirty-Six. Her Bernie-needs-a-love-life campaign would kick into the stratosphere if Diane ever spotted the new neighbor.

But it turned out the object of Diane's attention wasn't Number Thirty-Six at all.

"Morning Mrs. M."

"Morning, Freddy." I gave a quick wave to my on-again, off-again landscaper.

The day was freakishly beautiful for January, and he'd no doubt decided it was as good a time as any to thin out the gardens.

His wrinkled chinos, hooded sweatshirt, and scuffed work boots made him look more like an Old Navy model than the guy responsible for keeping the weeds at bay.

I pressed my palm to Diane's back, shoving her pregnant girth toward the car.

"Sorry to hear about you and Mr. M," Freddy said.

I smiled and shook my head. "That's life, but thanks."

Diane planted her heels and ground to a stop, staring back over her shoulder to where Freddy worked, pulling dead sections out of the front flower bed.

"He's checking you o-ut." Diane stretched the last word into two syllables.

"No, he's n-ot."

"Please," she whispered as we climbed into her car. "He asked about Ryan. He's trying to get a read on the situation."

I rolled my eyes. "The only thing he's trying to get a read on is whether or not he's going to lose a client. I could be his mom."

"Only if you had him when you were ten."

I had to admit the guy had the most stunning gray eyes I'd ever seen. Yet, in all my years of talking to Freddy, I'd never sensed the certain…something…I sensed in Number Thirty-Six.

As best I could tell, Freddy was somewhere between twenty-five and thirty, but still well below the bottom range of my potential dating pool.

Diane and I slammed our respective doors, but she failed to start the ignition, shifting her focus to Freddy's taut backside instead.

She lifted her sunglasses and arched one brow in his direction. "You know, the whole older woman, younger man thing is in nowadays." She turned the key and her minivan hummed to life.

"Oh, that's me all right. Sexual trendsetter." I yanked the seat belt across my chest.

"I believe the official term is *cougar*." Diane enunciated clearly as if she suspected the entire concept might be over my head.

She suspected correctly.

"So not me. Can we go now please?"

When we reached the mall, Diane headed straight for the most expensive anchor store.

"You do remember I'm unemployed, right?" I asked.

"That'll change." She gave a dismissive wave.

What was up with her and the waves? Had the pregnancy hormones morphed her into royalty?

She grabbed my hand and dragged me across the parking lot and into the store, making a beeline for the shoe department. Apparently, she'd run a reconnaissance mission before she picked me up.

"There."

She pointed to a display of lush leather boots. The type that hugged your legs and gave you curves even if you'd never possessed a curve in your life.

I, however, had never worn anything sexier than snow boots. Granted, they had sported fluffy collars and tassels, but they couldn't hold a candle to these babies.

These boots screamed sex. Loud and clear. S-E-X.

"I don't think so." I shook my head and scanned the area for the nearest emergency exit or restroom. I'd take either.

"Try them on." She waved to a sales clerk as she ignored my pleas for mercy.

Before I knew what hit me, Diane had pushed me against a bench. The backs of my knees hit the seat, and I went down like a house of cards.

The sales clerk wasted not a moment. She piled boxes next to me on the bench and on the floor to either side of my legs. As she worked, Diane wrenched the clogs from my feet.

"Careful. Those are my favorites."

Diane wrinkled her nose and turned to the clerk. "Anything in red? Let's start there."

"Red?" I squeaked. "You expect me to wear red boots."

She thinned her lips and tipped her head to one side. God help me, there was a lecture coming.

"Do you want to feel alive?" Her eyebrows arched.

I nodded.

"Do you want to feel powerful?" Her brows snapped together.

I nodded again.

"Do you want to feel sexy and desirable?" She nodded, and I kept nodding, having learned to fear this side of her in first grade.

At this point, even the clerk was nodding.

There was no way in hell I was making a clean getaway.

I held up a single finger. "One pair. One."

Diane clapped as if Marc Jacobs had died and left her his entire spring collection.

The clerk carefully unwrapped first one red boot and then the other. Having always been a sucker for the smell of leather, I clutched one to my chest and inhaled deeply.

Oh, my.

I swallowed down the lump in my throat and slipped my foot into the boot, savoring the fit and feel of the soft leather as I pulled the zipper up, slowly guiding it to the spot where the boot stopped just below my knee.

Diane clutched one hand to her chest and sighed. The clerk thrust the matching boot into my lap.

Once I stepped into the second, I pushed myself to my feet and took note of the moment.

The sleek style caressed my legs, the smell of new leather left me dizzy, and the red color oozed vitality. I, however, found myself totally incapable of walking a straight line in three-inch heels.

"You'll get used to them," Diane said.

This time Diane and the clerk gave dismissive waves in unison.

I'd managed one lap down along the benches to peek in a mirror and was headed back to where Diane and the clerk stood waiting when Diane gasped. Loudly.

My heart jumped into my throat and I scurried toward her—a move that was neither easy nor pretty. "What? Is it the baby?"

"No." She shook her head, eyes wide, and tipped her chin none too subtly toward the men's side of the shoe department. "That guy's checking you out."

I flashed back on her earlier comment about Freddy. "You have some serious checking-me-out issues."

But when I stole a glance at the gentleman in question, he *was* checking me out. Matter of fact, he smiled and gave me a quick nod.

I tripped over the edge of the mirror then somehow managed to steady myself against a rack of sling-backs. An odd sense of lightness washed through me. The fact I'd caught some stranger's attention rocked me to the core.

I boldly decided to test the theory, walking from one mirror to the other, adding a little sway to my hips as I went back and forth. Back and forth.

My admirer stood his ground, not stepping away until I sank back down onto the bench.

I could see only one way to handle this situation. After all, the boots obviously possessed magic powers.

I looked up into the sales clerk's eyes and smiled. "I'll take them…in every color you've got."

We left Nordstrom weighed down by four pairs of boots and my clogs. I'd put the red boots to immediate use and proudly strutted along with my purchases. Yet, even the challenge of balancing several heavy bags while wearing heels didn't prevent what happened next.

I stopped abruptly outside the window of a hair salon and studied the trendy, sleek-looking women inside as my own explosion of curls reflected back at me in the glass.

Thoughts of Dad's cryptogram messages danced through my brain, mixing with Diane's challenge to feel alive.

My common sense dulled by the smell of leather and the nagging desire to change my life, I walked inside and asked for a new look. Even worse, Diane found what she termed the perfect style in a folder of photos.

Lost in the moment, caught up in the promise of a new me, I told the stylist to go for it.

Forty-five minutes later, the new me staring back from the mirror was not the sleek, sexy woman I'd envisioned, but rather a young boy with a really bad haircut.

"Holy sh—"

"Short." Diane yelled. "Fabulous." She clapped her hands, apparently wanting to spare the stylist my true reaction.

Red splotches, however, had blossomed all over her face. She might be putting on a good show, but deep down, she knew she was about to suffer a slow and painful death at my hand.

Sure, the haircut had been my idea, but every woman knew drastic hair choices were not to be made while high on the power of new boots. Diane's role should have been to talk me down from the ledge. Instead, she had not only helped me climb up, she'd pushed me over.

Hell, she'd driven me to the mall.

There wasn't a court in the state that wouldn't find her guilty of abusing the laws of friendship.

I stared at my reflection in the mirror, fighting the urge to gather up the discarded clumps of hair and run screaming toward the nearest wig maker.

"It's sassy," Diane said as we headed for home.

I shot an evil glare in her direction. "Don't you dare tell me I look sassy, or cute, or hip, or whatever other bullshit you've got up your sleeve." I leaned over the console to make sure she heard me clearly. "I look like a prepubescent boy. So *not* what I was going for."

Diane's lips quirked into a smile, but she quickly pressed them tight.

"I saw that." I sank back into my seat, arms crossed.

"What?" she asked.

"You smirked."

"Gas." She patted her stomach. "Awful heartburn today."

Her voice faltered on the last word and a burst of laughter slipped across her lips.

My only response was to narrow my gaze, hoping the sheer intensity of my sulking would intimidate her into silence. No such luck.

"Here's what I'm thinking."

That particular phrase, when uttered by Diane, had always signaled impending doom.

She'd spoken the words once in junior high, moments before we were arrested for climbing through the window of an abandoned estate home—an estate home inhabited only by ghosts—or so she'd thought.

She had uttered the phrase again on the day we'd doused our heads in peroxide and spent ten hours on the beach in the blazing July sun.

I fell for the phrase later that same day when she convinced me over-the-counter hair color would correct the resultant Day-Glo orange hair I'd shoved up under a ball cap.

If I remember correctly, my hair had finally settled into a deep shade of lavender.

History had taught me to pay attention when Diane had one of her ideas. Doing anything else was just plain stupid.

"Start over again from the beginning," I said, knowing I'd already missed part of her spiel.

She frowned, shot me a glance, and then refocused on the road.

"Speed dating," she said.

Speed dating? Wasn't my speed separation, speed grieving, and speed baldness enough to hold me for a while?

I pressed a finger to my left eyelid to still a sudden twitch. "No." I spoke the word forcefully and with conviction. Diane never missed a beat.

"I've already signed you up." Her tone grew bright and cheery, as if the higher and faster she talked, the less likely I'd be to grab the wheel and crash her van into the curb.

"You what?" The few hairs left at the base of my neck pricked to attention.

"Signed you up." She maneuvered the minivan into my driveway. "You start next week. New Year, New You." Again with the hand wave. "All that good stuff. You'll like it, you'll see."

"*Like* it?"

She nodded, blinking a half dozen times in rapid succession, a sure sign she realized just how close to snapping I was.

I pushed open the passenger door, gathered my bags, and climbed out. I took great satisfaction in the fact the entire neighborhood rattled when I slammed the door shut.

Diane's smile had grown by the time she lowered the window and leaned to shout out at me. "Your welcome packet should be here any day. You're going to thank me, you'll see."

I stooped down to speak through the window, dropping my voice to a low growl. "If you're so freaking excited about speed dating, why don't you go?"

"Please." She sat back against her seat, patted her belly with her right hand, and wiggled the ring finger of her left hand in my direction. "I'd stick out like a sore thumb."

I pointed at my head. "Like I won't?"

"Sassy," she called out, but I was already in motion, headed straight for the safety of my house.

I was completely focused on whether or not I'd ordered anything from the hair re-growth infomercial I'd seen a few nights earlier when the most wonderful sound captured my attention.

The heels of my new boots clicked sharply against the front walk.

Alive. Powerful. Sexy.

I smiled.

My hair might have looked like shit, but from the knees down, I was hot.

A long, low whistle stopped me in my tracks, but a strange sense of disappointment slithered through me when I spotted the source.

Freddy.

Who had I hoped for? Number Thirty-Six?

"You look incredible, Mrs. M."

Even though the sun had begun to slip, a sheen of perspiration covered Freddy's forehead and a smattering of dirt clung to his arms where he'd peeled off his sweatshirt and worked in his snug-fitting T-shirt.

I shook my head and laughed a bit, wondering if I had enough cash to give the guy a big tip. "Thanks," I called out as I pushed open my front door and stepped inside.

It had been a *long* time since anyone had told me I looked incredible.

I stole another glance at Freddy as I shut the door.

Diane might have been wrong about most everything today, but she'd been right about one thing.

My landscaper was one fine specimen of the male gender.

I fought the urge to channel Demi Moore and focused on a more urgent matter.

Speed dating.

I muttered expletives and planned Diane's demise as I climbed the stairs, headed for my bedroom. When I caught my reflection in the hall mirror, I froze, my homicidal thoughts going silent.

What would I think if I didn't know me? If I saw me on the street? Or at the mall?

I didn't look half bad…if I squinted hard enough.

Maybe Diane was right.

Nah. I shook my head, sneaking one last glance at my reflection as I stepped away.

Even if she had been right, admitting so would only result in additional interventions. She'd already breached the worlds of skin care, footwear, hair, and dating.

I shuddered to think what might be next.

Lingerie? Alcohol consumption? Sugar intake?

What Diane didn't know couldn't hurt her. Hell, it couldn't hurt me. Any more of her interventions and I might lose the ability to recognize myself.

I stretched to catch my reflection in the mirror over my bureau.

Maybe, just maybe, not recognizing myself wasn't such a bad thing.

Maybe it was exactly what I needed.

And maybe Diane had known that all along.

"You will do foolish things, but do them with enthusiasm."
—Colette

CHAPTER FOURTEEN

— —— ——

*"DWPXDOLPDL OX YKIY XYOVV, XZIVV BWODL YKIY
RLVVX XW VWCJ YKL ZWHPOPT ISYLH."*
—HIVNK UIVJW LZLHXWP

I ignored my answering machine all weekend. Diane called several times to check on me…and my hair. I began to feel guilty for ignoring her when she called to squeal over my letter to the editor after it ran in Sunday's paper.

Number one, she was a great friend, always had been. Number two, it wasn't as if she held me down while the stylist cut my hair within an inch of its life. I did have *something* to do with Friday's events.

So, there I sat bright and early Monday morning wondering just how late Diane was sleeping these days. I owed her an apology but didn't want to wake her up to deliver it.

When Poindexter nosed the back door, I never thought to listen before I let him outside.

He'd no sooner cleared the back steps when I heard the drone. Had to be a 737. Or bigger.

"Shit." I shoved my hands up into my hair—yet another reminder of my near baldness.

Poindexter was off like a shot, bounding across the yard. He barked up at the sky without a care in the world, without a thought as to how quickly Mrs. Cooke would dial my number to deliver her latest lecture on dog control.

I stood poised with my hand over the phone, ready to try out the new answering machine message I'd been practicing.

Then the doorbell rang. That noise, I hadn't been prepared for.

I shuffled toward the front door and smoothed the front of my sweatshirt. At some point in the rebirth of my life I imagined I'd have to toss out this particular article of clothing, but I wasn't ready for that day. Not yet.

I peered through the peephole and groaned. Mrs. Cooke stood on my front step, smiling brightly.

"Bernie?"

Apparently I'd groaned louder than I thought.

I considered using the answering machine even though she'd stopped by instead of calling, but hadn't I lied to the woman enough over the years? Plus, the whole idea of an answering machine attached to the front door was far-fetched, even for me.

Besides, if not for Mrs. Cooke, Number Thirty-Six might never have saved Poindexter the day he escaped through the back door.

Truth was, I owed Mrs. Cooke a thank-you, not another round of avoidance.

I sucked in a deep breath and pulled open the front door, stunned to find myself staring down into a plate of cinnamon buns.

Saliva puddled in my mouth as I stood transfixed by both the heavenly scent rising from the plate and the sight of freshly baked pastries, ripe for the taking.

"I felt like baking," Mrs. Cooke said with a smile. "I was hoping you hadn't had breakfast yet."

Gooey caramel syrup dripped over the sides of the buns, pooling around the lip of the plate.

Breakfast? Who the hell cared about breakfast? Didn't everyone know cinnamon buns weren't just for breakfast anymore?

"Are they still warm?" My voice cracked on the last word.

Mrs. Cooke nodded knowingly. She had me exactly where she wanted me.

"Won't you come in?" I asked.

I delivered an awkward "thank you for looking out for Poindexter" as I led her to the kitchen. I'd grown so used to thinking of the woman as my nemesis I found it difficult to think of her, well, as my neighbor. Simply that. My neighbor.

"Oh," she said, her eyes widening as her focus zeroed in on my hair.

"Too short." I winced. "I know."

"Nonsense." She reached up to touch a strand and smiled. "It's lovely for the New Year. And it shows off your cheekbones. Don't take this the wrong way, but I always wanted to tell you to get your hair out of your face."

You. My mother. Ryan and just about everyone else in my life.

I forced a smile. "Thank you. Let me get us some coffee."

Fortunately, the coffeemaker had just finished its brew cycle. Mrs. Cooke moved toward the back door as I reached to pull down two mugs from the cabinet.

"What is it he's doing, dear?" She pointed through the glass to where Poindexter was now chasing plane number two. "I must admit he looks quite pleased with himself."

"He's chasing airplanes."

"Airplanes?"

She obviously hadn't believed this explanation when I'd delivered it in the past. Maybe it was one of those phenomena in life you had to witness to appreciate.

"Chasing airplanes," she repeated. "Isn't that the darnedest thing?"

I nodded. "Cream? Sugar?"

"What about bows, dear."

Bows? I squinted. "Bows?"

"For your hair."

I blinked, shoving the sudden image of me with bows at my temples out of my head. Not pretty.

"I'll think about that," I said very slowly. "Thanks."

"Black." Mrs. Cooke pulled out a chair and made herself comfortable at the kitchen table.

"Black bows?" My gaze narrowed so severely I was sure my eyes must be nothing more than slits.

"Coffee, dear." She smiled. "I take it black."

We chatted about the weather and our holidays and my new employment at the skating rink. When she pressed for information about how I was coping, my heart squeezed.

"I'm okay," I answered. "Really...okay."

Mrs. Cooke nodded without saying a word. She had that same I-can-see-right-through-you look my mother often used. Amazing.

"Well"—she pushed to her feet—"I'm sure you have things to do. Just holler if you ever need someone to talk to."

"I can't thank you enough for the visit, and breakfast." I gestured to the half-eaten plate of cinnamon buns as I scrambled to my feet. "This has been a real treat for me."

She paused to lean against the counter. "I'm proud of you, dear."

I frowned. "Proud of me?"

She nodded. "For the article in yesterday's paper. Not many people take the time to say what they think, but you did."

She pushed away from the counter and headed toward the front door. I stood frozen to the spot, weighed down by my intake of cinnamon buns and stunned into a state of disbelief by Mrs. Cooke's words.

"So, you read it?" I asked after several seconds of silence.

Mrs. Cooke was halfway to the front door. "I cut it out and taped it my fridge." She waved as she let herself out. "Words to live by, dear. Did you ever think you have a gift?"

I shook my head even as I mentally nodded. Dad had always told me writing was my gift, as had my fifth grade teacher, and my ninth, and my twelfth. Yet, I'd spent a lifetime setting aside one of the things I loved most.

I launched myself into motion, holding open the front door as I waved good-bye. Mrs. Cooke made her way down the front walk, toward her house next door.

A flash of red caught the corner of my eye. A red truck. Pulling into my driveway.

Freddy.

I winced.

Mrs. Cooke had come bearing sticky buns, but Freddy had no doubt come bearing an invoice for the work he'd done.

As much as I loved how beautifully he kept the five gardens I'd insisted on putting in two years earlier and then never maintained, I couldn't afford to keep paying him.

The savings account was only going to go so far. Until I got a salaried job, things like landscaping fell into the disposable category. Poor Freddy had to go.

I stifled a sigh. Maybe that was all right. Maybe the time had come to get a little dirt under my fingernails.

He smiled as he headed toward me, wearing dark blue jeans and a tweed jacket that made him look much older than he'd looked the last time I'd seen him.

His gray eyes danced and my stomach did this odd little thing where it balled up into a knot. Then my mouth went dry.

Too many cinnamon buns. Obviously.

Freddy's lips quirked into a crooked grin as he stepped up onto the front step. "Still say you look incredible, Mrs. M."

Considering I stood there without makeup, wearing a sweatshirt so ratty one cuff hung limp instead of encircling my wrist, Freddy either had a crush or he wanted something.

"Too short." I shook my head.

He reached out to touch a strand of my hair and a shiver danced across my back. Maybe Freddy wasn't so young after all, or maybe it had been way too long since a member of the opposite sex had reached out to touch anything of mine.

I studied the lean lines of his face. If I stared hard enough, I could almost imagine a hint of crow's feet around his eyes.

"Sexy." He uttered the word so softly I wasn't sure whether I'd imagined it or not.

"Want some coffee?" Much to my embarrassment, my voice climbed three octaves on the last word.

Freddy followed me into the kitchen.

I let Poindexter in the back door and turned to face Freddy.

Neither of us reached for coffee. Instead, we stared at each other, a palpable tension spiking to life between us. The memory of his voice ricocheted through my brain.

Sexy.

And Freddy…well…Freddy leaned so close I could smell the clean scent of soap on his suntanned skin.

He pinned me against the kitchen wall and brought his lips to mine. Shivers of delight raced through my every nerve ending and heat ignited in regions that hadn't felt heat in years.

Either I was seriously turned on, or I was having the mother of all hot flashes.

When Freddy slid his hands up under my sweatshirt and cupped my breasts, I thought my knees might give out completely. I gripped Freddy's shoulders and held on for dear life as he trailed kisses along the length of my neck.

The next thing I knew I was in his arms, being carried toward my bedroom. Not only was the guy an incredible kisser, but he obviously possessed superhuman strength.

We peeled out of our clothes and for once in my life I wasn't self-conscious about my waist, my hips, my thighs. None of the *assets* about which I typically obsessed.

The blatant lust in Freddy's eyes was enough to make any women feel like a supermodel.

He pressed me back against the pillows and I pushed aside the rumpled comforter.

I reached for him, ready for him to take me now. I couldn't believe how much I wanted to feel him inside me. Wham, bam, thank you, ma'am.

But instead he dropped his mouth to my neck, nibbling a path to one breast, then the other, suckling, kissing, driving me wild. When his mouth found my stomach, I writhed beneath him, unable to control my body's response to his touch.

When Freddy slid his hands up under my rump and lowered his mouth between my legs, I moaned, quite sure I was about to experience sex like I'd never experienced it with Ryan, when I heard his voice.

Ryan's voice.

"Bernie?" He sounded so close he must have been just outside the bedroom door. "The front door was open. Are you all right?"

I said nothing, too stunned to speak. Surely this was all a dream. Otherwise, I was experiencing the most surreal morning of my life.

"I came to clear out my office," Ryan continued. "I took today off. I didn't think you'd mind."

Mind? Why should I mind? Oh, maybe because I was *this* close to a mind-blowing orgasm with a man—a younger man—who actually seemed to desire *me*.

"How old are you?" I whispered to Freddy.

"Twenty-four," he mumbled as he shifted his mouth to my inner thigh.

Oh, my.

"Do you know how old I am?"

He shook his head. "Thirty maybe?" His words were barely audible. "And you're hot."

I was beginning to harbor serious feelings for the guy.

"Bernie?" Genuine concern tinged Ryan's tone.

"Hide," I mouthed to Freddy, who planted one more kiss on my stomach before he dashed for the master bathroom.

"I just threw up," I hollered to Ryan. "Give me a minute."

"Oh." A long silence followed. "I'll wait downstairs."

Nothing sent a man running in the opposite direction faster than vomit.

I left Freddy in the bathroom, wrapped my faded yellow robe around myself, and went downstairs. Ryan had settled into the recliner and sat flipping through my mail.

"There's nothing for you there."

He dropped the envelopes, guilt plastered across his face. His expression grew serious as he straightened to his full height. "You're really red. Do you have a fever?"

I felt my face grow even hotter. "Something like that. Listen, I already packed up your office, but maybe you could come back at a better time?"

He nodded. "Sure thing. Where's Freddy? His truck's in the drive."

I had to think fast. Definitely not something my brain was up to at the moment. I spotted the top of Poindexter's ears, hiding behind the china cabinet.

Smart dog.

"Um…I think Freddy took Poindexter for a walk."

Ryan made a face as if he didn't believe me for a second.

"I asked him to."

"Oh." He nodded.

I faked a little gag. "I don't feel so hot."

His eyes grew huge and he bolted for the door. "I'll give you a call later to see how you are. I can get my stuff another time."

"Thanks," I answered. But he'd already cleared the threshold and was halfway to his car.

Coward.

Five minutes later I watched Freddy's truck pull out of the drive.

He'd still been ready for me when I returned to the bedroom. Matter of fact, I don't think I'd ever seen a man quite so *ready*.

But on the way back up the stairs, I realized Ryan wasn't the only coward.

I was a coward, too. Too much of a coward to take a tumble in the sheets with my twenty-four-year-old landscaper, no matter how amazing his eyes were or what sort of tricks he could do with his tongue.

I was forty-one, for crying out loud. Forty-one.

I knew better than to jump into bed with the first warm body I could find. Didn't I?

I was standing in the doorway, clutching the neck of my robe when I heard a voice.

A deep, rumbling, masculine voice.

"Maybe you're right, Number Thirty-Two."

I winced, praying right then and there for the ground to swallow me up. Instead, I straightened, facing my cat-walking neighbor head-on.

"Right about what?"

Number Thirty-Six shrugged as he hesitated for a moment, then he resumed his walk, tipping his chin toward the tailgate of Freddy's truck.

"Maybe everyone does have an agenda."

When he glanced back in my direction, I'd like to say his face was expressionless, or teasing, but it was neither.

Number Thirty-Six looked disappointed.

I straightened, giving a brief thought to defending myself, to telling him Freddy meant nothing, to telling him to mind his own business.

I thought about saying a lot of things, but instead I merely pushed the front door closed without saying a word.

As inexplicably guilty as I felt, I decided I didn't owe Number Thirty-Six an explanation. The man had brought me a Christmas tree. So what?

Did that entitle him to pass judgment on my pathetic sexual almost-escapade with the landscaper?

I thought not.

Though as I headed back to the kitchen to eat every leftover cinnamon bun I could cram into my mouth, my guilt morphed from a tiny simmer to a full-out boil.

Number Thirty-Six.

Disappointed.

Damn the man.

"Conscience is that still, small voice that yells so loud the morning after."

—Ralph Waldo Emerson

CHAPTER FIFTEEN

— — —

*"HJKZ SFCSYF EJGF J ICCR JPH PK YPAF, WDN ACB VCHF
BFJVCK NEFZ KFGFB SDYY NEF NBPIIFB."*
—*DKQKCMK*

My UPS driver arrived first thing the next morning with an abso-
lutely-not-concealed-in-a-brown-wrapper box emblazoned with
the words *Dating Now*. I had to give him credit for trying to hide
his grin as he waited for me to sign his computerized tracking
contraption.

I supposed he figured I'd ordered just about everything else a
woman might need in life. Why shouldn't I order up a date?

Sadly, I actually bought that theory myself for a moment or
two.

The box was larger than I'd imagined the membership materials would be, so I grabbed my coffee mug and headed for the
kitchen table.

Thirty minutes later, I sat elbow deep in paperwork and pro-
motional materials, all touting the features and benefits of speed
dating—the Dating Now way.

No matter how many times I flipped through the colorful
leaflets and slick brochures, my gaze kept returning to one thing.

My appointment card.

You have a date with destiny.

Apparently I was to meet "destiny" this coming Friday night at seven o'clock in the Sunset Room of the Atlantic Grille. Somehow the whole idea of speed dating in the Sunset Room of anything was a bit too cliché for me.

But there were better things to worry about. Like, what would I wear?

I took a swig of my tepid coffee. The boots were a no-brainer, but what would I wear with them?

There was always the option of wearing nothing but the boots, but I imagined that if the Dating Now people wanted nudity, they'd call themselves *Naked Dating Now* or *Nudity Now* or something more...well...naked.

I shook off the thought and shoved every piece of paraphernalia back into the box. I had days to obsess about my upcoming date with destiny. For now, I had more pressing matters.

Like the to-do list I'd avoided since my dad died.

Sure, I'd sent copies of Dad's death certificate to every organization under the sun, but this was different.

This was the list that read: revise Mom's will, help Mom change car title, bank account, house deed, utilities, and credit cards to her name only.

There was more to it—a *lot* more to it.

But the plan for today was to start small. Today, my mother and I planned to upgrade her cell phone from the one I'd given my parents eleven years earlier as a Christmas present.

The morning had grown unseasonably warm by the time I headed south toward my mother's house; so much so, in fact, I felt inspired to do something I rarely did.

I stopped off at the cemetery.

I avoided going there more often than not. Call me a bad mother, call me whatever you want, but visiting that spot never failed to rip out my heart and leave me raw and emotionally void for days.

I pulled the car to the side of the lane next to the big black tombstone I used as a landmark and climbed out. I carefully navigated the path toward Emma's grave, my dad's grave, my grandparents' graves.

My steps faltered when I spotted the flowers—fresh arrangements on all three graves. In addition, a well-worn teddy bear sat tucked against the side of Emma's stone.

Who on earth would have left this?

I reached for the little guy, stroked his nose, and wondered how long he'd been keeping Em company.

As far as I knew, Ryan had only been back twice since our daughter's funeral. Once on what would have been her first birthday and again at Dad's funeral.

I'd put my money on my mother. She'd no doubt been up early and had taken advantage of the gorgeous weather.

Yet, the teddy bear had been here a lot longer than since this morning.

A flicker of guilt whispered through me.

I should stop there more often. I should sit and talk or think or pray. But I just plain didn't have it in me.

The cemetery wasn't where I wanted to be when I thought of Emma.

Each time I knelt there, I pictured her tiny, white coffin covered in a spray of flowers. I remembered our friends and family leaving the graveside while I stayed behind, unable to walk away for the final time.

I remembered Ryan's words as he'd reached to pull me back toward the car.

"She's not here," he said.

He was right. She wasn't there. Not in spirit, anyway.

I pushed myself up from my knees and stared at the sky. A pair of birds soared past and I realized Emma was everywhere.

Everywhere I wanted her to be.

With me. With Ryan. With my mom.

"Take care of her for me," I whispered to my dad's tombstone before I turned to walk away.

I usually sobbed as I drove through the huge iron gates of the cemetery, angry at the world. Angry at God for letting Emma die. But today was different. Today, I smiled, picturing Emma cradled in her granddad's arms.

Maybe I'd turned the corner on my grief.

Lord, I hoped so. My acceptance phase was long overdue.

I clung to my peaceful state of mind as I pulled into my mother's driveway. I even maintained my Zen-like calm as I looked over the master list of things we'd yet to take care of.

"Boy, this is some list." I shook my head as if my statement was news to my mother.

"I realize that, Bernie." She slid the list out from under my fingertips. "So, we'll start with the cell phone and go from there."

I nodded, suddenly flashing back on the flowers and the teddy bear at the cemetery.

"Were you at the cemetery today?"

Mom shook her head. "Your brother was."

Mark? Mr. I-refuse-to-talk-about-dead-family-members?

"There were flowers on the graves and a teddy bear on Em's." I squinted at her. "Mark did that?"

She nodded. "He goes once a week."

She could have knocked me over with a feather. "Since when?"

She gave me a slight smile. "I told you everyone grieved differently."

True. She had a point there, but I wasn't about to let go of this particular conversational thread that easily. "How do you know he went today?"

"He came by to try on your dad's jackets." She shuffled through a stack of papers as if she could distract me from what she'd said.

Nice try.

I moved in for the kill. "Which ones did he take?"

Her only response was the shake of her head.

A mix of anger and frustration tangled inside me. Anger at the hurt I read in my mother's expression. Frustration at the fact my brother refused to do this one simple thing.

Sure, he could put flowers on a grave, but he couldn't look in the closet, pick a damned jacket, and take it home.

"He didn't take any?"

"No." She tapped the list. "We'd better get going."

I knew better than to force the issue.

After all, my niece's birthday was coming up—the perfect opportunity to tell my brother exactly what I thought.

In the meantime, I refocused on Mom and her quest for a new cell phone.

Once we reached the store, selecting an upgrade for my parents' outdated plan took less than five minutes. Everything was going fine until the sales clerk asked for the one thing I hadn't anticipated.

"Do you have a copy of the death certificate?" She blinked, eyes bright, as if that was a question people asked every day.

I winced.

My mother swallowed.

"We just need to change the name on the account to my mom's." I gave the woman my brightest smile. "Surely you can do that without the death certificate."

The woman shrugged. "Sorry."

My mom sniffled and I spun around to look at her.

She struggled to compose herself even as tears glistened in her eyes. I knew better than to reach for her, knew that would only make things worse.

"Thank you." She forced the words, her voice tight with emotion. "We'll come back another time."

The sales clerk's features fell slack, suggesting she might have a heart beneath the pat smile and unfeeling questions.

"I'm sorry," she said softly. "I'll get you a form. You can fax it to me, if that would be easier."

My mother nodded. I nodded. The sales clerk nodded. Then she disappeared into the back room.

I reached for my mother's arm, but she spoke before I made contact.

"It's all right, Bernie."

"No, it's not." Anger began to simmer inside me. "It's not all right, Mom. Dad's dead and this sucks." I jerked my thumb toward the exit. "I feel like walking over there and screaming out into the parking lot. Everyone out there should take a moment to acknowledge how much this sucks."

She looked at me then, smiling through her tears. "I'm sure they have their own problems, honey."

I stared at her, completely in awe of the woman who had lost her soul mate yet soldiered on, who found a way to smile through her tears.

We didn't say much on the way home, having decided to return to home base and try *the list* again later.

I glanced at each car and pedestrian we drove past.

They have their own problems, honey. My mom's words echoed in my brain.

I knew she was right. I knew everyone had a story. I mean, how could they not?

The woman walking her dog had a story. The man driving the car behind me had a story. Even the neighbor picking up trash along the curb had a story.

Everyone had something they were trying to survive, or achieve, or overcome. No one was immune to loss or heartache or aspirations or struggle.

That was how it worked, this thing called life.

The only way to avoid life was to avoid *living*.

And while I couldn't speak for everyone, I felt fairly confident speaking for me and for Mom.

She'd say every moment with my dad had been worth the pain she felt right now. Worth the lonely days and nights she'd endured since he died.

She'd say she wouldn't have changed a thing.

I let that realization sink in for a moment, and then I thought about my life, knowing there wasn't a thing I would have changed either.

Not a moment with Ryan or Emma or Dad.

Sure, I would have taken a few more moments with Emma, but the time we did have together shaped me. Every second touched me, changed me, altered the course of my life forever.

No. I shook my head.

I wouldn't change the past.

Not even if I could.

At seven o'clock sharp on Friday night, I sat at my assigned table in the Sunset Room of the Atlantic Grille.

Turns out Diane had worried even more about my outfit than I had. She'd delivered a carefully chosen ensemble, covering every wardrobe item and accessory from top to bottom.

The classic herringbone pencil skirt stopped at my knees, showing off the full glory of *the boots*. The sweater she found hung long, yet nipped in enough to give the illusion of a waist, which I sure as hell didn't possess at this stage of my life.

The earrings were a bit much, dangling sterling silver hearts that weighed about five pounds each. I thought about leaving them behind, but I'd never put a thing past Diane in thirty-five years.

She pressed them into my palm, assured me they looked *fabulous* with my newly shorn hair, and then shoved me out the door.

So there we sat, me and every other Dating Now wannabe, cooling our heels, waiting for the *experience* to begin.

I seized the opportunity to size up the room and quickly realized the world of speed dating attracted all types.

I shouldn't have been surprised, but for some reason, I'd expected a room full of beautiful people. Instead, I sat in the middle of a room full of normal people.

Some average. Some not so average. Some plain. Some gorgeous. Some short. Some tall. And some—based on the years showing in their faces—who were looking to make their final love connection.

The Dating Now staffer reviewed the procedures with us before she announced the start of the first date. We had five minutes to acquaint ourselves with the person sitting across the table from us. At five minutes, the staffer slapped her palm down on one of those bells you ring at the deli counter when you begin to wonder if anyone actually works in the store.

At the sound of the *ding*, the men shifted one table to their left and each new date repeated the process.

Ding. Shift. Repeat.

Ding. Shift. Repeat.

I was fine with this entire concept, knowing I'd be out of there in an hour and a half max, when I saw *him*.

Of all people.

I watched as he made his way around the room, moving from table to table in five-minute increments. His hair was cut shorter than I remembered, and his glasses were nowhere to be seen. Contact lenses, no doubt. No. Check that. Corrective surgery.

Only the best for him.

My palms grew clammy as he neared. I managed not much more in my conversations than to repeat my name and job—or lack thereof—like a soldier rattling off her rank and serial number. I made eye contact with no one.

The only person I focused on was *him*. He moved closer and closer, smiling and chatting to each potential victim as if he were the most charming man on the face of the earth.

I thought about jumping to my feet and telling each woman he encountered to run for her life. I might have done it, too, had his gaze not captured mine as he made the turn, headed straight in my direction, one table away.

His mouth pulled into a tight smile—more of a smirk, actually. I swallowed down the ball of disgust and angst in my throat and braced myself. The poor guy currently seated across from me showed genuine concern.

"Are you all right? You look a bit flushed."

Flushed? I was flushed all right.

Flushed at the thought of facing the man I thought I'd never see again after I'd told him to shut up, once and for all.

But there he stood, lowering his six-foot-six frame into the seat across from me, reaching out to shake my hand.

Blaine McMann.

The boss from hell. Or should I say, former boss from hell.

I hugged myself instead of touching his hand and tried to arch a brow. Based on experience—and the amused look on Blaine's face—I'd succeeded in doing nothing more than squishing up one side of my face.

"I see you lost your hair along with your mind," he said.

I sneered. I wasn't sure I'd ever sneered before, but I sure as hell sneered then.

"Listen." Much to my chagrin, he kept talking. "We haven't got much time." He tapped his watch. "Now that our professional relationship is out of the way, what do you say we hit the sheets?"

When I gagged this time, there was nothing fake about it.

I waved frantically, doing my best to snag the attention of the Dating Now chaperone. She was at my side instantly, phony expression of sincerity plastered across her flawless face.

"Did you need something?" she asked.

"I'd like to pass."

"Pass what?"

"Him." I jerked my thumb at Blaine's nose.

"Why that"—she hesitated, blinking as if no one had ever asked the question before—"that would create havoc."

"Havoc?" I couldn't believe my ears. "Look, I paid good money for this. All right, I didn't, but someone else did, and if I want to pass, I think I should be allowed to pass."

My voice had climbed to a minor shriek while the Dating Now woman's tone dropped to little more than a whisper, a desperate whisper.

"You only have three minutes left." She leaned close, shot a glance at Blaine, then moved closer still. "If you don't care for this gentleman, why don't you just sit here quietly?"

Care for this gentleman? I *loathed* this gentleman. This gentleman had been the bane of my existence for more years than I cared to remember.

Blaine smirked. "I don't see why you're so upset. You sure as hell don't look like you've been getting any." He sat back against his seat. "You know you want it."

This time, I didn't hesitate. My boots and I were up on my chair before I could say *not a snowball's chance in hell*. I teetered precariously over my assigned table.

Blaine scrubbed a hand across his face and muttered. "Here we go."

"Don't you ever"—I pointed my finger in his face—"talk to me or anyone else like that again." I found my center of gravity and planted my fists on my hips. "You self-centered, arrogant, conceited piece of shit. I wouldn't sleep with you if you were the last living slimeball on the face of the earth."

Ding, ding, ding.

The Dating Now hostess had gone paler than pale. She gently reached for my elbow and tipped her chin toward the floor. "Time's up."

As I climbed down, doing my best to ignore Blaine's self-satisfied smirk, a smattering of applause broke out on the far side of the restaurant. Before I knew it, every woman Blaine had visited, without exception, stood clapping.

His smug expression shifted to one I'd never seen before. If I wasn't mistaken, Blaine McMann was embarrassed.

Embarrassed.

I hadn't thought it possible.

The warm satisfaction that burst inside my belly filled me from my head to my toes.

Maybe I'd been wrong about speed dating.

Though the admission didn't say much for the state of my social life, this was the best night I'd had in a long, long time.

On the way home I stopped off at my favorite café, deep in the heart of Genuardi's. I ordered up a grande chai latte and went to work.

If the *Courier Post* had published my first letter, maybe they'd publish a second. Who knew? Maybe somewhere out there readers were attacking their papers each morning, breathless with anticipation in the hope of knowing how my life was going.

Regardless, I decided the time had come to chase at least one dream—my writing.

Perhaps I had a bit too much caffeine, and perhaps the whole Dating Now incident had gone to my head, but damn it, I was going to write the best letter to the editor ever written.

An hour later my prose sat complete, sentences scrawled in my favorite purple ink, a flawless masterpiece extolling the virtues of stepping out of your comfort zone, no matter how small that first step might be.

After all, if Diane hadn't encouraged me to buy the boots, chop my hair, and speed date, I wouldn't have experienced the glorious moment of victory when I finally put Blaine in his place.

While I might not have taken a single one of those steps on my own, I had taken them.

Me.

Not anyone else.

Steps were steps.

Steps were good.

Steps were the only things that were going to save me. They were the things that were going to carry me forward, out of my old life and into my new one.

I felt so empowered by my writing I pulled Dad's book out of my purse. I'd started keeping the cryptograms with me, eager to reveal each remaining word, every message Dad had chosen for me.

It took only moments to solve the puzzle I'd started earlier that day.

The guy who manned the counter tapped me on the shoulder. "Ma'am, store's closing."

Ma'am.

Wasn't that always the way? Just when you were filled with a heady sense of empowerment brought on by sassy hair, sexy boots, and a cryptogram message, someone called you *ma'am* and brought your ego crashing back to earth.

I gathered up my notebook and tossed my empty cup in the trash. I headed across the parking lot toward my car, boot heels slamming confidently against the asphalt, determined to type up my letter and e-mail it the moment I got home.

Ma'am or no ma'am, I was taking steps.

Forward steps.

I had no intention of turning back.

"Many people have a good aim in life, but for some reason they never pull the trigger."

—Unknown

CHAPTER SIXTEEN

— —— ——

*"LFGWG IWG QCQGJLB XFGJ GUGWALFKJZ ZCGB XGDD;
VCJ'L OG TWKZFLGJGV, KL XCJ'L DIBL."*
—YRDGB WGJIWV

Much as I would never admit this to David, I looked forward to
my afternoons at the skating rink.

There was something about the hustle and bustle of the daily
practices and skating lessons that made me smile. Not to mention
the fact I'd convinced myself shivering in the freezing cold envi-
ronment burned extra calories.

On this particular day, I'd been assigned the task of running
the snack bar, a job I actually enjoyed because it gave me a chance
to interact with everyone at the rink.

Also, I'd discovered I could skim a jumbo chocolate chip
cookie or two off the top each day, unbeknownst to David. I convinced myself my actions fell more into the quality assurance
camp than into outright thievery.

Quite honestly, I couldn't help myself.

Willpower had never been one of my strengths. The summer
between my sophomore and junior years of college, I'd managed
a Candy Kitchen in Bethany Beach, Delaware.

The store featured a make-your-own-sundae bar, homemade chocolates, and fudge.

I'd packed on fifteen extra pounds before the end of June.

When I drove home for my birthday, the first words out of my mother's mouth fell short of anything warm and fuzzy.

She threw open the front door, watched me scramble out of my glow-in-the-dark-yellow Chevette, and frowned. "You've got thighs."

Sadly, those same thighs had been with me ever since.

Back at the rink, the team mothers tended to congregate inside the shelter of the snack bar seating area, clutching their coffees or teas or sugar-free hot chocolates.

An oh-so-trendy hockey mom sporting flawless makeup and chunky blond highlights ordered a decaf mocha latte. Was she kidding?

I blinked my focus out of the past and into the present, poured a cup of coffee, dumped in some hot chocolate, and handed the drink to the woman. She studied the cup suspiciously but didn't say a word.

During a lull in the snacking activity, I stood at the counter and rested my chin on my fists, staring at a team of teenage boys running through ice hockey drills.

I squinted when I spotted Ashley standing at the railing, deep in conversation with a boy who stood a half foot taller than she did.

I cracked a smile and began formulating my plan to tease her when Ashley gave the kid a shove. Hard.

Then she spun dramatically on one heel and stomped in my direction.

Obviously not the young love encounter I'd imagined.

"He's a Neanderthal," Ashley said with a dramatic roll of her eyebrow-less eyes as she breezed behind the counter and poured a tall cup of hot chocolate.

I blinked. "Big word, Ash."

She scowled at me. "He *is* a Neanderthal, Aunt Bernie. Their *mascot*." Her tone dripped with impatience. "They're called the Ice Men."

I bit down on my lip to keep from snickering. Somehow I was fairly certain laughter in any form would not be appreciated.

"Interesting." I nodded, doing my best to shake the sudden mental picture of a team of fur-draped cavemen taking to the ice.

"And then he said, 'Nice eyebrows.'"

Ashley gestured grandly, and I did my best to focus on her words, hoping I hadn't missed anything vital during the moment my imagination had taken over.

"So I said, 'nice eyebrows,' too."

She nodded, pointing to the bald area above her eyes. "I mean he does have nice eyebrows. His costume brows are pasted on, sure, but they're very authentic looking."

I nodded, working hard to project how seriously I was listening to her.

"He and his buddies all started laughing"—she patted her chest—"at me." She blinked back sudden moisture and all humorous thoughts fled my brain. "Then I remembered I don't have any eyebrows."

Ashley dropped her gaze to the carpet, and I reached out to squeeze her shoulder.

"They're jerks, honey. Immature jerks."

"But that's just it, Aunt Bernie." She lifted her watery gaze to mine.

My head was swimming at this point. Obviously I'd lost the ability to follow teenage thought processes a long time ago. "What?"

"He's not a jerk. He's really cool, and I thought maybe he liked me."

I winced on her behalf, feeling her pain, but before I could say another word, she spun on one heel and breezed out of the snack bar, Styrofoam cup in hand.

"Ashley," I called after her.

To my surprise, she slowed to a stop and turned to face me.

I closed the gap between us and tipped up her chin with my fingertips. I studied the expanse of smooth skin above her now tear-filled eyes. The faintest trace of brows had returned, and a sudden thought popped into my head.

"Let's go to the bathroom." I grabbed her hand and steered her toward the restrooms.

"I don't have to go to the—"

"Yes, you do." I nodded, unwilling to take no for an answer.

A few minutes later we stood side by side, studying my work in the scratched and blurry mirror.

"Don't I look like an old lady?" she asked, leaning forward to study the pale brows I'd drawn on with my eyeliner.

I shook my head no, while thinking that yes, she might resemble some washed-up star of film and stage, but at least we were on to something here.

With the help of the right tools—and makeup kiosk employees, heaven help me—we could manage a temporary fix while we waited for the Ashley's real brows to return to full strength.

I sank my teeth into my new mission and grinned at Ashley's reflection in the mirror. "How do you feel about a trip to the mall after work?"

Ashley and I parked at the entrance closest to the costume store in the mall for two reasons.

The spot was the farthest away from the coffee shop where the security force hung out, and the costume store offered the perfect opportunity to hide my identity before I took Ashley to face Brittany and Tiffany of Rediscover You fame.

I'd assigned Ashley the task of picking out a pair of funky glasses for me while I lovingly stroked the synthetic locks of a hot pink wig.

"Subtle, Aunt Bernie. Real subtle."

I didn't bother glancing at Ashley as she sidled up next to me. I could sense her eye roll; there was no need to see it.

"What?" My voice climbed an octave or two. "Too over-the-top?"

When she snapped her tongue, she sounded just like her mother, and I smiled.

No matter how hard we women tried to become anything but, when all was said and done, we were our mothers. In most cases, this was a good thing.

I smiled at Ashley and she narrowed her brow-less gaze at me.

In Ashley's case this was a very good thing. Mothers didn't come any better than Diane, when she wasn't scouring clearance racks.

Diane.

I swallowed and dug around in my purse for my cell phone. She'd kill me. Ashley and I hadn't even told David where we were going when we left the rink. As far as he knew, I was taking Ashley home and nothing more.

Diane was right. I had a whole lot to learn about the parenting life.

I frowned when Diane's ring clicked immediately into voice mail.

The woman felt as strongly about her cell phone as she felt about discount designer purses, so I found it difficult to believe she'd turned off her phone. Maybe the battery had run down and she hadn't noticed.

I left a message, snapped my phone shut, and shrugged. "Not answering, but at least she'll know where you are."

Ashley gave a dismissive shrug of her own and lifted my hand from the wig. She tipped her chin toward my head and grinned.

"Don't you think your haircut is disguise enough?"

My haircut.

The kid had a point.

The last time the Rediscover You dynamic duo had seen me, I'd sported my typical wild tangle of curls. They'd never recognize me in my prepubescent-boy pixie cut.

I couldn't help but notice the twinkle in Ashley's eyes. I hadn't seen her this happy since I'd witnessed her inhaling a can of peas. I couldn't help but feel a bit suspicious.

"What?" I asked.

Her smile widened and I was struck once again by how quickly she was growing up.

She handed me a pair of deep-red librarian glasses.

"Oh." I reached for the frames, slipped them on, and squatted down to study my reflection in the small mirror anchored to the counter.

If I didn't know me, I'd think I looked...cool.

"What do you think?" I straightened the frames and waited for Ashley's answer.

"I think they'll never know what hit them." She grasped my elbow and squinted, the corners of her eyes turning serious. "Thanks for doing this, Aunt Bernie."

My heart squeezed a bit. "Anything for you, Ash. Anything."

And I meant it.

At that moment, studying the light and hope and gratitude in Ashley's eyes, I realized I loved this kid as if she were my own.

I threw my arm around her shoulder and pulled her tight against my side. "I love you, sweetie."

"Aunt Bernie." She drew my name out into about fifteen syllables. "Someone might see us."

I bit my lip and laughed. "Duly noted." I waved the glasses in front of her nose. "Let's pay for these and go get you some proper eyebrows."

Things at the Rediscover You counter went fairly well, if I do say so myself. I was in rare form. That's to say, I bit my lip whenever one of the makeup twins said something that made my teeth hurt, which was often.

Ashley, on the other hand, handled Brittany and Tiffany like a pro. Based on some of the high school girls I'd seen at the rink, I imagined she had a lot of experience dealing with the perfect girls of her generation.

Brittany and Tiffany, as we'd established the day of the first Rediscover You encounter, viewed themselves as beyond perfect. Theirs was a perfection to outshine all others, making them eligible for the ultimate in perfection recognition.

They'd been chosen to teach, in their case, the art of makeup.

I gave myself a mental slap. I needed to let go of the past and move beyond my first impression of these girls.

They were being lovely with Ashley, and based on Ashley's smile—and perfectly natural-looking brows—she had become one very satisfied customer.

By the time I paid for Ashley's supplies, I convinced myself I might have been wrong about the dynamic duo. As Ashley turned for the smoothie stand and I tucked my wallet back into my purse, I almost felt friendly toward Brittany and Tiffany.

Until one of them spoke.

Loudly.

"Excuse me."

I pivoted, plastering on my best smile.

Tiffany waggled a finger in my direction. "You know, you need to actually *use* the recovery cream in order for it to work."

I bit down on my lip and sucked air through my teeth, trying to summon up every ounce of restraint I could.

Brittany wrinkled her nose and nodded. "And red is so not your color. Who picked out those glasses?"

Ashley grabbed my elbow at the precise moment I stepped toward the kiosk counter.

I held my ground, looking from Brittany and Tiffany's sneers to Ashley's pleading expression then back again.

In the end, I chose Ashley. How could I not?

"Thanks for stopping me," I muttered as we put space between us and the kiosk from hell.

"Thank you, Aunt Bernie." Ashley stopped for a second, gracing me with a smile that lit her every feature, including her new brows. "*You're the best.*"

You're the best. I grinned to myself.

The kid might be a bit biased and blinded by kiosk shopping, but her words were exactly what I needed to shove the Rediscover You twins out of my mind once and for all.

I dropped Ashley at her house, surprised to find no cars in the driveway. Best I could figure, David had stayed late at the rink and Diane had found a clearance rack…or two…or three.

I waited until Ashley gave me the all-clear wave from inside the front door before I headed home.

The message light on my machine greeted me, blinking its silent plea. *Press me. Press me. Press me.*

So I did.

David's words spilled out of my machine, tight and emotional. At just six months pregnant, Diane had started bleeding.

He'd met her at Cooper Hospital and she'd been admitted to Maternal ICU.

The gravity of his words hit home just as the phone rang.

The message cut off as I answered the incoming call.

"Aunt Bernie." Ashley started talking before I could fully press the phone to my ear, let alone speak. "It's Mom. I—"

"I'll be there in five minutes, honey." I focused on using my most soothing tone of voice, even though my insides had gone into full-out panic. "She'll be all right. You'll see."

As I shot Poindexter an apologetic look and raced for the front door, I could only pray the words I'd spoken were true.

"There are moments when everything goes well; don't be frightened, it won't last."
    —Jules Renard

CHAPTER SEVENTEEN

— — —

"MKAOXMP WXSRL F AOXMP LK XMARMLRDZ XM AOR
EREKVZ FL AOR GXLO AK WKVPRA XA."
—EXNORD IR EKMAFXPMR

My insides coiled into a tight knot as I searched for a parking space inside the Cooper Hospital garage, urging my car to climb higher and higher, up ramp after ramp.

I slipped into a restricted space between a minivan and an SUV. So much for compact cars only.

I scrambled out of the driver's door while Ashley catapulted from the passenger side. When I spun around to face the bank of elevators, I hesitated, flashes of the past hitting me so strongly I could smell them. Taste them.

How many times had Ryan and I taken the same set of elevators after a prenatal ultrasound for Emma? How many times had we hung our heads, weighed down by the growing signs that something was wrong. Horribly wrong.

As Ashley and I pushed the DOWN button and waited, I looked over my shoulder at the cutout in the building's exterior wall, remembering the time I'd stood in that very spot looking down at the concrete jungle below.

On that day, I'd cried for Emma. Cried for Ryan. Cried for me.

I'd cried for the dreams and joys and life events that were never going to happen.

A car had pulled into a nearby parking space, and as Ryan took my hand he said, "Would you get a load of those clowns?"

I looked up in time to see the car's occupants. Two adults in full clown regalia—red noses, fuzzy wigs, brightly colored costumes—obviously on their way to the children's wing.

I smiled even as tears slid down my face, finding their way into the corners of my grin.

Ryan anchored an arm around my shoulders and tugged me toward the car. But more importantly, he made me smile.

He was the one person that could make me smile during that terrifying time in our lives.

Ryan and I had understood each other, yet somewhere during the five years since, we'd become two strangers who once shared a life-changing experience. Nothing more.

"Aunt Bernie? Are you all right?"

I shook myself free of the memory and nodded to answer the frightened tone of Ashley's voice. I reached for her hand and held on tight as the elevator doors slid open.

In the lobby, we signed the visitor's log before we headed for the security guard at the end of the hall.

I kept hold of Ashley's hand until the second set of elevator doors slid open, depositing us in a hallway filled with hushed voices, worried families, and tension.

MICU. Maternal Intensive Care Unit.

I'd hoped never to have reason to be here again, yet there I was. The smells and sounds and memories threatened to send me screaming.

My own bloody show had happened at the beach with a houseful of company.

"There's lunchmeat in the fridge," I'd called out as Ryan and I headed to the hospital. "Don't forget your suntan lotion. We'll be right back."

Now it was Diane's turn, and as Ashley and I stood side by side, fighting to keep our composure, I prayed Diane's preterm labor would turn out far different from mine.

Ashley and I walked to the nursing station. I gave our names, asked where we could find Diane and David, and when we could see them.

While we waited, a doctor straightened away from one of the telephones, the stiff set of his slender frame sending the past crashing over me.

Dr. Platt.

He glanced in my direction, but not a flicker of recognition crossed his stern expression.

He didn't so much as bat an eye, and why should he? It had been more than five years since he had made my life a living hell. Yet, even now, the sight of a bulky binder tucked beneath his arm made my blood run cold.

I could picture him standing in the door to my MICU room as if it were yesterday, cradling his binder, flipping pages, studying test results and case notes.

"We're building a case."

I often thought about knocking him against a wall and pounding my fists into his chest as if Emma's diagnosis and death had been his doing. As if he'd believed so fervently she wouldn't live, that she hadn't.

I stared at his back as he walked away, wondering if it was too late for me to attack him.

"Bernie?"

David's voice captured my attention, shifting my focus out of the past and into the present, where it needed to be.

Where it needed to stay.

I braced myself before I stepped inside Diane's treatment room, giving Ashley's hand one last squeeze before she shifted to her father's side. David tucked his arm around her protectively and reached up to touch her cheek.

The same fear gnawing at my insides glimmered in Ashley's eyes as she lifted her gaze to her dad's. When he pulled her into an embrace and whispered reassuring words in her ear, I realized I'd always expected the worst of David. I'd never given him a moment's worth of credit, even though he was the man in whom my best friend had put her hope, her faith, her love.

Was I such a small person I couldn't accept he might have a human side?

We no sooner stepped inside the room than footsteps sounded behind us. Without looking to see who had entered, I crossed to Diane, sharing an unspoken greeting. Her frightened gaze locked with mine. I took her hand and pressed a kiss to her forehead, her skin moist with sweat.

"The heartbeat's slowing with the contractions."

I recognized Dr. Platt's voice instantly without turning around. Apparently, fate had sent the man of my nightmares to care for Diane.

"We need to start the medication. It's nasty stuff, but we have no choice." He spoke softly to David, but not so softly fear didn't splash across Diane's face.

"But she'll be all right." David's tone had gone grim, worried. "I mean, both of them will be, right?"

"We'll do our best," Platt answered. Binder pages rustled as he flipped through his notes. "We're also going to administer a shot to help mature the baby's lungs."

"How long will this take?" David asked. "Are we talking hours?"

"We're talking days, Mr. Snyder."

"Days?" David's tone morphed from worried to incredulous. "We've got a family business to run."

Anger took possession of my body and my mouth at that point, and for two reasons. One, David's expression made it clear his concern for the rink had suddenly taken precedence over his concern for Diane. Two, Dr. Platt and David were speaking as if Diane wasn't in the room.

"Maybe you should include the patient in your conversation." I spoke loudly enough to interrupt the hushed tone of their exchange.

David's eyes shimmered with impatience and warning. The doctor merely got right to the point. "And you are?" he asked. But before I could utter a word, recognition flashed in his eyes and he pointed at me. "Trisomy eighteen, right?"

Beside me, Diane gasped as if she'd felt the knife go through my heart.

I shook my head, forcing myself not to go for the doctor's throat. "My name is Bernadette Murphy." I took a step toward the man, even though Diane had fisted her hand into my sleeve and was hanging on for dear life. "My daughter's name was Emma Murphy, and yes, she was born with Trisomy eighteen.

"She lived for five days. Five days"—I pointed at him sharply— "you said she'd never have." I jerked a thumb at Diane. "This is

Diane Snyder, and I'd suggest you not only learn her name, but you also include her in your conversation."

We stood in silence momentarily, and I thought perhaps the man might offer an apology or ask how I'd been since the moment five years earlier when my daughter's life had slipped away as I held her in my arms.

Instead, Dr. Platt said nothing, dropping his focus back to the chart in his hand.

"The nurse will get you set up," he said as he headed for the door.

David scowled and turned back toward Diane, scrubbing a hand across his eyes. "I can't believe this. We've got an open house tomorrow at the rink."

Diane's eyes closed, and the pain that washed across her face was not physical.

I stepped soundly into David's personal space and jabbed my index finger into his chest. "Do you try to be a total dick, or does it just come naturally?"

His cheeks puffed out, my question leaving him momentarily speechless.

"*Bernie.*" Diane's tone rang with intensity. She'd released her grip on my sleeve after Dr. Platt's departure, obviously not anticipating her husband would become my next target.

"No." I shook my head, moving in a tight circle around David, who turned with me like a wrestling opponent anticipating my next move. "You want to say the same thing"—I stole a glance at Diane—"don't you?"

She bit down on her lower lip, shot a quick look at David, and then shook her head.

"Yes, you do." I nodded, hot determination ready to spill out of my every pore. "Don't you think that if I had backed Ryan against the wall a time or two and told him to go to hell, he might still be around?"

Diane's and David's faces scrunched into matching frowns.

"We're all too polite." I gestured wildly above my head. David ducked then moved behind Diane's IV stand for protection.

"We stuff what we feel until we don't feel anything at all." I jabbed a finger in David's direction. "Tell him what you really want to say."

Diane's face grew paler, if that were possible. "Well." She bit her lip again and winced, as if she thought herself despicable simply for thinking whatever it was she was thinking.

"Tell him," I repeated.

David glared at me. "Just because you screwed up your own marriage is no reason for you to screw up mine."

"Oh, shut up." The uncharacteristic sternness of Diane's voice silenced David. It silenced me. Hell, a hush fell over the entire unit.

She pushed herself up on one elbow and turned her head to meet David's shocked stare. "David. Go to hell."

For the first time since they had opened the ice rink four years earlier, David let the doors remain locked during Diane's second day in the hospital.

Dr. Platt put Diane on magnesium sulfate, a nasty drug that slows everything in your body. It succeeded as far as her labor went, but poor Diane looked like hell. Her nurse kept a large box fan pointed directly at her, and David kept the cold washcloths coming.

I saw a side of him during those two days I'd never seen. Maybe he'd finally come to his senses, or maybe Diane's outburst had been enough to anchor him to what really mattered.

His family.

We all slept there the first night—David, Ashley, and I. A bit before noon the next day, I raced home to take care of Poindexter. I'd been home once during the night, but the poor dog couldn't be expected to hold it forever.

Number Thirty-Six was out front walking his cat when I pulled into my drive. Did the man never do anything else?

"What do you do for a living?" I blurted out the second I cleared my driver's door.

"Good morning to you, too." He grinned, sending my insides tilting sideways. "Rough night?"

"You enjoy asking me that, don't you?"

He shrugged. "Well? Was it?"

I nodded. "A friend of mine went into preterm labor."

His grin faded instantly. "Sorry. Damn. Give me a second while I pull my boot out of my mouth."

"It's okay." I rubbed my eyes. "I need to let poor Poindexter out before I head back to the hospital."

"Tell you what"—he stepped close and his cat rubbed her face against my shin—"let me take Fluffy home and I'll come back for Poindexter. I'll take him for a run. He can spend the day with me. He can spend the night with me too."

Lucky dog.

I shoved that errant thought out of my mind and focused on the truly important part of what Number Thirty-Six had said.

"You named your cat Fluffy?"

"Don't worry." He smiled. "I'm secure in my masculinity."

Oh, I wasn't worried. I was merely amused.

"And what is it you do for a living?" I repeated my question.

"I keep an eye on you." Amusement glimmered in his dark gaze. "I'll be right back."

Embarrassment burned in my face as he turned for his house. I pushed open my front door, and Poindexter looked up from his spot at the top of the steps. Apparently he'd been standing guard. Either that, or he'd barely made it off the bed once he heard my key in the lock.

I bustled him toward the kitchen and out the back door. The poor thing made it to the edge of the patio and not an inch farther before he lifted his leg.

The drone of an airplane sounded overhead. Poindexter wrapped things up and took off, sprinting across the yard, barking like a maniac, racing back and forth. Back and forth.

When a hand brushed my shoulder a few minutes later, I shrieked, jumping at least a foot into the air.

"Sorry." The rich rumble of Number Thirty-Six's voice assured me I wasn't under attack by an ax-murderer, but his proximity did nothing to slow the beating of my heart.

"You scared the crap out of me." I took a sideways step, moving clear of his reach.

"You didn't answer when I knocked." He grinned. "I had to make sure you weren't lying somewhere unconscious in need of resuscitation."

I tried to swallow, but the move became impossible at that particular moment. As I watched, he took in my small kitchen, studying the place as if memorizing every detail.

"Nice." He nodded toward the coffeemaker. "Thought you didn't drink coffee."

"I don't." I wracked my brain for a believable answer. "I keep it around for…company." I smiled, nodding my head. "Company," I repeated. "Want some?"

He shook his head slowly. His gaze locked on mine, and the intensity of his stare sent heat climbing up my cheeks. The message in his eyes was clear.

He didn't believe a word of my story.

His lips quirked before he broke eye contact and refocused on the back door. Poindexter charged back and forth across the yard, barking with abandon.

He tipped his chin. "We could all learn a thing or two from your dog."

"Like what?" I moved next to him but stayed far enough away to ensure our arms didn't touch. "Aiming high?"

Number Thirty-Six shook his head then met my questioning look. "I was thinking more like not worrying about what anyone else thinks."

Was it my imagination or was he visually measuring the length of my nonexistent hair?

"He's true to himself," he added.

"He's a dog."

A quick shrug. "Doesn't matter. He's got a better grip on life than most of us do."

"What is it you do?" I asked again.

"Take care of your dog." He opened the door and whistled. Poindexter came running, screeched to a stop, and sat on Number Thirty-Six's command.

When he lifted his paw to shake, I rolled my eyes and headed for the dog's bowl. "I'll pack his things. Thanks again for your help."

"It's what neighbors do."

"Well"—I shook my head—"I owe you one." I frowned, thinking for a second. "Actually, I owe you two. Or three."

He gathered Poindexter's paraphernalia into his arms, stopping to speak softly next to my ear as he passed. "I'll make a note of it, Number Thirty-Two."

"I thought you said you didn't have an agenda?" I called out. My heart beat at a ridiculous rate as I watched the two of them head down the sidewalk toward Number Thirty-Six's house.

"Maybe I changed my mind," Number Thirty-Six said.

And even though he didn't break stride or turn around to deliver the line, I could picture the grin on his face just as clearly as if he had.

Late that night, I drove Ashley home. Diane and David had decided she needed to be in her own bed, and since Number Thirty-Six had things with Poindexter under control, I figured I could keep Ashley company.

David wanted to stay with Diane, even though they'd discontinued the mag sulfate and were ready to start a second drug that would allow her to come home if her contractions remained under control.

"Aunt Bernie?"

I smiled at the tone of Ashley's voice. The kid had used the same prefavor pitch since she'd spoken her first words.

"What do you want?" I glanced at her in time to catch her frown. I patted her knee. "I'm teasing. What?"

"Can we stop off at the convenience store?"

"Peas?" I asked, shaking my head.

"Mm hm." She sat quietly for a moment, trailing one finger along the edge of the door. "I'm pretty sure we're out of them."

Well, I had to admit the last two days merited peas if ever they'd been merited.

"Peas, it is," I said as I clicked on the car's turn signal and changed lanes.

"Thanks, Aunt Bernie."

But her words were dulled by the sound of a blaring horn. Another driver had moved into the same lane, at the same time, without use of a turn signal.

My middle finger flipped into the air of its own volition. "Nice driving, asshole."

Beside me, Ashley giggled.

Shit.

"Uh, sorry about that, honey."

She shrugged. "No biggie."

But I realized suddenly there was a lesson to be learned here.

"Listen," I started in on my rationalization. "I'm not saying it's right to swear or give other drivers the finger, but what just happened is a good example of expressing yourself."

I sneaked a peek at her and was rewarded by her smirk of disbelief. She gave me the adults-are-so-stupid face. "You cut him off."

"Minor detail." I shook my head, not wanting to lose my train of thought. After all, I was about to make a major point. "Take you and the peas. If you expressed yourself more, you'd need less peas."

"But peas are good for me," she answered.

"In theory." I turned my head to check for rogue drivers before I turned into the all-night convenience store lot. "But stuffing your feelings is never good."

"Like Mom never telling Dad to go to hell?"

I winced. Perhaps I wasn't teaching this kid using the best examples, but I held my ground, nodding. "Just like that. Only you don't have to swear to express yourself."

I slid the car into an open space, shifted into park, and cut the ignition.

Ashley wrapped her fingers around the passenger door handle. "I just need to stop stuffing my feelings?"

"That's it." I shrugged. "Basic concept. Got it?"

"Got it." She tipped her chin toward the storefront. "Peas?"

"Peas," I answered, following her into the store, remaining close on her heels until she turned down the canned food aisle, and I headed for the candy racks.

Peas.

The kid might grasp the concept of self-expression, but one thing was perfectly clear.

She had zero appreciation for true comfort food.

"Nothing fixes a thing so intensely in the memory as the wish to forget it."
—Michel de Montaigne

CHAPTER EIGHTEEN

——— ——— ———

"VZXY TQER FY QPWYDERBBW FHULIHDW, FQR ZR TQER
FY VZMYW XBDIHDW."
—EØDYP LZYDLYCHHDW

When Sunday arrived, so did the opportunity I'd been waiting for—my niece's first birthday party.

I picked up Poindexter from Number Thirty-Six and dragged my faithful companion along for two reasons.

First, he could stand to learn a thing or two about the art of confrontation.

Second, his dog-cousin, Buster, not only graduated at the top of his obedience class, but he had the certificate and T-shirt to prove it.

I arrived late as usual, screeching my car to a stop. I scrambled to grab Elizabeth's present and climb out of the car in one motion.

I opened the back door and Poindexter sat staring at me, not moving a muscle.

"Come on." I waved dramatically toward the house. "Let's go."

He didn't exactly shake his head, but he did make a general motion that clearly communicated his disinterest in going inside.

He'd spent the night there on more than one occasion, and I couldn't help but wonder what sort of trauma he'd suffered. Of course, with Poindexter, a raised voice constituted trauma.

I reached into my pocket for the treat I'd brought along. Number Thirty-Six had assured me Poindexter would be putty in my hand as long as he knew I had these little goodies.

I pulled out a red gummy piece of I-don't-know-what shaped like a miniature steak.

Poindexter gave me a single brow arch.

I'd be damned.

I waved the treat in front of his nose, pointed at the house, and worked up my most authoritative tone of voice. "House. Now."

He was out of the car and up on the front step like a shot.

I did my best to hide my dismay, figuring a blatant display of surprise would do nothing for the success of any future doggie commands.

I handed over the treat then rang the bell.

My mother answered the door, and I leaned in to kiss her cheek.

"Welcome to the zoo," she said with a smile, but the light in her eyes let me know she was in heaven.

Mark and his first wife had never had children, even though he'd always wanted a houseful. When he'd married Jenny, who was no less than ten years younger than he was, she'd been pregnant within the first year.

Elizabeth was their youngest.

I found the birthday girl in her high chair, clearly the center of attention at a table full of sugar-crazed children. Mark was in the process of lighting the cake's single candle but managed to give me a quick chin tip.

"Bernie."

"Mark."

I wasn't sure whether the chilliness between us stemmed from the fact I had missed most of the party or whether it was just our usual chilliness.

Buster's nose hit my knee, and I reflexively bent down to pat his head. My fingers connected with hard plastic, and I frowned, dropping my focus to the dog's level.

He wore a bright blue helmet, some sort of high-tech contraption more commonly seen on the Tour de France, if I wasn't mistaken.

"What's wrong with Buster?"

"Nothing." Jenny breezed into the room with a second helmet in her hand.

I never ceased to wonder how she kept up with her life. I found myself tired just watching her buzz around the party, juggling toddlers, adults, food, and tantrums.

My mother always said people adapt.

If that was the case, I felt I'd adapted fairly well to being a slug. But not Jenny.

Her cheeks were flushed with color and her eyes sparkled as they always did. Full of life.

"Has he been having seizures?" I asked, my brain working to figure out why on earth poor Buster needed headgear.

"Nope." Jenny moved toward Poindexter, whose eyes had taken on a distinct gleam of panic.

"What are you doing?" My voice climbed several octaves.

"It's for his own good."

With that, Elizabeth's sippy cup flew into the air, landing squarely on Buster's head. Without the helmet, I imagined the cup full of milk would have hurt like hell. With the helmet, the dog merely blinked before he resumed begging.

I looked at Poindexter and shrugged. "When in Rome, buddy."

As Jenny strapped on the orange helmet, Poindexter's big, brown eyes bore right through me.

No wonder the poor thing had wanted to stay in the car.

I leaned down to his level and whispered in his ear. "I'll make it up to you."

By the time he'd snarfed down five pieces of cake, he'd gotten over the whole helmet aversion.

As for me, I stopped after two pieces, choosing to drop back a bit from the center of activity. I leaned one hip against the kitchen counter, shifting my attention from the party table to the beautiful afternoon outside.

As the party progressed, I could say I tried to talk myself out of a confrontation with my brother, but that would be a bold-faced lie.

The truth was, I couldn't wait to get him alone, to corner him. The problem was going to be how to do that surrounded by fifteen toddlers, Jenny, my mother, and two dogs in safety helmets.

Yet, as fate would have it, the attendees began to topple like little exhausted dominos. Hyped up on birthday cake and peanut butter and jelly sandwiches, they slowly succumbed, their blood glucose levels plummeting before my eyes.

One by one they were carried out by politely smiling parents who no doubt couldn't wait to return the favor at their child's next party.

When Jenny disappeared upstairs carrying a party-weary Elizabeth in her arms, I made my move.

My mother vanished into the kitchen, trying to clean up the party mess in order to help Jenny. I supposed I should have done the same thing, but instead I stalked Mark like a lion working a desert watering hole, trailing him out into the backyard and the waning warmth of the afternoon sun.

He'd snagged a bottle of beer from the fridge as soon as the last guest left and took a long swallow as he turned to face me, his eyebrows pulling together. He lowered the bottle and pursed his lips.

"Spill it." He gave a quick shrug, daring me with his angry expression.

"What the hell does that mean?" I asked, as if I didn't know exactly what he meant.

"It means you've had a bug up your ass since you walked in the door, and I'm guessing it's got nothing to do with making your dog wear a helmet."

I squinted at him, raising my hand to shield my eyes from the slant of the afternoon sun. "You have to admit it's a bit much."

"It's been a long day. Get to the point, Bernie."

His tone angered me. His stance angered me. At that particular moment in my life, his breathing angered me.

Was this what we'd missed all those years we hadn't lived together as brother and sister? Maybe all the time I'd spent regretting our lost opportunities for sibling bonding would have been better spent being thankful we lived apart.

Apparently, proximity didn't bring out the best in either one of us.

"Why won't you do it?" I asked, waving one hand wildly into the air.

"What?" He tipped his beer bottle to his lips, his gaze narrowing.

"You know exactly what." I took a step closer. "Why can't you go to Mom's house and pick a damned jacket?"

He blinked, surprise splashing across his features.

What had he expected me to say? Surely he knew he'd let Mom down. He'd let her down ever since that first moment we'd stared into Dad's closet together.

"Are you kidding me?" Now it was Mark's turn to step closer. "That's why you're so pissed off at me?"

I nodded. "Can't you see you're hurting Mom? Why won't you do it? Don't you want one of Dad's jackets?"

He blinked again. "I do, I'm just…it's just…"

"Are you scared?" I could tell by the way his features tensed I was treading on dangerous turf. "I can't believe you're scared."

He frowned then, taking in a deep breath then slowly releasing it.

I knew the trick. Hell, I'd patented the trick.

My brother was stalling for time to think. Well, I wasn't about to give it to him.

"Did you ever stop to think you're doing a fair amount of hurting Mom yourself?" he asked.

His words took me by surprise, and this time, I blinked. "*I'm* hurting Mom?" I patted my chest. "I'm helping Mom."

"How?" One corner of his mouth pulled into a smirk and I fought the urge to smack it down. "Are you helping her by getting divorced, losing your job, or going through some short-haired, boot-wearing transformation?" He gestured at my head and then my feet.

"At least I'm there for her." I straightened, my voice climbing at least three octaves.

"Are you?" He had the audacity to laugh. "Because the last time I was at her house, you were nowhere in sight."

"Oh, and when was that?" I asked. "When you were finally helping her sort Dad's jackets?"

"Stop it."

This time, Mark and I both blinked.

"Both of you." My mother's voice was sharper and angrier than I'd ever heard it.

Mark and I turned to face her. Instant shame washed through me at the sight of her flushed cheeks, bright with anger. She might sound big, but at that particular moment, she looked small. Very, very small.

And standing in my brother's backyard arguing on my niece's first birthday wasn't helping anything.

I should have apologized. I knew this. But I didn't. Instead I jerked my thumb at Mark as if we were back at home during the years before he'd moved out.

"It's his fault. If he'd just face the fact Dad's gone, we could all move forward."

I never expected the tears that sprang into my mother's eyes.

"Nice going," Mark muttered.

My heart rapped against my ribs, guilt reaching deep inside me and squeezing. "Mom, I'm sorry—"

She held up one hand and turned, headed back into the kitchen. Jenny appeared in the doorway and intercepted her, placing one hand flat against Mom's back as she steered her out of sight.

"Nice going," Mark repeated.

"Oh, shut up." I shook my head, angry with my brother and furious with myself. I crossed the yard as quickly as I could, stepped into the kitchen, unhooked Poindexter's helmet, and headed for the front door.

I never stopped to say good-bye or to apologize or to bang my head against the wall.

I felt pretty certain any one of those actions would have been acceptable at that particular moment.

Instead, I headed for home, feeling like an ass.

I needed to drop off Poindexter before I went into work, but when I reached my neighborhood, cars lined the street and strains of "Hot, Hot, Hot" blared from the open windows of Number Thirty-Six's house.

I stood, transfixed, as six older women danced their way around Number Thirty-Six's house, their grass skirts swaying, Hawaiian shirts all but glowing in the afternoon sun. The day was seasonably chilly for late winter, but to look at the smiles on the women's faces, you'd think they'd been transported straight to the Big Island.

Uninhibited joy lit their expressions, and I wondered when in my life I'd learned to hold back.

"How's your friend?"

Number Thirty-Six's voice sounded close, and I jumped a foot. Who was this guy? Batman?

"Better," I answered, "Thanks again for taking care of Poindexter."

I turned to face him, my gaze held momentarily by how good he looked with a peach hibiscus behind his ear. Not many men could pull off the look, but Number Thirty-Six? Well, I'd come to realize the man could pull off just about any look out there.

"Your party?" I asked.

"My mom's." His grin spread wide, and I tried to remember a time I hadn't seen Number Thirty-Six happy. "I'm just the host."

I looked back at the party and sighed. "You're a good son."

"She's a great mom."

"Her birthday?"

Beside me, he nodded. "Her eightieth."

My heart fell to my toes. How Daddy would have loved a party like this for his eightieth, if only he'd lived a little longer.

Number Thirty-Six touched my elbow lightly and a jolt of awareness shot through me. "There's a piña colada over there with your name on it."

I moved toward my house, breaking our contact, pulling away from the party and Number Thirty-Six, when a very large part of me wanted nothing more than to don a grass skirt and dance the night away. But the local hockey league had a late afternoon game and I'd offered to man the snack bar.

Thank goodness. Otherwise, I might be forced to sit home and think about how awful I'd acted at Mark's house.

"I have to work." I forced a bright tone into my voice. "But you have fun."

"How about a cup of coffee, then?" he asked, his eyes widening with the taunt.

I grinned, giving a slow shake of my head. "Never touch the stuff."

He laughed as he turned back toward his mother and her guests. "So you keep telling me, Number Thirty-Two. So you keep telling me."

By the time I got to the rink, I'd rehashed the scene at Mark's house so many times my forehead hurt from frowning.

David was nowhere to be found, but players and families had begun trickling in from the parking lot.

Ashley sat in the snack bar, nursing a large Styrofoam cup of hot chocolate.

"Where's your dad?" I asked.

She wrinkled her nose. "What's wrong with you?"

Was I that transparent? I waved off her question dismissively. "Nothing."

One perfectly applied pale brow arched subtly. "Sounds like you're stuffing your feelings."

I couldn't help but laugh a little. I'd forgotten how dangerous new information could be during the teen years.

"I had a little argument with my brother." I shrugged. I neglected to add the fact I'd made my mother cry and I'd stormed out of the house like someone more the age of…well…Ashley. "Where's your dad?" I repeated.

She drew in a slow breath, took a dramatic sip of her chocolate, and slowly shook her head from one side to the other, sending her perfectly glossy hair swinging. "You won't believe it, but there's a sale at Macy's. He said he'd be back in time to lock up."

I sank into a chair.

A sale at Macy's? David?

I made a face.

Ashley threw her hands up in the air. "I think he's channeling Mom or trying to keep up her reputation while she's in the hospital, or something."

"Did you see her today?" I asked.

Ashley nodded. "Most of the afternoon." Her features brightened, her eyes dancing. "I think she's coming home tomorrow. And we had the best talk." Another shrug. "Probably the meds making her nice."

More like the scare making her realize all she had to appreciate.

I reached out to ruffle Ashley's hair and she expertly dodged and blocked my hand. "Do you know how much time it takes me to look like this?"

A laugh bubbled between my lips. "Just testing your reflexes."

Forty-five minutes later, the ice was a wreck from the game's first two periods and I'd inhaled so many chocolate chip cookies

I thought I'd explode. I'd been staring into space for who knew how long when Ashley popped around the corner, startling me so much I squeaked.

She grinned, an ornery, up-to-no-good grin.

"What did you do?" I asked, immediately expecting the worst.

She frowned, and I could read her unspoken thoughts. I was acting like a grown-up. Imagine.

"Want to run the Zamboni with me?" Her inflection climbed through the roof.

Zamboni.

I'd tactfully avoided all talk of Zamboni operation since my first few days at the rink. I had no intention of revisiting the topic now.

"Nope." I spoke the word sharply, turning to wipe down the already spotless counter.

"I can teach you, Aunt Bernie." A slight pause. "Please?"

I scowled, obviously having spent too much time around Ashley's father. "You want to teach me?"

She nodded, visibly encouraged by my question. "You know you want to do this. Face your fears and all that stuff, right?"

I reached up to rake a hand through my hair, knowing the short waves would be left in a disastrous tangle, but not caring.

Face my fears.

The kid was good.

"Who's going to drive, you or me?"

"Me." She slapped her chest. "You can ride with me. I'll teach you every step."

"What about the snack bar?"

"We'll put up a back-in-ten-minutes sign." Obvious excitement shimmered in her eyes. If the kid was this enthusiastic about teaching me how to drive the death machine, how could I say no?

I pressed my lips together then forced out one word. "Okay."

Ashley clapped, then spun on her heel. "Let's go."

I quickly scribbled the note for the snack bar and followed, dread simmering deep inside my belly.

My father always said I could do anything, especially something other people already knew how to do. Certainly, driving the Zamboni-from-hell fell into that category.

I mean, thousands of people probably knew how to drive a Zamboni, right? And you didn't hear about Zamboni deaths all that often, so chances were good I'd survive to talk about this.

But several minutes later, as the big machine lumbered across the ice and the cold rink air slapped me in the face, I longed for a barf bag.

I hadn't realized precisely how terrifying the machine was until I sat down next to Ashley on the freezing cold vinyl seat.

Terrified didn't come close. I was petrified.

"Isn't this easy?" Ashley screamed as she maneuvered the machine around the ice, following a precise pattern as the overhead sound system played Muzak.

"Piece of cake," I answered, lying through my teeth.

"You want to steer?" she asked.

I dramatically shook my head no, but I was too late. Ashley let go of…everything…and climbed onto the seat.

We were at center ice, headed straight for one of the team benches. The cave man mascot stood staring down the machine as the Zamboni lumbered closer and closer. He planted his fists on his fur-covered hips and furrowed his perfect brows.

I should have known Ashley had ulterior motives.

She widened her stance, solidifying her balance.

I reminded myself to remember her technique the next time I jumped on a chair to assert myself.

I frantically scanned the controls, working to bring the death machine to a stop, while Ashley went into action.

"Hey, asshole," she hollered at the precise moment there was a lull in the Muzak.

An audible gasp filtered through the rink. The cave man straightened, apparently well aware he was the asshole in question. I cringed as Ashley proudly gave him the finger, for the entire rink to see.

"Here's what I think of you and your eyebrows. Matter of fact, you and your eyebrows can kiss my—"

I leaned on the Zamboni's horn, drowning out Ashley's final thought. She dropped back onto the seat next to me, pride shining in her every feature.

At that particular moment, I was aware of three things.

One, I was a natural at operating the death machine.

Two, Ashley had apparently overcome stuffing her feelings.

And three, Diane and David were going to strangle me with their bare hands.

"It's funny," Diane said, biting back a grin as I walked into her hospital room the next morning, "I always thought I'd be the one to teach my daughter to give someone the finger."

I winced.

"You know, I realized I wasn't even mad she made an obscene gesture in front of the entire rink," Diane continued.

"No?" I dropped my purse to the floor and leaned down to kiss her forehead. I couldn't help noticing her overnight bag was packed and ready to go.

Diane shook her head. "I was mad I missed it."

I squinted, not sure where to go with my side of the conversation.

The corners of Diane's eyes grew a bit sad. "If anyone should be encouraging her to make vulgar hand gestures, it should be me."

When my brow arched this time, it worked. Call it shock. Call it what you will, but Diane's words had snapped my left brow to attention.

"I've neglected her. I can't let my entire world revolve around this baby." She lovingly rubbed her baby bump. "I need to get Ashley back."

Her gaze lifted to mine, tears pooling along the rim of her lower lashes.

"You never lost her," I said softly, shaking my head. "Not for a second."

Diane sniffed. Loudly. "You sure?"

Was I sure? "Absolutely. You're her mom. No one's ever going to change that. Not even good old Aunt Bernie teaching her to express herself."

"I got a little out of control with the purse thing," she said, squishing up her features.

I shrugged. "Blame it on the hormones."

A knock sounded at the door and I tensed, imagining Dr. Platt popping in to make one last visit. Instead, a brilliant smile lit Diane's face. I turned to see David and Ashley walking through the door.

"Shouldn't you be in school?" Diane asked, though the joy painted across her features made it clear she was delighted Ashley was there.

"We wanted to bring you something first." A sheepish grin slid across David's face—a look I hadn't seen since the night he and Diane met. I could still remember each of their expressions. I can also remember thinking *this is it*. And it was.

Ashley handed Diane a large box.

"For me?" But Diane had already begun attacking the ribbon and paper even as she asked the question.

The paper fell away and she hoisted the lid from the box, reaching inside to pull out a bag. She gasped, moisture shining in her sparkling eyes.

In her hands, she held a fabulously stylish diaper bag, suede with an embroidered heart and the word *love* spelled out in rhinestones.

Some might call the bag gaudy or over-the-top. I thought it was one of the most beautiful things I'd ever seen.

"Dad picked it out," Ashley said, her voice softer than I'd heard it in thirteen years. "By himself."

The tears glistening in Diane's eyes trailed wet paths down her cheeks, slipping into the lines of her smile. "I love bags. How did you know?"

David beamed as he moved beside her, wiping first one cheek and then the other. "Lucky guess."

Ashley and I both looked at the pale tiled floor to hide our grins, and when we returned our gazes to Diane and David, they were kissing like a couple of high school kids.

"I feel sick." Ashley slapped a hand over her mouth, but she couldn't fool me.

Hope sparkled in her gaze. Real hope. The kind of hope I'd been afraid she'd lost for good.

"I'm sorry I was such an idiot when you were first admitted," David said softly to Diane. "I was scared."

I hooked my arm through Ashley's and pulled her tight against my side. She was looking up at the ceiling, apparently unable to stomach such a public display of affection from her parents. But, no matter how far up she tipped her chin, she couldn't hide the smile turning up the corners of her mouth.

A bubble of warmth burst inside me, spreading outward to my fingers and my toes.

Diane and David and Ashley were on the mend. Sure, it had taken a crisis to set the change into motion, but wasn't that often the case?

Who knew, maybe the bun in the oven knew exactly what he or she was doing.

I never saw Dr. Platt again. He didn't say good-bye, and he wasn't at the nursing station as we left.

Part of me still wanted some sort of admission from the man, some sign he had a heart beneath his robotic exterior. But the man had never said anything that wasn't negative during that awful time in my life five years earlier. Why should now be any different?

After all, life wasn't a Hollywood movie, and not every ending provided closure. Sometimes an asshole was just an asshole, and sometimes a doctor who didn't believe in miracles was just a doctor who didn't believe in miracles.

I watched as David and Ashley bracketed Diane's wheelchair as her nurse pushed her toward the lobby.

Dr. Platt might not believe in miracles, but I did.

And maybe that was all that mattered.

"Life must be understood backward, but it must be lived forward."
—Søren Kierkegaard

CHAPTER NINETEEN

"HJR HEKHJ UW HJR XLHHRE OP HJLH ZUK LDVLZP BMUV
HJR EOTJH HJOMT HU QU. HJR JLEQ YLEH OP QUOMT OH."
—TRMRELD MUEXLM PFJVLENBUYW

I went straight home after leaving the hospital and spent much of
the day reliving the argument with my brother. I wrote another
column, this one about acting like a jerk and not being woman
enough to admit it.

I hadn't heard anything after I e-mailed my last letter to the
editor, so writing this one probably served no purpose. The process was cathartic, just the same.

I'd just pushed SEND on my e-mail when the doorbell rang.

I welcomed the interruption, yet surprise slid through me at
the sight of a smiling Number Thirty-Six standing on my front
step.

"It's a beautiful evening. I thought maybe you and Poindexter
might like to stop over for coffee."

I pressed my lips together, raking a hand through my hair.
Was this guy for real?

I shook my head. "What part of 'don't touch the stuff' is trip-
ping you up?"

Even as I said the words, I realized the house still reeked of the pot I'd made while writing.

Number Thirty-Six grinned—a great, crooked grin that made it clear he saw right through me. "The part where I don't believe you."

I shrugged.

A vertical line formed between his brows. "How about walking? Do you walk?"

"Of course I walk," I answered defensively.

What kind of question was that? But then it hit me. He'd tricked me. And I'd fallen for it.

"I mean—" I stammered a bit, trying to figure a way to backpedal out of my answer.

Number Thirty-Six didn't give me time to say another word. He brushed past me, headed for the back door with a decidedly smug gleam in his eyes. "Great. I'll grab Poindexter and we'll go."

Number Thirty-Six opened the back door and Poindexter bounded inside, headed straight for the front door as if the two of them had done this a thousand times before.

I stood, rooted to the spot as Number Thirty-Six brushed past me, looping Poindexter's leash over his shoulder.

I pointed. "Aren't you going to put that on?"

"Doesn't need it." He shook his head and grinned. "Watch and learn."

I glowered at him, not in the mood to have the fact he'd turned my obedience-school-drop-out mutt into Super Dog rubbed in my face. I followed anyway, pulling the front door closed behind me as Poindexter bounded across the front yard then sat on the sidewalk, waiting for instruction.

Sonofa—

"Poindexter. Walk." Number Thirty-Six's voice rang so authoritatively I instantly understood why the dog listened to him and not to me.

I hurried to catch up, walking quietly behind them as Number Thirty-Six barked out commands for Poindexter to heel, sit, stay, and walk. I had to admit I was impressed.

I'd spent countless hours with local pet trainers, dog food store clerks, and veterinarians, when all the while the obedience answer had taken up residence two doors down, in the form of Number Thirty-Six.

My stomach did a little flipping action I could have lived without, but I quickened my pace to catch up to Number Thirty-Six. Poindexter walked calmly in front of us.

"I'm still nervous about the no-leash thing."

He shot me a sideways glance, and the corner of his mouth quirked. "Amateur."

I narrowed my gaze on him. "I'm sorry, were there some professional dog training credentials you haven't yet shared with me?"

His crooked grin grew wide. "It's all in the voice. That's all you need to remember."

I blew out a laugh. "It might be all in your voice, but it certainly isn't in mine."

"Sure it is." He stopped, tipping his chin toward Poindexter. "You go. Make him listen to you."

I swallowed, my pulse quickening ridiculously. I couldn't believe how nervous Number Thirty-Six's suggestion made me. I mean, this was *my* dog we were talking about. Surely I could control him.

Couldn't I?

"I forgot to bring his treats," I said.

"Don't need them." Number Thirty-Six spoke so authoritatively I almost believed him.

But when a pair of squirrels crossed our path, Poindexter was gone in the blink of an eye. Tearing across one front yard and down the side of another, headed for the street just as a small car careened around the bend.

"Poindexter!" I screamed, the scene unfolding before my eyes as if I were powerless to stop the inevitable.

"Give him a command." Number Thirty-Six spoke sharply, his own anxiety blatant in his usually unflappable tone.

"Stop! No! Poindexter!"

I broke into a run, measuring the trajectory of the car's path against the direction of my dog's sprint. The car swerved, narrowly missing the first of the squirrels. Poindexter cleared the curb, headed directly into the path of the car's unforgiving bumper.

"Sit!" Number Thirty-Six's voice boomed from beside me. "Now!"

Poindexter dropped like a shot as the sound of squealing tires filled the air. The car came to a standstill mere inches from my beloved dog's suddenly motionless form.

I dropped to my knees, tears stinging my eyes. "Holy shit."

"He's all right." Number Thirty-Six placed his palm on my shoulder. I slapped it away as I stood up, the force of my anger taking me by surprise.

"No thanks to you." I waved to the car. "I'm sorry." Then pointed at my dog. "Get over here now."

He sprinted to my side as I turned toward Number Thirty-Six, glaring at him, reaching for the leash.

I yanked it from his shoulder and snapped the clasp onto Poindexter's collar. I leaned down, making full eye contact with the dog. To my surprise, he held my gaze, not shirking away to avoid the conflict sure to come.

I waggled my finger at his nose. "If you ever do that again, I will kill you myself. Do you understand?"

I straightened, pulled the leash short, and stepped off toward home, wanting as much distance as possible between myself and Number Thirty-Six.

"He listened," Number Thirty-Six called out after me. "You didn't give him the right command. And next time, don't run after him."

I couldn't believe my ears.

I spun on him. "Are you fucking kidding me?" I sounded like the wicked witch on speed, but didn't care. "Don't you know he's all I have? *All* I have. What the hell were you thinking? Why can't you just believe me that the dog doesn't listen? Why can't you just leave this alone?"

I turned back toward home but stopped and turned to deliver my parting shot. "Why can't you just leave *me* alone?"

His features fell as if I'd slapped him, but I didn't care.

I didn't need Number Thirty-Six. Poindexter didn't need Number Thirty-Six. We'd been just fine before the guy moved onto the street and into our lives. We'd be just fine again without him.

By the time I reached home, pushed Poindexter inside, and slammed the door shut behind us, I almost had myself convinced I was right.

❧

Two hours later, I was still so angry at Number Thirty-Six and at myself there was only one thing to do. I marched into the kitchen and began a drawer-by-drawer search for chocolate.

The old me had stockpiled the stuff by the bagful; the new me hadn't allowed myself to buy any in weeks.

Idiot.

Drawer after drawer, I came up empty-handed, until I pulled out the drawer next to my work desk. The thing was loaded to the brim—not with full bags—but with wrappers, empty bags, shreds of foil, paper, and traces of crumbs.

I had never seen such a pathetic display of zero willpower in my life. I stared at the evidence and frowned. Who had I been hiding these from? Myself?

I scooped the mess out of the drawer and retraced my steps, dumping the load on the kitchen table. Poindexter's tail thumped noisily against the floor. He'd once devoured a small box of gourmet chocolates and had lived to bark about it.

Because of that, I imagined he'd never been a big believer in the whole dogs-can't-eat-chocolate mantra. I studied the mess of empty wrappers and cringed. I hadn't left a morsel for him to worry about.

I swept the entire mess into the trash can and poured myself a large glass of water. I chugged down the contents, trying not to gag as the last gulp splashed into my stomach.

I glanced at the clock. Wasn't there some sort of diet rule about waiting twenty minutes when you thought you couldn't live without inhaling something?

Twenty minutes.

I thought about the day I'd had. The week I'd had. Hell, the last several months I'd had.

I could do twenty minutes. All I needed was a distraction.

I scanned the kitchen and spotted exactly what I needed—the long-forgotten bead shop bag I'd tossed onto the counter during my search.

Even though I knew I had no future in jewelry, I had spent a small fortune on supplies all those months ago.

I hadn't looked at the bag since. Matter of fact, I'd completely forgotten about it. Until now.

I drew in a deep breath and sighed. This was sure to be an exercise in futility, but if playing with beads kept me from running out for chocolate, more power to the beads.

I carried the bag to the kitchen table and worked slowly, methodically, setting out the tools I'd purchased, the beading wire the young woman had told me was the be-all and end-all of bracelet design, the cards touting simple patterns to follow, and the beads.

First, I dumped out a bag of purple beads, then a bag of lime green beads. Different. Spring-like. Bright. I used a placemat to keep the glass beads from rolling away, positioning them, lining them up by size, then alternating patterns, but still I wasn't pleased with the results.

Finally I dumped out the contents of every bag of beads I'd purchased, keeping everything separated by color.

I stared at the piles, waiting for some sort of inspiration.

I stared.

I squinted.

I blinked.

I placed a round bead here, a square bead there, an oval bead here, yet nothing looked right and everything looked wrong.

Whatever I'd learned that night at the bead shop had left my memory completely.

I glanced up at the clock. Five minutes left before the drug-store at the corner shut for the night. If I wanted to inhale a jumbo bag of M&Ms, it was now or never.

I thought about refilling the water glass again, really I did. Matter of fact, I was still thinking about doing just that as I screeched the car to a stop in front of the store and launched myself into a full-out sprint.

Hours later, queasy from too much sugar yet lulled into complacency by the chocolate, I passed the pile of beads on the kitchen table on my way to let Poindexter out one last time before bed.

I thought about attacking the bracelet project again but decided against it.

In the words of the great Scarlet O'Hara, tomorrow was another day.

As far as I was concerned, tomorrow was plenty soon enough.

Poindexter was out back barking before I even had a chance to get the coffee started the next morning. I'd stumbled downstairs in the throes of a sugar hangover to let him out, then stumbled back upstairs to get dressed.

I peeked out my bedroom window, watching the dog race back and forth across the yard. Based on the level of his frenzy, the planes must be coming in for landing no more than thirty seconds apart.

I prayed Mrs. Cooke would forgive me for another early morning wake-up call as I stared into my closet. Reaching inside, I pulled out a pair of yoga pants that had never seen a yoga class in their life. Then I plucked Dad's shirt out of the closet, pulling it over my head without undoing the buttons.

Turning toward the mirror, I pictured my father in the shirt, the deep red stripes weaving in and out of blue and green and gold, the plaid bold and comfortable. I could see his smile as if he were there with me, beside me, *alive.*

The past faded into the present and a tremble started deep within me, shaking me from the inside out. I sank to the floor, not even trying to quell the overwhelming sense of sadness that surged through me. But when the doorbell rang, I welcomed the interruption.

No one in his or her right mind would stop by this early, but based on my current mental state, any company would be good company.

Mrs. Cooke stood on the doorstep, a covered plate in one hand, a thermos in the other.

"I heard Poindexter so I brought over some breakfast for you, dear." She spoke the words cheerfully as she breezed past me, headed toward the kitchen.

She unscrewed the top of the thermos, took two mugs from the cabinet, and poured coffee in both. Then she uncovered a dish of homemade muffins.

I leaned against the doorjamb, taking in the sight, wondering if I still might be asleep and dreaming.

When she opened the back door and called Poindexter in, I pinched myself.

Poindexter gave Mrs. Cooke a warm greeting, and she rewarded him with a dog biscuit from the pocket of her cardigan.

Morning people.

How did they do it?

"You really shouldn't have." I gestured toward the counter and to Poindexter. "But, it's awfully nice."

She pulled out a chair and tipped her head. I followed her directive obediently, dropping into the chair as she set a stack of napkins and the plate of muffins in the center of the table. I took a long swallow of coffee the instant she handed me the mug, then squinted at the woman.

"Why?"

The corners of her eyes crinkled with kindness as she patted my hand. "A little birdie told me you've got a lot going on."

My squint morphed into a frown.

She read my unspoken question, nodding her head. "Aidan."

"Who?" I straightened.

"Aidan." A mischievous grin lit her face, her pale eyes dancing. "I believe you call him Number Thirty-Six."

Oh, *that* Aidan. I slid lower in my seat, ashamed of myself.

"I'm afraid I wasn't very nice to him yesterday, Mrs. Cooke."

"Call me Sophie, dear." She pulled out a chair and joined me, plucking a muffin from the plate and peeling back the paper cup in which she'd baked the pastry.

"Sophie," I repeated, testing out the feel of her name. I liked it. "Anyway"—I shook my head—"it was awfully nice of him to let you know."

"He's a nice boy." She nodded.

Yeah, when he wasn't sending my dog out on suicide missions without a leash.

We sat in silence for several long moments, sipping our coffee and eating. There was something in Sophie Cooke's eyes I couldn't quite put my finger on. If I didn't know better, I'd swear she knew I'd been more than a little harsh with Number Thirty-Six.

I decided to test out my theory.

"I might have been worse than not very nice," I said softly.

"I know, dear."

"You do?"

She nodded, a mischievous twinkle dancing in her gaze. "I may have cracked my window open to hear a bit better."

My mouth fell open as I sat back against the chair.

"Mrs. Cooke." I teased.

"Sophie."

"Sophie," I repeated. "You were eavesdropping?"

She gave a slight lift and drop of her slender shoulders. "A woman's got to get her excitement somehow." The corners of her mouth pulled into a smile, lighting her features.

I smiled in return, ran a hand through my hair, and sighed. "I really was mean, wasn't I?"

She nodded.

"Do you think I overreacted?"

Another nod.

"What should I do?"

She blinked as if the question were a no-brainer. "You could always talk to him, dear. Go apologize. I'm sure he's sorry for pushing you and Poindexter a bit too hard."

I narrowed my gaze, and she nodded.

"He doesn't bite, last time I checked."

Too bad.

The image of his hurt expression when I'd told him he needed to leave me alone flashed through my mind's eye.

Shame on me.

Sophie's kind gaze narrowed. "He knows you're under a lot of stress, dear," she said as if reading my thoughts. "I wouldn't worry too much about what happened."

She reached for the placemat covered in beads that I'd shoved aside to make room for our impromptu breakfast.

"What are you working on?" She traced a finger over a red piece of round glass, then a turquoise square.

I reached for a second muffin, but pulled my hand back. After the calories I'd inhaled last night, a second muffin was most definitely out of the question if I ever wanted to wear anything other than yoga pants and big shirts again.

"I wanted to make a bracelet." I shrugged. "But I'm having a difficult time picturing the finished product."

"Beautiful colors," she said as she pushed back her chair. "Looks like a rainbow, doesn't it?"

I stood to give her a thank-you hug as she headed for the front door, but I couldn't help but stare over her shoulder at the placemat full of beads.

A rainbow.

I'd be damned.

Sophie was right.

After she headed back home, I stood over the kitchen table and stared at the piles of colored beads. Reds. Purples. Greens. Blues.

I pulled one bead of each color, lining them into a single row, not worrying about matching sizes or shapes or textures. I poured another cup of coffee then cut a long length of wire, setting the instruction card next to me as I settled down to create my masterpiece.

An hour later, I'd started and stopped and woven and unwoven the bracelet more times than I could count. I wanted to create a masterpiece symbolic of my life—my new life—but all I succeeded in doing was making a mess.

I pushed aside the beads I was working with, mixing them with all of the other beads spread out on the placemat. Frustration bubbled up inside me and I slid everything back into the store bag, mixing colors and shapes and sizes. I sealed the bag and dropped the entire mess back into the drawer.

I pictured how Mrs. Cooke's eyes had brightened at the sight of the beads, thought of how she'd encouraged me to apologize to Number Thirty-Six.

But I knew better.

I slid the drawer shut, drew in a deep breath, then sighed.

Sometimes, the best course of action was to walk away. To admit defeat and quit.

Simple. Effective. Painless.

But as I headed for a hot shower, I didn't feel effective at all.

I felt like a quitter, and I didn't like it.

I didn't like it one bit.

"The truth of the matter is that you always know the right thing to do. The hard part is doing it."
—General Norman Schwarzkopf

CHAPTER TWENTY

— —— ——

"RI FSV PVEFS QY KRIFVD, R YRITMMA MVTDIVP FSTF FSVDV
KTU KRFSRI NV TI RIBRIORLMV UJNNVD."
—TMLVDF OTNJU

A few weeks later, George Clooney fed me grapes. The tips of his fingers brushed my lips as he dropped each juicy morsel into my waiting, hungry mouth.

He reached up and ruffled the top of my hair. "You look cute as a boy."

Cute.

Even in my dreams, I couldn't get things right.

Ding-dong.

George tipped his head to one side. "Must be Aidan. He's bringing over the brownies."

Ding-dong.

"Aidan?" I asked lazily.

George nodded. "Number Thirty-Six."

Oh. *Aidan.*

With that, George morphed into Number Thirty-Six, all tousled hair and sexy grin.

My nerves simmered to life inside me, but I slapped them away, reminding myself there was no room for nerves in a dream this good.

I focused on relaxing as the doorbell sounded again.

Number Thirty-Six winked and I wondered what kind of brownies he'd brought to the party.

An icy-cold wet nose nudged my cheek, but I swiped it away. *Ding-dong.*

Another nose nudge. Another swipe.

This time, a paw on my chest.

"Poindexter," I muttered, willing myself to stay in the dream. "If you could see what I see, you'd let me sleep."

Ding-dong.

I frowned, blinking open my eyes.

That last chime most definitely was not part of the dream.

I blew out a sigh of regret, bid a silent farewell to George, Number Thirty-Six, and the brownies, and reached for my robe.

Poindexter gave my cheek a quick lick, and I gave his neck a squeeze as I pushed myself off of the bed. "Good boy." *I think.*

I'd just slid my bare feet into my bunny slippers when the doorbell rang yet again.

I squinted at the clock. Six thirty in the morning. Whoever this was, he or she meant business.

My stomach did a slow sideways roll.

Someone was at my front door, ringing the bell insistently, at six thirty in the morning.

A phone call this early in the morning meant bad news, but a house call had to mean…I shook my head, refusing to let my thoughts do anything more than focus on making it to the front door.

When I peered through the peephole and saw Diane, blotchy-faced and obviously upset, my stomach's sideways roll morphed into a full-out tilt. A knot formed in my throat and squeezed.

In one smooth motion, I yanked open the door, grasped her arm, and pulled her into the foyer.

Her eyes had grown to the size of saucers, tears swimming along the edges of her lower lashes.

I studied her, forcing my lips to form one word. "What?"

Myriad thoughts flew through my mind in the time it took her to answer. The baby. David. Ashley. Ashley *and* David. Their house. The rink. All of them. None of them. And wasn't Diane supposed to be under baby house arrest?

"It's Ryan."

Ryan?

I'm fairly sure I stopped breathing momentarily. I knew for a fact my heart stopped beating.

You can tell yourself you don't care about someone until the moment you think they might be hurt, or sick, or worse.

The full force of how much I still cared about Ryan hit me like an oncoming locomotive—headlight beaming, horn blaring—knocking me backward until my heels hit the bottom step and I sank onto the stairs.

"Is he…?"

I held my breath waiting for her answer.

Diane nodded. "A daddy."

A daddy?

I shut my eyes, hating myself for how quickly the tears came, stinging behind my closed lids.

"Girl or boy?" I asked without opening my eyes, but I pulled myself taller, as if a stiff spine could fool anyone, including me, about how much this hurt.

"Girl."

Diane spoke the word in barely more than a whisper, wedging herself onto the step beside me, squeezing her very pregnant body between the wall and me. She wrapped one arm around my shoulder and pulled me close.

Poindexter tiptoed down the steps behind us to investigate. He typically hid after I answered the door to make sure whoever stood on the other side posed no threat. Then he appeared.

Had the visitor been a burglar, ax-murderer, or door-to-door magazine salesperson, he'd be beneath the bed upstairs by now.

Instead he sat behind me, his furry chest pressed against my back as he lowered his chin to my shoulder, tucking his head against my neck.

"Is she all right? Healthy?" An irrational fear tugged at my insides as I asked the question.

"She's fine."

I nodded, happy for that much. "What did they name her?"

Diane shook her head against mine. "I don't know. Ryan called David, but he didn't say anything more than she was here."

She was here.

Ryan's new daughter. Ryan's new life.

I had thought I'd be prepared for this. After Emma's death and Dad's death, I hadn't expected this particular moment in my life to be quite as painful as it was, but the deep, throbbing ache in my heart was almost more than I could bear.

"Well," I forced a note of levity into my voice, even though I knew I'd never fool Diane. "I should have known it would take more than a designer purse sale to get you out of bed this early."

My voice broke on the last word, and a guttural sob punched through my facade of control.

Diane tightened her grip on me, anchoring my head against her neck. Poindexter moved even closer, until I felt like a sandwich filling, pressed between the woman and dog who probably loved me more than most everyone else in my life.

And even though my heart hurt at the mental image of Ryan cradling his new daughter, my head knew I'd survive.

"It's going to be all right, Bernie," Diane whispered. "I promise."

I nodded. I knew she was right, but for the time being, I was content to stay exactly where I was. Safe. Protected.

I could face the world later.

After all, I was fairly sure it wasn't going anywhere.

I called out sick to the rink, though based on David's voice, he didn't believe a word of my elaborate fictional disease description.

Matter of fact, he sounded sympathetic and concerned.

I scowled.

The whole new in-touch-with-his-emotions David might take some getting used to.

I decided to pull a movie marathon.

Why just wallow in my sadness? Why not watch one sappy love story after another to fully reinforce the fact there wasn't a sign of true love or romance to be had in my life?

After the Dating Now fiasco, I'd let my trial membership lapse, which left me with just about zero prospects for a love match. And even though he'd been quite friendly in my dream, I hadn't had a single Number Thirty-Six sighting since I'd verbally attacked him over Poindexter's near-death experience.

I had just slipped into another blissfully deep sleep when the doorbell rang.

I was beginning to see a pattern here.

I wiggled out from beneath Poindexter's limp body. The dog was either one hell of a deep sleeper or one hell of a good actor. If I had to bet, I would have gone with the latter.

When I spotted Ashley through the peephole, I warmed instantly. Unless the kid was on the run and looking for a place to hide, I was happy to see her.

Hell, I'd be happy to see her even if she was on the run.

She brightened when I opened the door, blessedly saying nothing about her Uncle Ryan's new baby.

"Dad was going to let you drive the Zamboni all by yourself." She bounced past me, headed straight for Poindexter and the sofa.

Let me? "Let me?"

She nodded, her penciled-in brows lifting in an effort at sincerity. "Builds character, you know."

I couldn't help but smile. "So I hear."

She plunked down next to Poindexter, hoisting his furry chin off of the cushion and onto her knee. He lazily studied her before thumping his tail and snuggling in close.

"I wish we had a dog," she murmured then lifted her intense gaze to mine. "Did you know dogs do whatever you say and love you no matter what?"

"Really?" I felt a smile spread across my face, a touch of lightness pushing against the darkness I'd felt since Diane's visit that morning. I tipped my chin in Poindexter's direction. "You might want to tell him that. I don't think he *gets it.*"

I made air quotes with my fingers and instantly frowned. So did Ashley.

Since when had I become an air quote person?

I shuddered, forcing myself to refocus on Ashley's sudden appearance at my front door.

"How did you get here?" I perched on the coffee table, patting her knee.

"Bus."

I was beginning to think the kid was up to something more than a social call. "You took the bus to come see me?"

She shrugged as if her actions were inconsequential, but I'd known this child since the moment of her birth. As much as I'd like to believe she'd gone out of her way simply to check on my well-being, I knew better.

"Where do your parents think you are?"

"Mall." She flipped through the stack of DVDs I'd tossed onto the coffee table, her head snapping up as she grinned at me. "Have any peas, Aunt Bernie?"

Peas. God help me. "What did you do?" I did my best to keep the suspicion out of my voice, but based on Ashley's sudden frown, I'd failed miserably.

"I didn't do anything." Her voice cracked on the last word.

I pressed my lips together, saying nothing, deciding to pass on any attempt at a single eyebrow arch.

"I skipped school," she muttered, bending to hug Poindexter.

Skipped school. Oh, how I remembered those days.

"You did what?" I pushed to my feet. "Why?"

A shadow washed across her face. "You sound just like mom."

Did I? Maybe I was making progress in my efforts to become an adult.

"That's not an answer."

She sucked in a deep breath and straightened, meeting my expectant gaze head-on. "The Neanderthal called me a clown."

Maybe the next time she pointed a Zamboni at the cave man, I'd hit the gas instead of the brake.

"What happened?"

"My eyebrows smeared."

I bit down on my lower lip to control any involuntary reaction my facial features might have.

"What do you mean smeared?"

"Smeared." She gave another shrug. "I sweat, Aunt Bernie. I'm only human. And when I wiped my forehead"—she made the motion as if to prove her point, trailing two pale streaks across her forehead—"they smeared."

Shit. She did look like a clown.

"I can't go back there."

"Yes, you can." I nodded. "We'll go back to the mall. Those little...*salespersons*...at the Rediscover You kiosk must have something waterproof."

Ashley's eyes glimmered with hope. "You'd do that for me?"

"Honey, I'd do anything for you." I leaned down to press a kiss to her smeared forehead before I used my thumbs to erase all evidence of the makeup pencil's remains.

"How about those peas?" Ashley's voice climbed three octaves on the last word.

I laughed. The kid was nothing if not persistent. "I never touch the stuff, but I know someone who might."

I reached for the phone and punched in Sophie Cooke's number. After all, she kept telling me to call if I needed anything.

Much as encouraging Ashley's pea craving went against every law of junk food I held dear, I knew how much these teenage years could hurt, even with eyebrows.

If the kid wanted legumes, I'd go to the ends of the earth—or at least next door—to find her legumes.

While I listened to Sophie say she'd be right over with the cans she'd purchased at last week's two-for-one sale, Ashley straightened up from the sofa, moving toward the mantle.

I watched her from the corner of my eye, my heart catching as she studied Emma's photo and traced one slender finger along the lines of my daughter's face.

My stomach tightened, the usual dread knotting inside me as I hung up the phone.

"What are all of those things on her face?"

Surprise flickered through me. Not that Ashley had asked the question. I had always known she would someday.

What surprised me was that whenever someone did ask the question, I was never as prepared as I thought I should be.

"She needed some help breathing, honey." I stepped to her side, pointing to the tape and tubing on her face. "She needed some oxygen after she was first born."

"And then she could do it herself?"

Ashley looked into my eyes, and the hope and innocence in her gaze stole my breath away.

I bit down on my lip and wrapped an arm around her shoulders, hoping she hadn't spotted the tears threatening in my eyes.

"No." I forced the word through my tight throat, wondering when it would ever get easier to talk about Em. "She never could breathe for herself, but she sure tried. She got better and better and then her heart gave out, honey."

Ashley said nothing, studying me, nodding slowly. "I'm sorry you never got to bring her home, Aunt Bernie."

I blinked then, forcing a smile, fighting like hell against the sting of tears in my eyes.

In one sentence, Ashley had summed up all my pain.

I never got to bring Emma home.

I wrapped my arms around Ashley's neck and squeezed. "Thanks," I said softly.

And then the mental image of Ryan holding his new daughter filled my brain and an inexplicable anger pushed against my sadness.

He'd replaced Emma.

He'd found another woman, another baby, another life.

Ashley pushed away from my embrace and narrowed her gaze on me as if she knew exactly what I was thinking.

"I think Uncle Ryan wanted the new baby because of how much he loved Emma, don't you think?"

The vise of anger and grief loosened its grip on my heart, and I stared down at the carpet for a moment.

Maybe Ryan hadn't been trying to replace Emma...or me. Maybe he'd been trying to recapture what we'd once had.

I looked up at the picture, at the look of sheer joy painted across Ryan's features as he'd cradled Emma in his arms.

Ashley was right.

Ryan hadn't been trying to replace our daughter at all.

He'd only wanted to feel that same sense of unconditional love again. One more time.

And suddenly, I couldn't find a shred of a reason to fault him for that.

"Can I see her memory box, Aunt Bernie?"

Ashley's question so surprised me, I audibly gasped.

"I'd like to see it, too."

Sophie's voice startled me. I hadn't heard her come through the front door.

She pointed back toward the foyer as she stepped into the room. "I knocked, but I guess you didn't hear me. I hope you don't mind."

Moisture blurred my vision, and I shook my head, swallowing down the lump in my throat. "Of course not."

She held up two cans of peas and waved them in the air. "Ta-da."

But then her focus locked on my face and I felt my features crumple, unable to hold my emotions at bay for another second.

Without saying another word, she crossed the room and wrapped me in a hug. I melted into her, not caring about the stream of tears that escaped, beating wet paths down my cheeks.

"Life has a funny way of working out, dear," she whispered against my ear. "Never forget that." She pushed me out to arm's length and gave me a gentle smile. "I'd love to see Emma's things." She spoke the words without an ounce of uncertainty.

"Really?" I blinked away the lingering moisture in my eyes.

I found it difficult to believe her. No one had ever asked to see Emma's things before today. No one.

I never quite understood if it was because they didn't want to remember what had happened or if they were too uncomfortable. Maybe it was because they were afraid to bring up my memories, my heartache.

"Really," Sophie answered.

Something glimmered in her eyes, and I realized she wasn't afraid of the box. Wasn't afraid of the memories.

Even more than that, I knew without a doubt it wasn't my heartache she hoped to bring back.

It was my joy.

I stole a glance at Ashley. Moisture shimmered in her eyes as she nodded at me.

"Okay," I said softly, returning her nod. I turned for the stairs, hesitating momentarily on the bottom step to take another look at these two women.

Sophie's eyes met mine, her gaze softening with encouragement and love.

Was this really the face of the woman who'd yelled at me countless mornings over Poindexter's barking?

Her eyes crinkled just the tiniest bit as if she knew exactly what I was thinking.

"I'll be right back." I heard myself say, and the next thing I knew, I was headed upstairs to retrieve my most private possession, ready to share my most painful—and my most joyous—memories with the lanky teen and the next-door neighbor who had become two of the most important women in my life.

I sat and stared for a long time after Sophie left and David came to take Ashley home. I stared at the contents of Emma's memory box, at her photo on the mantle.

Trisomy 18.

I remembered when the call came. I remembered the time of day, the smell of late summer coming in through the open windows, and I remembered the tone of Dr. Platt's voice.

I remembered the slick wall, cold behind my back as I slid to the floor in disbelief and shock.

And then we'd battled—Ryan and I—together as a team.

We'd fought for Emma's life, and for five days, we'd won.

I slowly climbed the stairs and headed down the hall to Emma's room, or rather, what would have been Emma's room.

I'm sorry you never got to bring her home, Aunt Bernie. Ashley's words reverberated in my brain as I peeked through the doorway.

An oversize plush bunny snuggled into the pillows on the bed where I'd always imagined I'd cuddle Emma on nights she couldn't sleep or got scared. Trailing pink and yellow tulips graced the fleece blanket on which Emma had rested at the hospital.

A rainbow of stuffed elephants, bears, and dogs lined the shelves, waiting for a little girl who would never come home, who would never cuddle them in her sleep. How many times had I touched their heads with fingertips that still remembered the softness of Emma's skin and the downy hair on her forehead?

She would have loved it here.

A sob pushed against my throat, and I pressed my fingertips to my lips to hold it back.

Ryan had never believed the prognosis. He'd always sworn the test results were wrong, the ultrasound findings were inaccurate. But me, I'd always known something wasn't right.

Call it mother's intuition—call it whatever you want to call it—I'd known Emma was sick. Sure, I'd believed in the miracle. I'd been convinced she'd prove the doctors wrong by being born alive, but I'd never been able to picture her coming home.

Had I failed her by not believing enough?

I squeezed my eyes shut, trying to conjure up the image of her face, her scent, the feel of her tiny body against my chest as I'd held her in the NICU. Then I refocused on where I stood.

The doorway to Emma's room. The doorway to what might have been.

I'd stood there countless times before. I'd sat in the middle of the floor with her belongings piled around me, intending to sort them, give them away, put them in storage.

But I never had.

I'd never been able to fully accept the truth.

Emma wasn't coming home.

I looked at my feet, blinking against the tears that came, watching as one fell with a tiny splash to the top of my foot.

When I lifted my gaze, refocusing on Emma's room, everything looked the same, and yet everything looked different.

I needed to let go.

And this time, I was ready.

By the time I had sorted and packed Emma's toys and clothes and blankets, my eyes were gritty with fatigue, but there was still one thing left to do.

Ryan and I were meeting at my lawyer's office in a few weeks to sign our property settlement papers. I patted a small box as I pushed away from the bureau in Emma's room, making a mental note to take it with me when I saw him.

I ruffled Poindexter's head as I passed him in the hall, gesturing for him to follow me when he wearily lifted his snout and squinted at me.

We padded downstairs together, I checked the lock on the front door as we passed, and I tossed him a few dog treats then let him out back.

The night was clear and cold, a bit colder than normal for this time of year, but early spring was like that around here. You never knew what kind of weather you were going to get from one day to the next.

Kind of like life.

I slid open the drawer where I'd stashed the beads and wire and jewelry tools, and plucked out the bag holding them all.

I let Poindexter back inside, locked the back door, and settled at the kitchen table, methodically spreading everything before me, this time seeing the pattern and color combinations as if they'd been heaven sent.

I took a deep breath, measured the wire, and snipped. I faithfully worked the pattern, over and over, stopping and starting, cutting the wire and beginning again, until I got it right.

I wove the beads into a simple pattern—a rainbow of colors and textures down the middle framed by seed beads the color of the sun down either side.

As I reached for my bedside lamp a long while later, I studied the play of color against my wrist, tracing my fingertip over each piece of glass.

I reached for Dad's book and flipped the cover open, searching not for a cryptogram to solve but instead for the words he'd written on the inside front cover, the sentiment he'd lived by, taught us, hoped we'd believe.

In life, you either choose to sing a rainbow, or you don't.

Maybe I'd taken my time in getting to this point. Maybe someone else would have bounced right back from life's curveballs without quitting a job and cutting her hair and almost sleeping with her landscaper.

But, I hadn't. And that was all right.

This was my rainbow. Mine alone. And maybe for me, the singing had finally begun.

"In the depth of winter, I finally learned that there was within me an invincible summer."
—Albert Camus

CHAPTER TWENTY-ONE

— — —

*"VX OPRX FQPAX VQP MLPV FQX VPJAF PZ YA SLC CPL'F
FYJL FQXHJ ZSEXA SVSG."*
   —*VSOMXJ WXJEG*

A decent amount of trepidation filled me as I pulled into my mother's drive on Easter Sunday. I hadn't seen or talked to Mark in the two months since our argument, and while I'd spoken to my mother plenty of times since that day, we'd avoided the issue, dancing completely around the topic.

We'd also avoided my mother's to-do list, or at least, I had.

Mark, Jenny, and the kids hadn't arrived yet, so I let Poindexter out into my mother's fenced yard then followed her into the kitchen.

I spotted a small silver object hanging from the waistband of her jeans and pointed. "What's that?"

"A pedometer." Mom gave the tiny device a pat. "Ten thousand steps a day and I feel like a new woman. You should try it, honey."

I bit my lip to avoid laughing. "I'll do that."

Then I opted for a subject change.

"I was thinking about your list." I swiped a pickle from the crystal serving dish while my mother wasn't watching. A move I'd perfected in grade school.

"It's done," she said.

"What's done?" I muffed the question through pieces of dill. So much for subterfuge.

"The list."

"Your list is done?" Was she serious?

"Mm hm." She nodded as she slipped a tray of dinner rolls into the oven.

"Since when?"

"Since I started attacking it item by item."

Without me. I cringed. "I'm sorry, Mom."

She spun on me, her brows crumpled. "For what?"

"Mark was right. I'm not here enough. I should be here. I should—"

"You have your own life," she interrupted me.

"But I—"

"And you should live it."

The doorbell rang just as she stepped toward me. She ignored the chime long enough to cup my chin in her fingertips.

"Live your life, Bernie. That's all your dad and I ever wanted for you."

I stood frozen in place, working to swallow down the knot of emotion in my throat as my mother headed for the front door.

"Don't you look handsome?" I heard her say.

"Is she here?" Mark asked.

Mark.

I drew in a fortifying breath. The time had come for me to say I was sorry. Hell, the time had come and gone. A good sister would have apologized weeks ago. But not me. No sir.

I heard Mark's approaching footsteps and opened my mouth to speak. When he cleared the threshold, sporting Dad's favorite jacket—navy blue with brass buttons, words failed me.

Don't you look handsome? My mom's words rang in my ears.

He did look handsome.

And he looked like Daddy. The sight stole my breath away.

Mark smiled, knowing the exact effect he was having on me. Sudden tears swam in my eyes and he frowned, reaching out to grasp my arm.

"Hey." He pulled me close. "This wasn't supposed to make you cry."

I tried to choke out a response, a word, anything, but nothing came.

Mark steered me toward the back door, a move my father had made countless times during my childhood. A moment later, we were sitting on the back step, the warm spring air caressing our cheeks.

"I wasn't ready for this before," he said. "I'm sorry—"

But I squeezed his hand, stopping him short.

It had taken me five years to face Emma's room. Mark had faced Dad's closet in only seven months.

"No." I forced the word through my throat. "I'm sorry. I was wrong. So very, very wrong."

He hooked an arm around my shoulders and pulled me close. I couldn't remember the last time we'd sat like this. Hell, I couldn't remember ever sitting like this.

"We were both wrong." The soothing tone of his voice washed over me, calming any tinge of anxiety I'd still held inside. "I think losing a father will do that to people."

"Make them crazy?" I asked.

"Yeah." He chuckled lightly. "Make them crazy."

"Nice jacket." I pulled at the hem.

"A little something I picked up," he teased.

"He'd be proud of you."

Mark's voice tightened then. "Think so?"

"Know so," I answered.

He gave my shoulders a squeeze.

"What do you think he'd say about your hair?" he asked.

I reached up to self-consciously smooth a strand. My hair had grown long enough for the uncontrollable wave to become… well…uncontrollable. Let's just say the effect left a lot to be desired.

And then we spoke the words together. "I don't care what anybody says, I'd wear it anyway."

We were still laughing as we stepped back inside, but just before we left the mudroom, he grasped my arm again, pulling me to a stop.

I turned to face him, my eyes widening.

"You've been through a lot, Bernie."

I shook my head. "No more than anyone else."

He nodded, his eyes narrowing. "I'm proud of you."

We stared at each other for a few moments, the silence comfortable, a bit like coming home.

"I cried for days when Emma died." Mark spoke the words so softly I thought for a moment I might be imagining them. Moisture glistened in his eyes.

I'd never seen my brother cry.

Never.

"Why didn't you tell me?" My throat tightened again, relief and sadness and grief washing over me all at once.

He sighed, the sound more shudder than exhale. "Because big brothers aren't supposed to cry."

I wrapped my arms around his neck, tears stinging behind my lids. "Yes, they are," I whispered the words in his ear.

"A bebe." A shrill little voice sounded just before a tiny pair of arms locked around my knees.

I pushed away from Mark, holding his gaze long enough to read the truce in his eyes.

I turned and hoisted Elizabeth into my arms.

"A bebe," she repeated as I pressed a kiss to her chubby cheek. My heart ached wondering how much she'd look like her cousin Emma might have looked.

"She's been practicing your name all week," Mark said, smiling proudly.

"And it sounds perfect." I gave Elizabeth a squeeze and reached my open hand for Mark's, sliding my fingers inside his. "Perfect," I repeated as the three of us headed back toward the rest of our family.

"We were at the mall," Diane said as she and Ashley let themselves in my front door later that evening.

I wondered briefly if the day would ever come that Diane didn't feel she could walk in without knocking.

I hoped not.

"Aren't you supposed to be on bed rest?"

Weeks had passed since the preterm labor scare, and, with the exception of mild cramping, Diane's pregnancy had continued along smoothly.

"We're close enough to term that I'm allowed to do light activities."

"Like going to the mall," Ashley chimed in, rolling her eyes.

Ashley's forehead captured my attention as I nodded in response to her statement. Her eyebrows were…perfect. I mean, truly perfect.

"Rediscover You?" I asked. She and I had never gotten back to the makeup kiosk, but she'd obviously found a solution to the smearing issue.

Diane shook her head. "We bought some things at the drugstore and did them ourselves in the parking lot. They look great, don't they?"

I stepped more closely to Ashley and reached out a finger to lightly trace her brows. I smiled. Her stubbles had almost grown in. Someday soon, the kid would have her brows back.

"Nice." I gave her a hug.

Ashley took a backward step and hoisted a paper bag into my arms. "Open it," she commanded.

I scrutinized the bag and frowned. "What is it?"

"Open it." Diane repeated Ashley's words.

So I did.

I unfolded the top of the bag, peered inside, and studied the vivid lilac shade. I reached into the bag, pulled out the thick cotton knit and shook out the sweatshirt.

A *new* sweatshirt.

I looked down at the ratty sweatshirt currently covering the upper half of my body and laughed. The cuffs were no longer attached and the zipper was on its last tooth, literally.

"Read it." Ashley's eyes grew even brighter.

Read it?

I turned the garment around and read the single word emblazoned across the chest in big, bold letters.

Goddess.

"Oh, shit." I slapped a hand across my mouth as I started to laugh. "I mean…shoot."

"Isn't it great?" Ashley didn't miss a beat, snatching the new sweatshirt out of my hands and reaching to unzip the one I wore.

I captured her hand in mine. "Excuse me?"

"We're burning it." Diane waggled her fingers at my zipper. "Get that off."

"Burning it?" My voice squeaked on the last word.

Diane pursed her lips and nodded. I'd forgotten just how bossy she could be.

But, I liked it.

A grin spread across my face as I looked down again at the sweatshirt that had been my faithful companion through most every moment of my recent metamorphosis.

Burning it.

I liked that idea a lot.

I unzipped my top, shrugged out of the offending garment, and let it drop to the floor in a faded gray puddle. Diane plucked the beyond-repair sweatshirt from the floor and headed toward the back door. Ashley stepped behind me, holding up the lilac sweatshirt as if the garment were a coronation robe.

I slid my arms into the new sleeves, savoring the plush feel of unworn cotton against my skin. I reached down to pull the zipper home, stepped in front of the hall mirror, and smiled.

Goddess.

Not even close, but I'd take it.

I laughed.

"Where are your matches?" Diane's voice rang out from the kitchen.

Matches.

Now, I might be a tad on the uncoordinated side, but the thought of a very pregnant Diane lumbering about in the backyard with a pack of matches made my blood run cold.

"I'll get them," I answered.

Several minutes later, we'd successfully fired up the barbeque pit. Diane held the old gray sweatshirt in her outstretched arms as if it reeked of disease.

"Anything you want to say?" she asked.

I reached for the shirt, plucking it from her grip. "Let me do that."

I dropped the sweatshirt on top of the fire, frowning momentarily when I thought it might extinguish the flames instead of catching them, but the fire's glow grew, sparkling through the beads on my bracelet.

I smiled, knowing exactly what I wanted to say. Exactly what I wanted to believe.

"To chasing rainbows." I hoisted up one of the three glasses of water we'd poured to celebrate the moment.

Ashley's forehead crumpled, but Diane beamed. Someday Ashley would know exactly what I meant. For the time being, she merely shrugged and took a sip of her water.

We watched as the flames licked up from the barbeque pit Ryan and I had used just once.

"Aunt Bernie, do you have any—"

"For the love of God, do not say peas." I shot Ashley a warning glare.

"Marshmallows?" She finished her question and shook her head. "Why would I want to roast peas?"

The three of us laughed, the sound of our happiness mingling with countless sparkles of light, lifting from the burning sweatshirt and dancing on the night air before fading away, leaving only the promise of things to come.

The drone of a plane sounded overhead, and Poindexter took off running, paws pounding against the yard, snout pointed skyward, his gaze fixated on the lights of a cargo plane circling for landing.

As Ashley headed inside to look for marshmallows, I did something I'd thought about doing countless times before.

I put down my glass and ran with my dog, racing back and forth across the yard, keeping the target in focus.

A single airplane. Poindexter's rainbow.

We chased until the plane was out of sight, then I dropped down onto the grass, laughing, pulling Poindexter into my arms.

If I wasn't mistaken, a silhouette moved away from the patio doors down at Number Thirty-Six.

And I smiled.

"We love those who know the worst of us and don't turn their faces away."
—Walker Percy

CHAPTER TWENTY-TWO

— — —

I woke early the day I was meeting Ryan at the lawyer's office. Matter of fact, I hadn't slept much at all.

We were to sign our property settlement at lunchtime. The division of property hadn't been difficult. For one thing, our house was pretty much the only thing we had. Sure, we'd been very careful about saving for retirement, and oddly enough that had been what helped me now.

Ryan kept his retirement funds intact. I got the house. We'd been making double payments for as long as I could remember, and the remaining principle was negligible. Even I could manage the payments, assuming I didn't work at the rink for the rest of my life.

I studied the clock and wished our appointment was early rather than later. I'd accepted the fact our marriage was really and truly over, I just didn't want to think about it any longer than I had to.

Realizing I had time to kill, I decided to get comfortable, make some coffee, and find a way to make the morning pass as quickly as possible.

When I reached for the security of Dad's shirt, I hesitated, my fingertips a fraction of an inch from the well-worn fabric. I lifted the sleeve and pressed it to my face, inhaling deeply. After countless launderings, all traces of Dad's scent were gone, just like Emma's scent from her lock of hair, her booties, her gown.

Dad was gone. Emma was gone. Neither was coming back.

I dropped the sleeve, smoothing the fabric before I closed the closet door.

I knew I'd pull the shirt out from time to time, but it had seen me through the worst of things. Maybe the shirt and Dad's book had been exactly what I'd needed to bring me there. To that moment.

I reached for the sweatshirt Ashley and Diane had given me and pulled it on. I caught my reflection in the mirror and smiled.

Goddess.

A laugh burst through my lips.

At least the kid believed in me. And Diane believed in me. Hell, Sophie Cooke and my family believed in me. I must be doing something right.

I touched my bracelet, tracing the outline of each bead, starting at the clasp and working my way around in a circle.

The rainbow wasn't perfect. Some segments of color were flawed and a few were misbeaded. A lot like me, actually.

Suddenly, I couldn't think of a talisman more perfect for my day—or life—ahead.

Ryan and I stood outside the lawyer's office, staring at each other awkwardly. The entire signing process had taken less than fifteen minutes, and now all we had to do was wait and watch our mailboxes for the official document.

The late April day had grown warm, and a hot wind wound its way down the sidewalk, tumbling small potted plants, whipping brightly colored flags, foretelling the storm to come.

I took inventory of Ryan's features as we stared at each other, the uncomfortable silence stretching between us. There were new lines at the corners of his eyes, and if I wasn't mistaken, he carried a little extra weight in his cheeks. His gaze lit with something I remembered from long ago but couldn't quite put my finger on.

I remembered how we used to laugh, how he would finish my jokes and I would finish his. I remembered how we used to be in sync, how we used to be in love.

When had we lost us?

Maybe we'd tried to get pregnant one too many times after we lost Emma. Or maybe we hadn't tried enough. Maybe trying for a baby wasn't the only thing we'd given up on. Somewhere along the way the unspoken thoughts had taken over. Lost in the silence, we'd let our life together slip away.

The corners of Ryan's eyes turned down. I realized signing the papers had hurt him as much as it hurt me.

I found comfort in the fact it pained him to walk away from us—from me—after all these years.

"You look beautiful, Bernie." His lips pulled into a crooked smile, but a shade of regret fell across his eyes. "Maybe this is what you needed."

"What?" I frowned.

"To be alone." His gaze widened. "Without me."

I shook my head and let a disbelieving laugh slide across my lips. "No."

Truth was, a part of me still wanted what we'd once had. I'd let our marriage die along with my spirit in the years following

Emma's death. It had taken losing Ryan and losing Dad to show me just how much I'd shut down inside.

Maybe I looked different because I'd finally given myself permission to live. Permission to survive. Permission to feel and love and laugh.

After all this time, I finally understood exactly what rainbow it was I needed to be chasing.

Me.

"Your toes are purple." Ryan's brows drew together, etching a deep line into his forehead as he glanced down at my feet.

In a toss-up between the boots and a new pair of strappy sandals Diane had given me, I'd gone with the sandals. After all, from the ankles down, I still had it all going on.

"Toenails?" I asked.

"Toenails," he repeated.

"What's your point?"

"You never painted your toenails purple when we were married."

I glanced down at my feet and shrugged. Not a what-in-the-hell-business-is-it-of-yours shrug, but rather a will-you-look-at-that sort of shrug.

I never did a lot of things when we were married.

I thought the words, but I didn't say them. Maybe I was a coward. But maybe, just maybe, I thought the words might hurt Ryan, and at that moment, hurting him was the last thing in the world I wanted to do.

After all, it wasn't Ryan's fault I shut down after Emma died.

It wasn't anybody's fault.

It just was.

"People change." I spoke the words lightly, downplaying their significance.

People did change.

I'd changed.

Soon I'd no longer be Ryan's wife. And while I'd always be Emma's mom, I was moving past the grief of being Emma's mom. I was ready to be me. To live my life. To be Bernadette Murphy.

And why not?

I stole another glance at my feet.

Anyone who wore purple toenail polish couldn't be all bad.

Ryan gave me a tight smile and began to turn away. I remembered the box and reached into the large tote bag I'd carried to hold my copies of our papers.

"Hang on a sec."

He hesitated, frowning at me slightly. When I handed him the small, wrapped box, surprise and curiosity danced in his gaze.

"For the baby," I said.

He blinked.

We hadn't spoken a word about his new daughter. It was probably better that way, but I wanted him to have what I'd brought him.

A pair of young mothers stepped away from a wrought-iron bench nearby, hurriedly pulling up the canopies on their strollers as the sky darkened.

I pointed toward the vacated bench. "There. Let's open it."

"You sure?"

Our eyes locked and held, and for a moment I could see our entire past played out in the depths of Ryan's searching gaze.

"Very," I said softly.

We settled next to each other, and he peeled back the wrapping paper, slipping a finger beneath the flap of the box to pry open the top.

The pale pink hippo sat inside, nestled in a bed of tissue paper.

"This is Emma's," he said softly.

"Was Emma's," I corrected. "I think she'd like her little sister to have it, don't you?"

Ryan's features pinched, and for the briefest of moments, I thought he might cry. Instead he straightened away from the bench and leaned down to press a kiss to the top of my hair.

"He plays Brahms's 'Lullaby.'" I explained as if he wouldn't remember, even though his expression made it evident he hadn't forgotten a thing.

I reached to pull the hippo's accordion-pleated tail. "Right here."

Soft music filtered into the warm air, and for a moment I found myself transported back to the day Ryan and I picked out the toy for the nursery.

The music came to a stop, and we stayed motionless, wordless, until Ryan returned the hippo to the box and closed the lid. "Thanks."

We stared at each other, and I nodded, unable to find my voice.

"See you around, Bernie." His eyebrows lifted slightly as he said the words, and my heart hit my toes.

I forced a smile as he turned and walked away, down the windswept sidewalk back toward the metered space where he'd parked his car.

"See you around," I whispered toward his back, my words lost on a sudden burst of moist air. In my heart I knew chances were pretty good I wouldn't see him around at all.

Ryan Murphy had really and truly walked out of my life and into his new one.

❦

There were two messages waiting for me on the answering machine when I got home.

The first sent my pulse into an excited frenzy. I absentmindedly waited for the second message as I reached for the phone to return the first.

Jim Barnes at the *Courier Post* wanted to talk to me about a regular column.

Regular.

Column.

He'd never heard back from me when he'd called about the second article, so would it be all right to run them both now? How soon would I be able to get him another, and when could I come in to the office to discuss whether I'd be able to provide them with something on a weekly basis?

Regular.

Column.

I longed to say the words over and over, tasting them, trying out the feel of them on my tongue.

Had I found a job by pouring my heart onto paper? If only Dad could see me now.

I laughed in disbelief just as the voice of the second caller cut through my happy oblivion.

"Bern, it's David. Diane's water broke. Ashley's with me at the hospital."

I was in motion, slamming down the phone, grabbing for my purse and keys, running, breathless, not waiting to hear the rest of David's message.

As I backed out of the drive and pressed down on the accelerator, I flashed back on the last urgent message from David. The one that came shortly after I'd e-mailed the second article to the paper.

Had there been other messages on the machine that day? I tried to picture the flashing light and how many times it had been blinking.

Had I missed Jim Barnes's call?

Chances were I had, but I could worry about that later.

I smiled.

Right now, the newest Snyder was about to make his or her arrival, and I didn't plan to miss a single second of the blessed event.

When I reached Labor and Delivery, Diane and David were nowhere to be found. Diane had been whisked to surgery for a C-section and David had gone with her.

I found Ashley sitting alone in the waiting room, pale as a ghost, frightened eyes huge.

"Aunt Bernie." Relief oozed from her words as I gathered her into a hug.

"Any word?" I asked.

She shook her head against my chest, and I stroked the length of her smooth, long hair.

"Everything will be all right," I whispered against the top of her head. "You'll see."

And then I prayed, with all of my might.

The nurse told me the baby's heartbeat had been dropping with each contraction. The doctor's call had been to get the baby out.

Ashley and I waited for what seemed like forever, but in reality was no more than an hour.

When David finally appeared, the happy news was splashed across his face.

Ashley pushed to her feet, and her father grinned. "You've got a little brother."

She launched herself into his arms. I kept my distance as they laughed and hugged. Sometimes I worried I took my place within their family for granted. Truth was, maybe they merely tolerated me.

My fears were squashed when David held one arm out to me, gesturing for me to move closer. I wrapped one arm around his back and another around Ashley, joining in the celebration of the newest Snyder's arrival.

"What are you going to name him?" I asked.

"Junior."

"Junior?" Ashley and I repeated at the same time.

"I'm kidding," David teased. "We don't know yet. If he'd been a girl we were going to name her Bernadette, but one of those is probably enough."

Call me crazy, but I thought he and Ashley laughed a little too hard at that moment.

I glanced at Ashley as we headed toward her mother's room. Her forehead puckered with concern, and she'd apparently forgotten to smooth her eyebrows in the rush to get to the hospital. The new hairs were long now and zigzagged across the space above her blue eyes like out of control caterpillars.

She caught me staring. "What?"

"Nothing." I shook my head.

As we stepped inside, a nurse was tucking Junior Snyder into his mother's arms. Tears of joy slid down Diane's cheeks.

David gently wiped the moisture from Diane's face then dropped a kiss first to her forehead, then to his son's.

There were many years in which I would have never thought this, but Diane was lucky to have him. Hell, look how lucky I was to have him—to have all of them.

I remembered the moments before Emma's birth and how badly I'd wanted to keep her inside me where she was safe. Those days seemed forever ago when I thought about how life went on without her, and for a time, without me.

Emotions welled up inside me and I choked on a mixture of joy, sadness, and hope. I hiccupped, and all heads turned toward me.

David left Diane's side long enough to reach for me. "You okay?"

Genuine concern glimmered in his eyes. I may have once fantasized about putting this man's head in an oven, but he'd turned out to be the real deal. A keeper.

I nodded. "I just thought of the perfect gift."

"Gift?" David's forehead furrowed.

"For Junior's crib," I said, picturing the blue elephant from Emma's room.

They'd come in a set of three. The pink hippo. The blue elephant. The yellow bear.

We'd carried the bear to the NICU, setting it next to Emma in her incubator. We hadn't known whether or not she could hear until the moment the bear played "Clair de Lune." Emma had turned her head, eyes wide with wonder, and she'd listened.

I'd keep the bear. After all, who knew what surprises life had in store.

As I watched Diane cradle her new son, happy laughter built inside me, nothing more than a slight bubble at first, building in intensity, growing until it tumbled out of me, spilling into the room.

"Bernie?" David took a step closer, concern plastered across his face.

"Junior," I said, my laugh growing stronger, my smile spreading wide across my face.

David smiled. Diane smiled. Before I knew it, the three of us laughed and cried while Ashley practiced dramatic eye rolls.

Life was funny…and wonderful.

Sometimes you had to wait a little while for the good times to kick in. But when they did, you realized every moment and experience that came before was necessary…necessary to bring you there.

The skies that had been threatening all day gave way during my drive home from the hospital. Rain slapped at the windshield, coating the glass with a thick sheet of water.

I could make out the shopping center to my left and realized it had been a while since I'd sat in the café, watching the world go by.

No time like the present to see what new inspiration I could find while studying Genuardi shoppers. After all, it looked like I had some columns to write.

I didn't notice the darkly clad figure racing across the parking lot next to me until we both reached the overhang running the length of the store.

I flattened my back to the wall, grimacing against the squish of rainwater in my sopping-wet sandals.

"Nice choice of footwear, Number Thirty-Two."

The rumble of his voice was unmistakable and the tightening of my belly undeniable.

Number Thirty-Six.

I looked up at him, relief washing through me at the sight of his smile. "I was going for bold and daring," I answered. "Not good?"

The rain pelted the awning over our heads, like applause in a too-small space—loud and out of control.

He laughed a hearty, from-deep-inside-the-soul laugh. The kind I hadn't heard in a long, long while.

"What?" I asked, as if Number Thirty-Six owed me an explanation for his joy.

He smiled down at me, tiny creases framing his eyes, laugh lines bracketing his sensuous mouth.

My heart tilted sideways.

"I was just thinking." The deep timbre of his voice tickled something deep inside me, a craving I'd thought long dead. The desire to be spoken to, whispered to, made love to. Not sex. *Love.*

I did my best to arch a brow. After all, two could play the neighbors-trapped-under-an-awning game. "Thinking what?"

His lips parted, exposing a wide grin. A great big, wonderfully uninhibited grin.

"Rain like this"—he tipped his chin toward the downpour— "we'll have to sing a rainbow."

For one very long moment, the world hushed around me. I saw nothing but the intensity of his gaze. Heard nothing but the reverberation of his words in my mind.

I thought of the inscription in Dad's book and what Mom had said the day she handed me the cryptograms.

I'm sure your father thought he'd have more time.

I thought about the puzzles he'd chosen and realized my dad's message may not have been complete, but wasn't that the beauty of life?

Wasn't that the beauty of learning and growing and stumbling and getting back up and trying again?

"Is that something you say a lot?" I asked Number Thirty-Six. "The rainbow thing?"

Number Thirty-Six frowned slightly and laughed. "No. It sort of popped into my brain just now. Funny, huh?"

"Funny," I said in a whisper.

It was all so simple, wasn't it? In the end, life boiled down to whether or not we chose to sing our rainbows.

If possible, the rain picked up in intensity.

For longer than I cared to admit, I'd been content to be carried—a loose twig washing downstream with the current.

I hadn't tried to swim to shore. I hadn't tried to buck the current. I hadn't tried, period.

But standing there, looking into Number Thirty-Six's face, I saw the possibilities and realized I was ready to risk giving everything I had to give.

"So what do you think?" he asked.

I blinked myself back into focus. Number Thirty-Six had been saying something while I'd been lost inside my head. "I'm sorry?"

He jerked a thumb toward the café sign at our back. "Buy you a cup of coffee?"

I stole another look at his laugh lines. At that moment, he looked like…well…he looked like someone I might want to know forever.

I smiled then. A real smile. The kind of smile that pulls you taller, straighter, brighter.

"Coffee sounds great," I said.

And you know what?

It was.

ACKNOWLEDGMENTS

There are countless individuals and moments that play a part in the life of a book like *Chasing Rainbows*.

There are the parents who believe in the power of your dreams, who encourage you to believe in yourself and reach for the stars. For Regina Steele, my mother, who never ceases to amaze and inspire me with her unfailing belief, encouragement, and love, thank you. I love you, Mom.

There are life events that alter your sense of reality. There are heartaches that teach you to survive and move forward. For Howard Steele, my dad, and for Emily Bernadette, my firstborn, I miss and love you both, but will carry you in my heart forever.

There are family members who support and celebrate with you on a daily basis, eat pizza when you're on a deadline, and forgive you when you need to write just one more scene. For my husband, Dan, and my daughter, Elizabeth Anne, this one's for you. I love you more than words can ever explain.

There are treasured friends who read and reread every word, encourage you to never give up, and cheer you when the dream comes true. For Anna Sugden, Sheila Raye, Janice Lynn, Beth Andrews, Tawny Weber, and every single pal at Writers at Play, thank you. You have been, and continue to be, the most wonderful part of this writing journey.

Finally, for Lindsay Guzzardo, Amazon Publishing, and Kindle Direct Publishing, without you this book would have remained a file, tucked away on a backup drive. Thank you for the opportunity and the belief.

ABOUT THE AUTHOR

A long time ago, in an elementary school far, far away, a very young Kathleen Long scribbled a story idea in her journal. Then she wrote another, and another. She added several poems, the lyrics to a song or two, a love letter to David Cassidy, and so on and so on.

While her early writings never saw the light of day, many of her later works did. And while she didn't end up with David Cassidy, Kathleen did marry her own Prince Charming. Together, they are raising one drama queen and one obedience-challenged border collie mix in a kingdom divided between suburban Philadelphia and the Jersey Shore.

The author of thirteen novels, Kathleen has been nominated for a RITA® and has won a RIO Award and two Gayle Wilson Awards of Excellence. Her additional honors include National Readers Choice, Holt Medallion, and Booksellers Best award nominations. She spends her time plotting her next book, bribing her little one to pick up her toys, and begging the dog to heel.

A CONVERSATION WITH KATHLEEN LONG

— —— ——

1. **What inspired you to write *Chasing Rainbows*?**

   Many of the key elements for *Chasing Rainbows* came directly from my life. I don't think that's unusual for an author. I believe that once authors have ideas in their minds for good stories, they pull details and emotions from their own experiences to bring the story to life for readers. That's truly what I did for *Chasing Rainbows*.

   Did I endure the loss of our infant daughter and my dad? Yes.

   Did I face down cosmetic kiosk clerks who, after I asked for prevention cream, said I needed *recovery* cream? Yes. (Did I jump the counter? No, but man, that scene was fun to write!)

   Do I believe a good pair of boots can cure most any problem? Yes. I'm shallow like that.

   Did I come to realize life's not perfect and there's always going to be a choice between wallowing and moving forward? Yes.

While much of Bernie's story is culled from my life, even more is not. The beauty of writing and creating is that the initial kernel of an idea—be it for a premise or a character—takes on a life of its own and grows into a fully formed journey for the author and her readers.

Chasing Rainbows gave me the opportunity to write the kind of book I'd always wanted to write—a bigger book that deals with topics important to women.

2. What is your favorite scene in the book?

Without a doubt, the most special scene for me is when Bernie finally faces her daughter's empty nursery, and packs away and sorts the items she's clung to for five years. I tear up every time I reread this passage because Bernie's actions embody the message of *Chasing Rainbows*. To me, it's symbolic of Bernie's choice to move forward and choose living over grieving. We all have heartaches, and the choice to move forward is ours alone.

3. What scene did you love writing? Is there a scene that was especially difficult to write?

Writing the cosmetic kiosk scene in which Bernie scales the counter and corners the sales clerks was more than a little fun to write. Perhaps Bernie's actions are a bit over-the-top, but I love her passion, her emotion, and the fact she does something that I'm sure many of us have fantasized about at some point in our lives.

As to which scene was most difficult to write—that would have to be Bernie's arrival at the hospital when Diane goes into preterm labor. Just as Bernie had to work through difficult memories upon her arrival in the MICU and seeing her former doctor, I found myself working through similar memories and anger while writing about it. This particular section of the book took me a while to create. While the names and personas are fictionalized, the descriptions and Bernie's memories are very true to life.

4. **Why cryptograms?**

"T PAFY FG T ATLWBL FP PTHK, WIU UATU FP GBU DATU PAFYP TLK WIFQU HBL."

You might be thinking, "What the heck?" Or, you might be thinking, "Oh, a cryptogram." Exactly what is that jumble of letters? The trick to solving a cryptogram puzzle is to slowly break the code. Does the T stand for A? Does the U stand for T? In this case, yes…and yes.

My father and I used to open the newspaper each morning and race to see who would uncover the cryptogram solution first. I loved the challenge, the shared moments, and the revealed quotes. For that reason, I decided to include cryptograms as a special story element in *Chasing Rainbows*. I actually have a journal full of cryptogram quotes my father compiled for me, much like Bernie's father leaves behind for her in *Chasing Rainbows*.

Bernie's journey is framed by these quotes. I loved the creative challenge of weaving the book's story threads together through them.

5. **What do you want the reader to walk away with after reading this book?**

The most distinctive thing about the main character is that she's not perfect. As a matter of fact, she's far from perfect. She makes mistakes. She thinks selfish thoughts. She fails. Yet, she reaches a point in her life at which she decides to get up and try again. She decides to move forward.

The book often quotes Bernie's father. "In life, you either choose to sing a rainbow, or you don't." I hope readers will take away the realization that no matter what might be happening in your life at any given moment, it's never too late to start singing.

6. **What is your writing process like? Do you write in the morning, the evening, or intermittently all day? Do you need music or total silence?**

Before my daughter was born, my time was my own. I primarily wrote in the early morning, but if I was in the thick of a story, I had the freedom to write for fourteen hours straight. I no longer have that flexibility, so I've had to relearn my process.

For a while, I tried to write late at night. That didn't work out very well. Now, I'm back to morning writing, working on my portable keyboard first thing each day.

As to the question of music versus silence, I used to need silence, but now I create a playlist for each story. I can turn on that music and the songs become white noise that allow me to immediately immerse myself in the world I've created.

7. **What is the hardest part about writing for you?**

For me, the hardest part of writing is starting the story. While I don't plot out every single detail of a book, I need to know where each character is headed and why. If I'm not fully immersed in the characters and their motivations, I find it difficult to write quickly, and I love to write quickly. Writing fast is the process that works best for me.

Once I have the foundation of the story ready to go, I'm set. It's that initial brain work that takes the most time, and considering I spend much of my time negotiating deals with a stubborn six-year-old, quality brain time is a precious commodity in my world.

8. **If you weren't an author, what would you want to be?**

I'd be a meteorologist! (Everyone who knows me just groaned, by the way.) I am *obsessed* with the weather. Is it going to storm? What's the temperature? Which way is that hurricane headed? How many inches of snow are they calling for?

One time when hubby and I were first married, we were late on paying the cable bill. As a punishment, the cable company flipped some switch which allowed us to receive only The Weather Channel. Punishment? I thought I'd died and gone to Heaven!

9. **Looking over all your books, what character are you most like?**

I am definitely the most like Bernie from *Chasing Rainbows*.

Sarcastic? Check. Difficult hair? Check. Still carrying around weight from fertility treatments? Check. Never took the belly dancing DVDs out of the cellophane? Check. Climbed a chair to yell at a boss? Check. Chase airplanes with the dog? Check.

Unlike Bernie, I am happily married and spend my time trying to keep up with our six-year-old. Who knows? Maybe Bernie will get a sequel someday.

10. What are you working on right now?

I'm working on a new women's fiction project, due out in early 2013. *Changing Lanes* is the story of Abby Halladay, a woman who's forced to move home to her parents' house after a case of terminal termites sends her packing. The story is full of quirky, small-town characters, poignant moments, and loads of self-discovery.

For all of Abby's efforts to hang on to what she thinks matters most—jobs, relationships, memories—she learns that in the end, life is a journey of letting go. Life is about letting life happen—the good, the bad, and the out-of-this-world amazing.

QUESTIONS FOR DISCUSSION

1. What do you see as the turning point that finally snaps Bernie back into action and puts her on the road to reclaiming her life and happiness?

2. What did you feel was the most poignant or touching scene in the book? Why?

3. What does Bernie's story tell us about grief? How do Bernie and her brother differ when it comes to grieving? What aspects of Bernie's grief can you relate to?

4. Has your worldview ever shifted following a loss or difficult time in your life? How do you think Bernie's worldview changes?

5. Do you think Bernie was ever too over-the-top? What was your favorite over-the-top Bernie scene? What's the craziest thing you've ever done out of grief or heartbreak?

6. The book makes reference to chasing rainbows and pursuing dreams. Do you have a dream you long to chase? What might be holding you back?

7. Bernie's mother discovers her father's book of cryptograms. Have you ever discovered a secret or treasure following a loved one's death?

8. Did you work any of the included cryptograms? What was your favorite quote from Bernie's father's journal, and why?

9. What do you think happens to Bernie and Number Thirty-Six after the book ends? Do you think they start a relationship? If so, do you think they stay together? Would you want them to?